Deceived

Also by James Scott Bell

Fiction

Deadlock

Breach of Promise

The Whole Truth

No Legal Grounds

Presumed Guilty

Try Dying

Try Darkness

Sins of the Fathers

The Darwin Conspiracy

Circumstantial Evidence

Final Witness

Blind Justice

The Nephilim Seed

City of Angels*

Angels Flight*

Angel of Mercy*

A Greater Glory

A Higher Justice

A Certain Truth

Glimpses of Paradise

Nonfiction

Write Great Fiction: Plot & Structure

Write Great Fiction: Revision & Self-Editing

*coauthor

Deceived

JAMES SCOTT BELL

ZONDERVAN.com/
AUTHORTRACKER
follow your favorite authors

ZONDERVAN

Deceived
Copyright © 2009 by James Scott Bell

This title is also available as a Zondervan ebook. Visit www.zondervan.com/ebooks.

Requests for information should be addressed to:
Zondervan, *Grand Rapids, Michigan 49530*

Library of Congress Cataloging-in-Publication Data

Bell, James Scott.
    Deceived / James Scott Bell.
      p. cm.
    ISBN 978-0-310-26904-5 (pbk.)
      1. Deception — Fiction. 2. Canyons — California — Fiction. I. Title.
PS3552.E5158D44 2008
813'.54 — dc22

                                                     2008033884

The author would like to thank the Alfred Publishing Co., Inc, for use of the song "Anything Goes," words and music by Cole Porter, © 1934 (Renewed) WB Music Corp. All rights reserved. Used by permission of Alfred Publishing Co., Inc.

All Scripture quotations, unless otherwise indicated, are taken from the *Holy Bible, New International Version*®. NIV®. Copyright © 1973, 1978, 1984 by International Bible Society. Used by permission of Zondervan. All rights reserved.

Interior design by Christine Orejuela-Winkelman

Printed in the United States of America

09 10 11 12 13 14 • 24 23 22 21 20 19 18 17 16 15 14 13 12 11 10 9 8 7 6 5 4 3 2 1

Deceived

Hey, Jon, thanks for the e-mail.

You're right, I've had TV people practically camped out in my front yard. There's even a movie guy wanting me to cooperate on a screenplay. He's the craziest. He actually followed me into the men's room at Ruth's Chris and wouldn't let me close the stall door! Says he's got two screenplays "in development" at the studios. Maybe he does, maybe he doesn't, but you don't corner a man when nature is calling. Know what I mean?

Still, that's all part of it. You and I know it's a juicy story, and I know you must be getting the same kind of calls.

Yes, I will do a paper on this. My specialty is cognitive psych, as you know, and that's why you called me in the first place. And you also know what's got me into so much trouble lately with my peers—introducing the concept of what I call "sin dissociation" to the academic discussion.

But from the research I've done, and the interviews, I know we have a biblical case right here. That's your department, of course, but remember—I was a year ahead of you in seminary. I get to pull rank, don't I?

Please, don't think there is any way you should have suspected this. Not under the circumstances. Especially not with the killing happening the way it did.

I'm attaching some notes. This is all just preliminary. I suspect the paper will take a good year. I've tried to put the events in chronological order and, every now and then, bring in the past to explain the present.

Let me know what you think. Your input will be invaluable.

It was good getting together with you. Hey, maybe you and I should do the screenplay. I mean, you live in LA. Isn't it required that everyone in LA write a screenplay?

Let's talk soon.

Ray

If there is to be any hope of recovery, we must recognize the unalterable fact that this is a spiritual malady, and as such requires a spiritual answer.

For too long, our profession has done real harm by failing to recognize the existence of soul and spirit, as well as the reality of sin and consequence.

But if we can attune our patients to listen, listen to what we may call the voice of God, that is ground for real hope and healing.

—From "Sin Dissociation" by Dr. Raymond C. Vickers

Saturday

The big, fat liar was dressed in yellow slacks, a yellow golf shirt, and a straw hat with a black band. He even had yellow socks to go with the black shoes. He looked like a ripe banana with feet.

He also looked like dead meat, Rocky thought, as she watched him take a full practice swing.

They were on the first tee at Woodley Lakes, a public course in Van Nuys. But Mr. Sawyer W. Pinskey was all decked out, like he was about to tee off at Augusta in front of a bank of television cameras.

Roxanne "Rocky" Towne smiled at the thought. Because, in a way, he was about to do something very much like that.

Pinskey took his stance again. Rocky kept her head steady as she observed from the golf cart.

He took a mighty swipe at a dandelion, then posed after the swing. As if he'd just hit one three hundred fifty yards and was listening for the approval of the gallery.

Rocky approved. Oh, did she ever.

As Pinskey waited his turn on the tee, Rocky, who did not play golf but was dressed like she did, approached the middle-aged man. He was about to take another practice cut when he looked up and saw her.

He nodded.

"Hi," Rocky said. She watched as Pinskey did what most people did the first time they saw her. He looked her in the eye—into her sunglasses, actually—then down slightly at her scar, then back up to her eyes.

Rocky interrupted his gaze. "I just took up golf myself, and I saw you practicing, and I was wondering if I could ask you a question."

He smiled. "Of course."

"I never seem to hit the ball very far. You look like you hit it a mile."

"Well, it depends." He chuckled. His big, fat lying face was ruddy and jowly. "If you don't get it in the fairway, it doesn't matter how far you hit it."

"Ah," Rocky said.

"But the secret to power is to take it back just a hair more than you think." He took his stance again. "Now watch."

Rocky watched.

In slow motion, Pinskey took his driver back, twisting around on his spine's axis. When he got the club to the apex, he held his position, his upper torso coiled. "See that?" he said. "See how my club is parallel to the ground?"

Rocky nodded.

"Now I just crank it a little more" — he twisted himself a little further — "and then start the downswing with a hip nudge." Pinskey gave it a full swing, the club whooshing through the air. He turned the other way on the follow-through and held the finish a moment.

Then he came back to start position. "That's all there is to it," he said. "Or as John Daly puts it, 'Grip it and rip it.' Pretty simple game, huh?"

"Oh, I'm sure."

A voice from the tee box said, "We're up."

Mr. Sawyer W. Pinskey, a senior investment management analyst with Merrill Lynch, stuck out his hand. "My name's Sawyer."

"Julie," Rocky said.

"Nice meeting you. Remember, keep it in the short grass."

Rocky nodded and watched as Pinskey joined his foursome — three other men about the same age, varying in their paunch factor. Pinskey led the belt-overhang competition, yet he moved with a certain confident elasticity.

Which was odd for a man who had supposedly suffered a spinal injury in a car accident in May.

Rocky trained her sunglasses on the tee box and watched the gentlemen take their various cuts. Pinskey was the last to play. He even gave her a wink as he teed the ball up. Then he stood back, surveyed the fairway, took a practice swing, and stepped up to the ball. He waggled the club once, then took it back and came through solid.

The ball took off like a bullet and rose, curved a little to the left, then hit the grass and rolled.

"Good ball," one of his companions said.

Pinskey, broad smile on his face, turned to Rocky. "And that's how it's done," he said and waved at her.

Rocky waved back.

She waited until the foursome chugged their two golf carts to the first ball, then got back in her own cart. She made a U-turn on the cart path and scooted back toward the clubhouse. She wouldn't be needing her cart anymore.

Because what Mr. Sawyer W. Pinskey did not know was that she had absolutely no interest in golf. He did not know that she was working for the insurance company. And he especially did not know that in her sunglasses was a nanocam that took digital video, or that his golf acumen was now memorialized and would soon be in the hands of insurance company lawyers.

Rocky Towne allowed herself a fleeting moment of satisfaction. She'd done a really good job this time. Working freelance, it was essential to do good work. You built a rep that way.

She needed a good rep. She needed the income.

And right now she especially needed to get back to the apartment. Back before Boyd got home.

Because he was going to be stinking mad at what she was about to do.

1:32 p.m.

"Come on, honey, what is it?"

"Just don't talk." Liz meant it, too. If he said another word, another soft-spoken, understanding word, she'd pick up a rock and throw it at his head.

They were hiking well inside Pack Canyon, his favorite spot, not hers. She walked reluctantly, silently, baking in the afternoon sun. It was a clear Saturday, the winds blowing away the haze that usually blanketed the city.

Arty bounded up a couple of boulders, a T-shirted mountain goat. "Come on up," he said. "You can see to forever."

Liz said nothing. She sat and looked the other way. Not to forever. To the scrub brush about a hundred feet below.

"Honey?"

She didn't answer. Let him sweat. Let him get it through his skull that he was being stupid.

She heard the clomp of his hiking boots descending.

If he tries to touch me now, she thought, it might get ugly.

He came around in a little semicircle and sat, facing her, on a rock.

"Sweetheart, please talk to me," he said.

She looked at him now and saw, for a brief moment, the man she wanted him to be. Tan face, thick brown hair that sprang from his head like Hugh Grant's. Blue eyes to die for. A package like that was supposed to have ambition, success, wealth — the winning ticket.

"What do you expect me to say?" Liz put on her cold stare.

"You could start with 'I love you,'" he said, "and tell me how charming I am."

"I'm not in the mood."

"Start with anything, then. Anything."

"You want me to say anything?"

"Please."

"You've changed," she said. "I don't like it."

He was silent a long time. He passed his hand over the surface of the rock. He looked up. Finally, he said, "You're right. I have changed. I thought you understood that."

"I don't understand," Liz said. She rubbed her hands on her shorts as if an ant was crawling on them. "I don't understand how someone can go from being one way to ending up a completely different person."

"That's the whole point," he said. "He wouldn't be much of a God if he didn't change you."

"Not your personality. Not the thing that makes you who you are. Made you who you *were*."

"There's a lot of the old me still here," he said with a smile. "I just don't think about the same things in the same way."

"Do you think about me?"

"Of course I do. I'm committed to you."

"Committed. Sounds so enthusiastic."

"I mean it in the . . . best way." He looked confused. Good.

"Then why're you making it so hard on me?" Liz said.

"I'm not trying to make it hard on you. I just can't go back to selling a product I don't believe in. Just can't do it."

Arty wiped his face with his right hand, then kept it over his eyes for a moment. Like he was trying to hide.

Liz said, "Have you thought that having a lot of money enables you to do good? Like buy food for poor people or something? Or maybe buy a nice car for your wife once in a while? Isn't that a good thing too?"

"Maybe."

"Maybe?"

"I just can't earn money from something that's wrong."

"What is wrong with a little entertainment?" Liz shouted *entertainment*, creating a small echo.

Arty didn't even blink. "Bikini Blackjack Babes is not entertainment," he said. "It's just this side of pornography."

"They don't take their bikinis off, do they?"

"It doesn't matter. It's the suggestion."

"This is really freaking me out, this whole thing, this whole change. I really, really can't stand it."

She sighed to the sky. Arty had quit RumbleTV a week ago, even though he was pulling down six figures. And he had quit because of one little game they produced for cell phones. It was a *game*! People played this thing for *fun*!

But no. His "faith" would not allow him to continue with a company that made such things. His "conscience" was bothered. It kept him up at night. Well, she kept him up that night he told her. She gave him one big earful, oh yes.

You don't know what it's like to be poor! You do not have any idea. You don't know what it's like to eat Hamburger Helper five nights in a row, and maybe if you're good, you get a Lemonhead for dessert. One Lemonhead! You don't know, so you go and blow a good thing. I hate you for that!

Arty was hurt now. She could see it in his body language. The way his shoulders sagged as he got up and started climbing again. Running away. The old Arty would have stayed and fought.

Six figures! He threw that all away for what?

"Honey, come up here," he called. "It's beautiful."

Oh please, please, please, shut up.

She did not go up. She went down. Down the rocks toward the scrub wedged in the hillside. It was thick down there. Maybe she could get lost. Maybe get Arty to come crying after her.

She almost fell. She cursed out loud. Loud enough so Arty could hear it. Loud and she took the stupid Lord's name in vain—that's what they used to say back home, anyway. If you said *God* except in prayer you were *taking the Lord's name in vain.*

What a stupid rule that was. Like what that skinny old man told her when she was a girl, about how there's the saved and unsaved, redeemed and unredeemed, and you can't change who's who. *Saints and ain'ts* the preacher said, his mouth turned down in tight-lipped emphasis.

Liz had known immediately which one she was in that old gasbag's eyes.

"Watch out down there," Arty called, concern etched in his voice.

Liz kept on. The rocks made a V a few yards away, a place where you could easily get stuck. Maybe if she went for it, Arty would follow her and get wedged in, and then she could slap him until he came to his senses.

Thanks. I needed that.

Yes, and then he'd wake up and think about *her* needs for a change. Wake up and get back to making money.

Wake up and be a man again.

Sure.

"Honey, please wait!"

She didn't.

Keep moving. That's what Mama always said.

Keep moving so they don't get you.

Keep moving or they'll lay you out.

She kept moving, got to the V and thought for a moment what it would look like if Arty was really and truly in there.

And then she knew exactly what it would look like. Because she saw a body.

"Honey, what are you doing?"

"Shut up." Liz said it without premeditation. Said it because she was going to control this situation. Arty would get all bothered and righteous about the body.

She needed time to think.

It was clear he was dead. She knew that without going down to see.

He was a motorcycle rider. His big, old Harley was on its side about ten feet from the body. His legs were bent and so was he. Like a pretzel of flesh and bone.

"Honey, are you coming back here or not?"

She ignored him and started to make her way down the rocks.

Let him try to follow, she thought. He can follow *me* now. He can bring up the rear if that's what he wants. He can run away from life if he wants. I'm not going with him.

Keep moving.

Liz wasn't the sure-footed goat Arty was, so she had to be careful. But as she quickened her pace she gained more confidence. Just before reaching the bottom of the—what was it? a gorge?—she felt like she could easily master these rocks. That she could jump and stride and go wherever she wanted.

She always knew she could master anything she put her mind to.

She reached the body. For a half-second she thought he might move. Maybe he wasn't dead after all. Maybe he was just hurt and needed their help.

But there was no sign of breathing. She reached out to touch his arm. He was as still and cold as stone.

He was a big man, wearing the least amount of helmet allowable by law. A glorified skullcap. Didn't do him any good, from the looks of things, because his neck was probably broken.

Face up he was, eyes open in death, skin the color of clamshells, a bit of dry tongue sticking out the corner of his mouth.

"Don't touch anything!"

Arty. His voice startled her. She turned. He was almost charging down the rocks.

Slip, will you?

"Is he alive?" Arty said.

"Does he look alive?" Liz spat the words like hot rivets. "Oh, that's terrible." Arty was now by her side. He looked up. "There's a dirt path right over there. I've seen kids on bikes there, and it's not good. He must have just gone right over. We need to call this in."

"Wait a second," Liz said. "We don't even know who this guy is."

"We don't need to."

"He's not going anywhere, Arty."

He looked at her like she was some strange creature he'd never seen before.

"I suppose we could look for an ID," Arty said.

"Good," she said. "You do that. Look in his pockets."

"Yeah."

He went to the body. Liz let him. She didn't care one way or the other about the man. Who he was didn't matter a bit. But the death was something different. Radically different. Beautifully different, in a way.

As Arty looked at the body, Liz checked the overturned Harley. A nice piece of machinery, with silver-studded black saddlebags.

Maybe the ID was in one of the bags.

"Don't touch that," Arty called.

She ignored him. She unbuckled the two straps on the up-facing bag, opened the flap, and bent over so she could look inside.

Some sacks, like stuffed gym socks, were inside. She fished one out. It was buff-colored canvas. She hefted it. It felt like a sack of marbles. It had a little zipper on top. She unzipped the bag.

"What is it?" Arty said.

"Get over here," she said.

● ● ●

"You're a young man," Mrs. Axelrod said. "Why aren't you married?"

Mac kept his head under the hood, pretending he didn't hear. "Almost got it, Mrs. Axelrod."

"How's that?"

Good. Subject changed. Mac gave the wrench a final turn, then pulled out from under the iron shell. He wiped the sweat from his forehead with the back of his hand. It was a scorcher today.

"Should fire right up," Mac said. "You want to give it a try?"

"No, you go right ahead. But a young man like you should be married. Why aren't—"

"I'll do 'er right now." He went quickly to the driver's seat of the '95 Buick, put the key in, and started it up. He hoped his automotive triumph would distract Mrs. Axelrod from asking the question again.

"It's fine now," Mac said, getting out. "If it ever—"

"Come up to the porch," Mrs. Axelrod said, waving her cane toward the house. "Got something I want to talk to you about."

"Can't it wait, Mrs. Axelrod?" He always called her that. It seemed respectful to the oldest living member of the congregation. She was eighty-seven and therefore had a full fifty years on him. Calling her Edie just didn't seem right.

"No, it can't wait," Mrs. Axelrod said, clipped and final. She'd have been a good prison guard. Give her a cane with an electric prod, and *zappo*. Even so, Mac liked her. She spoke her mind. You knew where you stood. She was short, plump, and colored her hair nut brown. She always wore dresses, which put her more than a little out of style in the laid-back canyon community.

Here, among ex-hippies, aging Baby Boomers, struggling artists, outlaw bikers, an assortment of young families—and ex-cons fighting to stay on the straight and narrow—Mrs. Edie Axelrod was almost like a queen.

She, along with her late husband, Elmer, had been one of two founding families of Pack Canyon Community Church. When she spoke, people at the church hopped to it. She did not abuse her position so much as assert it. She was the "keeper of the books," Pastor Jon told Mac once. "The Energizer Cornerstone."

And so, dutifully, Mac trudged to the front porch of the mini-Victorian that had been built in the 1930s. *Back then*—Mrs. Axelrod was fond of saying, almost as often as she saw you—Pack Canyon was little more than a couple of ranches and a notorious bordello for some of Hollywood's sneaky male stars. The canyon still had a little of that frontier feel, though after the Boomers discovered it in the 1980s, it got a little more suburban.

The site of the bordello now housed the Pack Canyon Market. You could shop for food there. Maybe pick up a can of peaches in the very room Errol Flynn once favored. That's the way store manager Henry Weinhouse liked to tell it, anyway.

Mrs. Axelrod had Mac sit in a wooden rocker. She sat in the other rocker next to a table. On the table was a pitcher of iced tea and two elegant, frosted glasses.

"Now then," she said, pouring tea for both, "have you given any thought to your future?"

Future? He hardly had a present. "I'm just glad to be alive and living in Pack Canyon."

"But where is your basket?" she said.

"Basket?"

Mrs. Axelrod tapped her cane on the wooden planks of the porch.

"Mr. Axelrod always said a man should put all his eggs in one basket, then watch that basket!"

"Sounds like a wise man," Mac said.

"I see a little Elmer in you."

Mac took a swallow of iced tea. He didn't know if he wanted any Elmer in him. He had enough trouble keeping Mac in check.

"Elmer was a man's man," Mrs. Axelrod said. "You don't find many of those around anymore, sad to say. Lots of men going to the beauty parlor now. I remember when men started to wear earrings. Earrings!"

"It's outrageous," Mac said.

"How old are you?"

"Thirty-seven, ma'am."

"Don't call me *ma'am*. You should be married. Have you ever been married?"

"Mrs. Axelrod—"

"Why aren't you? The sea is full of fish. All you've got to do is put some bait on your hook."

His head started throbbing. The right side. The side with the fragments. The hot claws would be coming soon.

"You do believe in marriage, don't you?" Mrs. Axelrod said.

"Yes, I do," Mac said.

"Well then, why—"

"I was married, Mrs. Axelrod. But, as you know, I did some time in prison."

Her eyebrows went skyward. "And your wife?"

"She decided she didn't want to be married to a con. Can't say as I blame her."

"But you're reformed," she said. "You are a Christian man now."

"That's an ongoing project, Mrs. Axelrod."

"I like you," she said.

"Well, thank you. I—" The claws sank into his head. His eyes watered. He had to get out of there before he started saying, or doing, things he shouldn't.

He had to call Arty.

Arty was the only guy who knew everything, the only one who understood.

Mac stood up. "I'm sorry, Mrs. Axelrod. I have to go."

"We're not finished talking."

"I'm not feeling too good." Pinpricks of fire heated his skull, and it started to implode.

"Come inside," the widow said. "Maybe the heat—"

"I'm sorry," Mac said, then ran down the steps and across the lawn. He heard Mrs. Axelrod hitting the wood with her cane.

• • •

"Rocky!"

His tough-guy voice. It turned Rocky's bones to sticks. It was the sound of beer and shots. Boyd did bad things when he chased whiskey with beer.

"Where are you?"

She continued to pack the suitcase. She didn't bother folding anything. This was not for a pleasure cruise. This was to get the heck out. Fast. Sort it all out later. If she stopped now, she might not do it at all.

Boyd Martin had a hold on her. When he was sober, he was more caring than any guy she'd ever been with—which wasn't so many, but by comparison he stood out. The others wanted one thing, and only wanted that as long as they didn't have to look at her face too much. Boyd, she always felt, wanted *her*.

When he was sober.

The first time he took her to dinner, he'd put his hand softly on her face, his palm over the scar that ran from the corner of her left eye in a half-moon to the corner of her lips. He said, "You're beautiful." The way he said it wasn't just a line. Or maybe she just wanted to believe it wasn't.

When he was sober, he could make her believe almost anything.

But when he drank, he was Mr. Hyde. And he made her drink with him. The drinking dulled the pain when he screamed at her, so she figured it was worth it. But it stopped being worth it last night. It was one too many episodes, like the shot that takes you from drunk to passed out.

All over horticulture.

She was reading a gardening book, late, when he got home from the poker game. Boyd played on Fridays at a house in South Pasadena.

He came into the apartment smelling of beer and cigar smoke. And he wanted her in bed. She said no, she had to read her book.

It was an excuse, but partly true. The one thing she looked forward to when they got married — someday — was having a house with a garden. She'd always loved plants and flowers. They were a way of making something beautiful, something she would never be. Gardening was a way to *feel* beauty, and ever since she could remember, that was what she wanted to feel.

Boyd grabbed the book, looked at it, cursed. She asked for it back and he slapped her.

The blow was stunning in its suddenness and in its anger. He had come close to hitting her before, and once pushed her down on the bed.

Now this.

He looked surprised for a second, then got a hard look and said, "This is an *apartment*, you dummy. We don't have no house for a garden, so quit reading about it." He threw the book across the room. It hit the table where they kept a cup of loose change. The cup spilled and coins hit the hardwood floor like a hard, metallic rain.

The sound of which only fueled Boyd's inner fire. "Clean that up!"

She cleaned it up because she didn't want to fight and because she wanted him to pass out before he asked her again to get into bed with him.

She knew she had to get out. As much as she wanted to still believe in him, she had to leave. Today.

But she hadn't expected Boyd to come home in the middle of the afternoon, hammered.

She faced him now. "Boyd, we need some time away from each other."

"Stupid thing t'say," he said.

She scooped her underwear from the top drawer of the bureau and tossed it in the suitcase.

"Stop!" he ordered. His six-foot-four-inch frame filled the bedroom door. Before his stomach developed its beer-soaked circumference, he'd been a pretty fair linebacker. Played one season for the University of Utah, then dropped out of school.

He'd been making good money working for a pool service, getting some Beverly Hills and Brentwood accounts. But the drinking, always the drinking. He'd been fired recently for downing shots of Jack Daniels, then falling into a pool and almost drowning.

Rocky said, "I think it's a good idea if we take some time to think things out."

"You can think right here."

"I can't."

He called her a name.

"I'm going to stay with Geena for a while," she said.

She turned to the bureau again. Boyd came up behind her, his boot heels banging the hardwood floor like muffled gun blasts. She whirled as he threw the suitcase over the bed. The contents spilled on the floor.

"You and me, we're gonna talk it out right here," he said.

"Boyd, don't."

"Chill, spill, take a pill."

He was going into his bad rapper routine. Boyd thought for a time he could make it as a buffer version of Eminem. He lacked only two things — talent and sobriety.

Speaking softly, Rocky said, "Baby, listen. Just some time to think. We haven't had that for a long time."

His eyes were flame red. He kept blinking. "You think you can do better?" he said.

"That's not what this is about," she said. "Look, let's set a date, next week, we'll go out to Miceli's and have dinner."

Maybe there was still a chance with him. She loved him, right? Wanted to love him. Wanted it to be right and to last.

"Don't go," he said and sat heavily on the bed. Little boy lost. That's what they were, two lost people who'd found each other. It wasn't good that way. At least one of them had to know where they were going.

She sat next to him and put her arm around his shoulder. He was shaking. "Come on, baby. It'll be good this way for a while. Just a while, huh?"

Boyd said nothing.

"I could try to get more work," she said. If she tried, she could get more files. Maybe even the singing thing would finally happen for her. She could dream, right?

"Don't go," he said.

"We'll talk soon."

"No, I mean it, don't go. No go, that's what I said."

He stood.

She stood.

"Let me call you tonight," she said.

He shook his head.

She put her hand on his cheek.

He slapped it away.

"Don't do that," she said.

"Let's go out somewhere," he said.

Rocky turned, shaking her head. She had to pick up the suitcase and start packing again. This was pointless.

"Wait." He closed the suitcase. "Let's cool off, huh?"

"I'm cool now."

"One hour. Will you give me one hour?"

"No."

He sat on top of the suitcase. "Now that's just not nice."

"Get off the suitcase, Boyd."

He smiled.

"Don't act like this," she said.

"*You* don't act like this."

He grabbed her wrist, pulled her and twisted her, so she sat on his lap. He kissed her, clumsy and hard. She turned her face away.

"Come on," Boyd said. His arms were around her, tight.

He kissed her again. She let him. Kiss it all away, she thought. All the bad. Make me believe we can make something out of this dirty, stinking mess.

His foul breath filled her nostrils. She thought she might retch. She pushed his chest, hard, and in doing so fell backward, sprawling on the floor.

"See?" Boyd said. "Don't fight."

He reached for her but she scrambled away. She got to her feet, grabbed her purse. If she didn't keep going, she thought, she never would. And in not going, she'd die a little.

She heard him grunting. Heard the boots on the floor. She rushed out the door before he could reach her.

She walked fast, up her dismal street toward Franklin Avenue. She caught a glimpse of the Hollywood sign. The noted landmark, the beacon of dreams for so many, now a mocker of her own dreams of being a singer.

What prospects did this town have for her anymore? And who was she kidding? Life was unfair, and she'd been dealt cards from the bottom of the deck.

She was eight when the dog mauled her. She'd been playing in the backyard, making houses for bees. They had bees who liked the blossoms of the apricot tree, and she thought she'd make houses on the ground out of leaves and sticks. She thought she'd get a little honey later and put a few drops inside. The bees would catch on and find a nice home, courtesy of Roxanne Julie Towne.

She heard the cracking of wood.

The Townes had a fence between their house and the Lloyd family. Mr. and Mrs. Lloyd were nice, but they had a son, Rick, who was fifteen and not very nice. He already had tattoos and a bunch of friends who made noise late into the night.

Now there was another crack, and a plank in the fence kicked up like a dancer's leg. Went back down, then up again.

A snout came through. A dog. A black dog. One she'd seen before and been scared of.

One that she wanted to stay away from.

It turned toward her, snarling. She always wanted to be friends with dogs. She loved dogs.

This dog didn't want to be friends.

It charged.

Roxanne screamed and tried to get up to run, but her foot slipped on the bee house.

Then the dog was on her. She could still remember the saliva and the teeth, but nothing else until she woke up in the hospital.

Rocky was almost to Franklin now. As she sometimes did, without wanting to, she thought about what her life would have been like without the scar. No kids shouting "scar face" at her. No spending her childhood and adolescence isolated in her own inner world.

Maybe she would have had a boyfriend, a senior prom, college, a recording contract, a movie even.

Yeah, she thought. And maybe unicorns dance on rainbows.

* * *

Liz waited as Arty came over and looked in the sack. She watched his face. It went from troubled to amazed in two seconds flat.

She smiled.

"I don't believe this," he said.

"Believe it." Even though she could hardly believe it herself. There it was—a jumble of stones that had to be diamonds, some loose, some set in necklaces and rings. Three other sacks just like it were also in the saddlebag.

"Jewels," Arty said.

Great observation! Liz wanted to scream. "Yes, jewels, and where do you think they came from?"

"I don't know."

"It looks real suspicious, doesn't it? I mean, these are probably stolen."

Arty said nothing. He was deep in thought.

"These are hot rocks," she said.

"How do you know that?" Arty said.

"Please, Arthur, you know I was raised in a pawn shop."

Arty nodded. "You're probably right. Don't touch anything. Let's call the police."

"Hold on a second," she said. "Think about this, okay? *Hot stones.*"

His head tilted back slightly, as if he sniffed a bad odor. "You are not seriously thinking that we can keep any of these, are you?"

"I'm just asking you to think for half a minute."

"There's nothing to think about, Liz. We have to do what's right."

"What's right? If these are stolen, they're insured. The owners won't care."

"The insurance company will."

"They're the biggest con artists in the country," Liz said. "Let them take a hit. They deserve it."

"And just what do you propose to do with stolen jewels?"

"It's not that hard," Liz said.

"What's not that hard?"

"To fence them."

"Liz! This is crazy talk."

Liz closed her eyes and tried to will Arty into submission. Or maybe he could just go away. *Forget me, forget the jewels, forget the body. Go away.*

She felt Arty's hand on her shoulder. She wrenched away from his hold.

"They're not ours," he said.

"Well, they're not *his*," she said.

"It just isn't right. We have to obey the law."

Liz sighed as loudly as she could. "That's the whole thing right there. Obey the law, obey God. Why don't you think about me?"

"I am thinking about you. About us."

"Right."

"What you're thinking is way too dangerous."

"Life is dangerous," she said. "Arty, listen to me, will you? You remember when you said you wanted to be worth two million dollars before you're thirty-five? That was a great dream, a great goal. I was down with it. But now you act like you don't care if we have any money at all. This could set us up."

"There's probably a reward," Arty said.

Liz said, "And maybe not."

Arty bit his lip, shook his head. "The longer we talk, the more we'll have to explain to the police. If we call them now, there's no problem. We'll have done the right thing."

Liz saw the phone on his belt. Without a moment's consideration, she snatched it.

She thought Arty would get angry. Maybe try to take the phone back.

"Go ahead," he said. "You make the call."

Soft and understanding. It grated on her to hear him talk that way. Soft and understanding wasn't the way you gained net worth. She started to climb. Back up the rocks, holding the phone, hoping Arty would stay with the body and never bother her again.

Divorce. Yes. She'd end it now. Bag someone else while she was still young. And hope he didn't have a religious conversion.

"Liz, where are you going?" Arty shouted.

She didn't answer.

"Liz!"

She surprised herself. She could really move when motivated. Even over rocks.

Arty kept calling to her, giving chase.

Now what? She was no match for Arty when it came to rock climbing. He'd get to her sooner or later. Probably sooner. If he put his hands on her, she knew she'd probably go a little crazy.

Maybe she was a little crazy now.

The diamonds were all she could think about. How much would they amount to when fenced? One heck of a lot more than she and Arty had now, after they burned through the last of the savings. More than they'd probably ever make legitimately with Arty on his new spiritual hayride.

Fencing the stones would be the challenge, but there were people she could track down, maybe back home, maybe here—

"Stop right now!"

Escape. That's what she needed. Escape from Arty, from this marriage that had skidded and crashed into a religious wall she never saw coming.

Escape and money.

She was at the top now, lungs burning, and Arty was only a few yards away.

Liz opened the phone and snapped it in two, then threw the pieces as far as she could. She heard the pieces clatter on some rocks.

Arty was watching, openmouthed.

"What did you just do?" he shouted.

Figure it out for yourself. She put her hands on her knees to catch her breath.

"Liz, this is nuts," he said.

She was too winded to reply.

"Let's go home and talk about this," he said.

"Shut ..."

"We can talk—"

"... up."

"—this out."

She felt his hand on her back. She straightened and hit it away.

"Okay," he said, "that's enough. Just stop it."

"Don't ... tell me ... to stop it."

"I am telling you," he said. "You're acting crazy. We are not going to take any of that stuff. We're going back to the house and calling the police before we get into trouble."

"We're in trouble now!" Liz flapped her arms once, like a large bird that couldn't fly. "We're in trouble ... because of you ... throwing away your job ..."

"I didn't throw anything away that would last, that would make us happy."

"Do I look ... *happy* to you?"

"Honey—"

"Find another name for me."

"Come on."

He took her arm. She took it back.

"Now look," he said. "That's enough. If you don't come with me, I'm going to the house myself and make the call."

"Good. You do that. I'll see to the diamonds."

"That's it."

When he grabbed her left arm this time, his fingers formed an iron grip. She tried to pull away, couldn't. He pushed her toward the trail.

Nobody does that to me. Nobody, nobody, nobody.

She swung a roundhouse right and cracked him in the jaw.

He let her go immediately and put his chin in his hands.

She watched his eyes. The way she used to watch her stepfather's eyes. The way she used to anticipate when it was coming. When he'd try to get her. His eyes would get mean.

Arty's eyes had that same look now. At least she thought they did.

Nobody does that to me.

In her body, every muscle tensed and flamed, as if she were a storehouse of fireworks with a torch thrown in, the hissing starting as the first rocket ignites.

Then, explosion. Blind pinwheel rage and Roman candle fear.

Her eyes closed. She felt her hands shoot out in front of her. Her right-hand fingers scraped his cheek. Her left pounded his chest.

She pulled back, readied another strike. The faintest part of her warned her to hold up, to stop.

She hesitated and opened her eyes.

Arty wasn't there.

• • •

"Where you been, MacDonald?"

Slezak was the last person Mac wanted to see. Especially in that made-myself-at-home position, waiting by his door. Slezak loved to wait. Or show up knocking when you least expected it.

Mac hadn't seen him as he pulled his pickup into the driveway. The little guest house behind the church was Mac's only home now. Pastor Jon waived rent in return for duties around the grounds and general fix-it tasks for the members. No, it wasn't much at all, but it was Mac's place. His, but not completely. Not as long as he fell under the jurisdiction of Gordon Slezak, parole agent for the California Department of Corrections.

"I need to get inside," Mac said. His headache pounded like a drill bit in granite.

Slezak said, "Let's get this over with quick, and I can be on my way."

"Just let me get something, okay?"

"Drugs again?" Slezak said. "Turn around."

"My head—"

"Turn around or I'll tag you for resisting, huh?"

Mac turned and put his hands on top of his head. Maybe if he squeezed his own skull he could keep the pain from overtaking him.

Slezak frisked him. Hard and slow, taking his sweet time.

"Empty your pockets," Slezak said.

"Please."

"Now. The more you talk, the less I like it."

Mac pulled a flat leather wallet from his left front pocket, then untucked the pocket completely. He had a plastic comb in his back left, and two quarters, a dime, and a penny in his right front. He already had his keys in his hands.

"Just hand 'em over," Slezak said.

Mac, with knots tightening behind his eyes, tossed the stuff on the chipped flagstone slab in front of the door. And knew he'd made a big mistake.

"Oh, now that is going on the report," Slezak said. "Yes, indeedy. Attitudinal adjustment is slow in coming, huh?"

"My head . . ."

"Sure. On the ground."

This was worse than prison. There, they didn't care enough about you to single you out, as long as you knew the rules. You could play by the book and they'd leave you alone.

On parole, it was your PO that decided the form and texture of your life. Daniel Patrick MacDonald had drawn the short straw and gotten Gordon Slezak, a middle-aged man who seemed to be in a prison of his own, venting on other people as his only escape.

Just be still, Mac told himself. Lie facedown in the dirt as Mr. Gordon Slezak goes through your wallet. Pray that you don't do anything stupid.

He prayed.

"You got a job yet?" Slezak asked.

Mac turned his face to the side. "Yeah."

"You didn't tell me. That's great news, huh? Whereabouts?"

"Odd jobs."

"Be more specific."

"For the church."

"Oh yeah, the church. You're sticking that one out pretty good, huh? Got 'em snowed, do you?"

Mac said nothing.

"What're they gonna say when you up and walk out, huh? Which you'll do. Then you can go pull a con somewhere else, where I'm not there to call you on it. But they'll know. They'll contact me."

Pause.

"You're clean here," Slezak said. "Your wallet's got moths." He laughed. "Up and at 'em. Let's take a look inside, huh?"

He had to let Slezak inside. In California they made you waive your Fourth Amendment rights when you got out of the joint. For all the time you were on parole, your PO could search you or your house or your vehicle without probable cause. All they had to do was show up.

Gordon Slezak loved to show up.

Mac sat down heavily in the old, cracked leather chair that had come with the place and waited. This shouldn't take long. His place wasn't much. One bedroom, one bath. A bed and this chair that had once belonged to Pastor Jon. Only a little more than they gave you at Soledad. But it was his.

Mac rubbed the sides of his head, keeping the flames down.

Slezak took his time, opening drawers, looking under cushions, keeping up a line of patter.

"Yep, you got that old reverend snookered," Slezak said. "You know what *snookered* means? My granddaddy liked that word."

Mac said nothing.

Slezak paused at the scuffed desk that served Mac as both dining room table and storage for odd papers. The PO opened the top drawer and rummaged.

"Yeah, the old man worked vice in Kansas City, did you know that? I ever tell you that?" Slezak opened a second drawer, put his hands in it. "The confidence men he brought in, the stories he'd tell. Taught me one thing. You can't trust anybody. You just can't. His own chief of police he brought down."

This guy is talking to himself, Mac thought. Or he might as well have been. All Mac wanted was for him to finish his show — because that's what this always was with Slezak, a show — and get out. Get out so he could throw down some painkillers.

Slezak had stopped talking. He was holding something in his hand, looking at it. "So this must be what's her name," Slezak said. "Aurora?"

Mac stiffened. It was the photo of his daughter taken five years ago, when she was two.

"That her name?" Slezak said.

You know her name. He'd play along. "Yes," Mac said.

"Pretty name," Slezak said. "Real pretty. Pretty little girl, too. When's the last time you saw her?"

You know that, too. "A few years," Mac said.

"She and the mother, now what was the mother's name again?"

"It's in your records," Mac said.

"Where'd they move to?"

Mac said nothing.

"She'll be just fine, the little girl," Slezak said. "Your wife remarries maybe, the girl gets a new dad. It's all for the best. Things have a way of working themselves out." He stopped talking then and lingered over the picture.

Mac clenched his teeth—a move that didn't help his head—and tried to think of something other than Gordon Slezak. What Mac got was a memory of Aurora being born, back before he went to the slam. It was a hazy memory, in part because he'd been high, in part because he kept trying to remake the memory so he wasn't high. So he could pretend he wasn't a jerk who lost everything before he even knew what he had.

He told himself once again to keep cool. He prayed to keep cool. Because if he ever had any hopes of seeing his daughter again, of getting a court to let him, he couldn't violate his parole and get sent back to jail.

Which seemed to be Gordon Slezak's one goal in life.

Why?

"Now the girl you impregnated," Slezak said. "What was her name again?"

Mac said nothing.

"Never married her. Am I right about that?"

Mac stared. Slezak knew he had married Athena. Yes, he had gotten her pregnant, but he also did what they used to do, what he thought was the honorable thing. He had married Athena and tried to make a go of it. Really tried.

And blew it.

"That's the thing about responsibility," Slezak said. "Most of you guys never learn that. You think you can go on through life day by day, no plans, no work. You know what that's called? Recipe. Recipe for disaster. Another phrase my granddaddy liked."

Slezak finally put the photo back in the drawer.

"Don't want to see you follow that recipe, Danny Boy. But if you do, I'll be right there to flush you down the toilet. You know that, right?"

Mac looked into Slezak's dull, gray eyes.

"Answer me," Slezak said.

Oh dear God, help me. Mac could feel it coming on again, one of the rages. Mac felt like the grip of rage was an enemy combatant. Pastor Jon told him the enemy was Satan.

Mac was beginning to think Satan was really one Gordon Slezak.

"I said, 'Answer me,' " Slezak said.

Mac fell to his knees, grabbing his head as he went down.

• • •

Red blood on buff-colored rocks. As if a child had spilled paint on a light brown surface.

That was the first thing Liz thought of. She wanted it to be paint, not blood that came from Arty's head.

Arty's body was facedown, legs splayed, twenty feet below the blood stain. A larger, darker blotch spread outward from his motionless head.

Maybe he could be saved. She could call 911 and ... wait ... there was no phone. She'd broken it. And by the time she got back to the house and made the call he'd be gone.

She could go down there and see if he was breathing, maybe put something around the wound to stanch the blood.

Or ...

She looked around and listened. No one.

Time to think fast. Time to take control. Fully now. No one to tell her what to do or how to do it or when.

Keep moving.

• • •

"Get up."

Slezak's voice, from a distance.

No, from above. Mac looked up. He felt like his head had been worked over by a nail gun. He must have fallen from the pain.

"I got to take something," Mac said. Tears were streaming down his face, and he was sweating.

"Get off the floor," Slezak said.

Mac could only see immediately in front of him, as if staring through a small hole in a fence.

Enough to get to the bathroom.

"Where do you think you're going?" Slezak said, his voice behind Mac now.

Mac ignored him. *Shoot me in the back if you want to. It'll be a relief.*

He got to the mirrored medicine cabinet, opened it, found the Vicodin. It was in his hand.

Then snatched away.

"What's this now?" Slezak said.

"I got a prescription," Mac said.

"Whoa, whoa, whoa." Slezak stepped out of the bathroom.

"You can't take those," Mac said.

"I wasn't told about this," Slezak said. "No, no, no. You can't be taking narcotics now, huh? I'll have to check with the doc about this. If it's cleared, you'll get these back. But not before then. May take a few weeks."

The bits of metal in Mac's head felt like they were shifting around. He grabbed his head and squeezed, then dropped to his knees on the bathroom floor. Tears from the pain continued to spill out. The desire to kill Slezak swelled so strong he could hardly fight it. He clenched his teeth to will it away but lost any capacity for will.

The front door slammed. Mac staggered to his feet and got to the window. Peeked out and saw Slezak driving away.

Back in the bathroom, he found aspirin, poured five into his hand and threw them into his mouth. He took water straight from the faucet, put his head back, and swallowed.

He went to his bed, fell on it, and waited.

Ten minutes later, the headache started to subside. But the nightmare remained. A bad dream named Gordon Slezak.

He needed to call Arty. He was the best friend Mac had now. He got his phone and hit the speed dial.

It went to voicemail.

"Need to talk to you," Mac said. "Call me."

• • •

When she got back to the apartment building, Rocky wished for once that she did believe in prayer. Because this would be a good time to get some help from above.

She hoped Boyd would be sober and remorseful. That had happened before. Then maybe she could reason with him. They could split up like responsible adults.

Would she ever consider getting back together with him?

It wasn't like she had a lot of prospects.

Her record in the boyfriend department was not exactly stellar. In high school she had been asked out twice. Once by Carl Day, who was into theater and who cancelled at the last minute for a reason Rocky never understood. It had something to do, so Carl said, with his tropical fish and walking like an Egyptian. What The Bangles had to do with aquatic life was never explained.

No doubt, Rocky would later reflect, it was the worst excuse ever made up by an overly creative type.

The other one who asked her out was Nicholas Grimes, a science whiz who looked like it, and who needed arm candy for the prom. Rocky was a junior and Grimes a senior and apparently the pool of senior fishettes had run dry.

After Nicholas got turned down by three other juniors, or so Rocky was told later, he landed on her.

At first her father refused to pay for a new dress, but he finally relented under her brother Arty's single-minded campaign on her behalf. Their mother had died eight years earlier, and Arty did his best to offer Rocky the advice their mother might have given her about what a guy liked. It basically boiled down to, *Be yourself and don't worry.*

She worried. And then got angry when Nicholas spent the first half of the prom with his science buddies talking about the relative merits of the Apple Macintosh versus the IBM Peanut.

No dancing.

When they finally got around to it, the dancing was ludicrous. Nicholas Grimes knew calculators. He did not know choreography. Rocky enjoyed dancing. But the more she got into it, the more Nicholas seemed to distance himself.

Nicholas asked Rocky if she could find a ride home. There was something going on at one of the other guys' house, and he had to go with them right away. "Thanks for coming," he said. "I had fun."

So much for romantic high school memories.

After that, she could count her boyfriends on the fingers of one hand. None lasted more than a few months.

Except Boyd. Coming after a gap of three years, he lasted longer because she thought he was her last, best hope.

Kind of wrong about that, weren't you, girl? Rocky unlocked the apartment door. She closed the door and waited for Boyd to respond to the sound.

No response.

Where was he?

She listened but heard nothing. Not even the sound of his heavy breathing.

Maybe Boyd had decided to avoid a scene and taken off. Good. That was probably the best thing all around.

Her things. Now was the time. Pack again and get out. Before he came back and they had to go through a whole ordeal.

She went to the bedroom, looked on the bed. Her stuff wasn't there. No clothes, no suitcase.

She looked around.

Nothing around the room.

She looked through the dresser drawers.

All her stuff was gone.

He'd taken everything.

Just to be sure, she searched the apartment. Maybe he'd packed and put the suitcase somewhere inside. But it wasn't there.

Maybe he put it by her car, which was parked in the back.

She took the stairs and went out the back of the complex, out to where her parking space was.

The back window of her car was smashed. Her ancient Volvo, which she named Sputtering Sue, was now as scarred as her owner.

Rocky caught a whiff of smoke. Not like someone barbecuing on their balcony. More like someone burning leaves.

Though here in the Los Feliz district, burning leaves was illegal.

She saw smoke coming from around the corner, where the Dumpsters were. Something told her there was a connection.

When she got there, another tenant, an old woman whose name Rocky didn't know, was rattling her walker.

"Who did this?" the old woman shouted. Her voice was like a nail scraping the Dumpster's shell.

Rocky didn't answer. She looked inside, saw the last bits of flame dying down, the charred remains of clothes, the unmistakable remnant of her suitcase.

"You know who did this, don't you?" the old woman said. "Let me tell you, there's going to be hell to pay. I won't stand for it. Hell to pay!"

• • •

As she emptied the saddlebag, a state of calm came over Liz. It surprised and pleased her. It was like something she'd once heard about, a Zen moment. In the midst of the most horrendous trouble, people were able to stay focused and peaceful.

In control.

It was exhilarating. As she worked, part of her was observing the whole thing, as if outside herself.

That had happened once before that she could remember. She was ten, and they were making fun of her like always. In the school cafeteria. She had mashed potatoes and gravy and red Jell-O and green beans. She was sitting alone, of course, nobody ever sat with her, but she had a highly developed sense of awareness. She could tell when people were making fun of her and getting ready to do things. Like throw dirt clods at her, which was one of their favorite pastimes when she walked home from school.

This day there was a little group of them, all boys. Laughing and pointing at her. Turning heads back to each other for a fresh insult.

She pretended not to see, but out of the corner of her eye she could. Her peripheral vision was acute. Maybe because she had to use it so much to protect herself.

And then one of them sauntered up to her table. Cal Sensenbrenner. The athletic one. Stocky, built, fastest runner in school. He said, "Hey, Lazy Lizzie, your daddy in jail again?"

"No." But he was.

"I heard he was in jail and drunk and he peed his pants."

"Did not!"

"Maybe he could come to career day. I wanna be a jailbird someday."

She didn't say anything. She looked down at her food.

"Answer me," he said and pushed her.

An explosion went off in her head. *Nobody does that to me. Nobody, nobody, nobody.*

She threw the tray. It got most of him. The rest ended up on the floor and on some shoes and on a couple of the other kids. They started swearing at her.

Cal swore loudest, picked up some Jell-O in his hands and mashed it in her face while everybody started cheering. While she was crying, Miss Brainerd waddled over and told Cal to cut it out and he cussed at Miss Brainerd.

"You shouldn't have done that, Elizabeth," Miss Brainerd said. "You broke the rules, you sure did."

Liz wanted to cuss, too, but instead she held her tongue and looked at the mess she made, and it seemed beautiful to her. Reds and greens and browns, like a finger painting. It was beautiful because she had done it. She had made trouble and stopped stupid Cal's face from having that stupid smile.

Now, feeling in control with two dead bodies near, Liz's movements were fast and sure.

Arty's body lay far enough away that no one could see it or her from the path. The biker had managed to get himself good and dead in an out-of-the-way spot, too. It was to her advantage, if she moved quickly.

She put the four sacks next to each other on the ground. Then she checked the other saddlebag. It was empty.

The dead biker wore a leather jacket. He wasn't going to miss it. His ashen-faced, blank-eyed stare looked somehow shocked at his own condition.

Liz started working the jacket off the inflexible body. That's why they call it a *stiff*, she thought. That's what Arty will be like in a couple of hours.

At that moment a jolt of regret and a little fear zinged through her. The jolt had a voice, and the voice said, Give this up. Don't do this thing. Go back and call the police and tell them everything that happened. It was an accident, see, and this elaborate plan you're coming up with has too many holes in it, don't do this thing . . .

"Shut up," she said out loud. That surprised her. What did she think she was doing? Responding to some real voice? *No, pack it away. Put aside any idea that you're guilty here of anything. You are not. You deserve this.*

But Arty didn't deserve what *he* got. He was a good guy, deep down. *He didn't know what he was getting when he proposed to you. You played him, offered your body at just the right time, withheld it after that until he was mad to have you.*

But Arty had brought this whole thing on himself. He should not have changed. He shouldn't have traded in what made him a man and a success. People like that didn't survive in this world. They ended up like this biker—and Arty.

She flipped the biker onto his stomach and got the other sleeve off.

From there it was no problem to pack the sacks in the jacket.

She began to feel better. No voice now, oh, maybe just a whisper, but it was overtaken by a sense of—what was it?—flow. Being carried along on a wave but also causing that wave. Surfing on an ocean of her own making.

Her mind was buzzing and alive.

Wait . . . Fingerprints.

That thought brought her up short. All that *CSI* stuff. She knew what she'd touched. She took some dirt in her hands and spit on it. She had a red bandana in her back pocket. She spread the mud around on the saddlebags, especially the metal parts, and wiped those places down.

Footprints.

It was mostly rock around here, just a little dirt where the body was. No problem there. She used the jewel-stuffed jacket to smooth over the prints her hiking boots made and backed away onto rock again.

She laughed. She was going to get away with it. At least the carrying-off part. That much was a high. The best she'd felt in years.

Control was intoxicating. Bring it on, more and more.

And keep moving.

Because somebody may happen along and spoil everything.

• • •

"He did *what?*"

"Keep your eyes on the road, Geena. Last thing I need today is an accident."

Rocky and Geena were heading into Silver Lake, Geena driving.

"Well then, *tell* me," Geena said.

"Let's wait until—"

"He set your clothes on fire? And you want me to wait? Here's a red light."

Geena stopped. The white dome of the Angelus Temple was just to the right. Rocky remembered something about it. Some woman evangelist had set it up in the 1920s, and here it still was.

"Smashed my car window, too," Rocky said. "I'll leave it there for

Exhibit A." She'd call in a report later. Now she just wanted to be away from the place, away from the vicinity of Boyd Martin.

The one thing he didn't get was her kit from the trunk. Her tools of the trade, which included a mini tape recorder, camera, binoculars, lock-pick set, and her nanocam in sunglasses. Her secret weapon. She could do so much with those, and they actually looked good on her.

Also, her laptop from the apartment. With these things, at least, she was still in business.

Geena said nothing. Rocky was looking straight ahead but she could see, from the corner of her eye, the unmistakable dropping of the jaw.

"I don't *believe* this," Geena said.

"If you'll just relax," Rocky said, "I'll go over the whole thing in gory detail. Let's go to Franco's." The bar near the freeway.

The light turned green, but Geena didn't move the car. "What if we go see Swami T instead?"

"If you mention any more swamis, I swear—"

The angry blare of a car horn cut her off. Geena gunned through the intersection.

Rocky held on for dear life.

• • •

Liz thought she must have gone at least a football field away from the dead biker. She came to a grove of knotty oak trees, the kind that used to be all over this end of the valley until they started mowing them down for houses.

But the Packers—what Pack Canyon residents liked to call themselves, Liz found out, and without any apology to Green Bay—put up a major stink when developers started getting too close. They won battle after zoning battle, and Liz could kiss them because this was all land she could use now.

There were lots of places to choose from, including a little creek bed. Here the water trickled by through a long trough of weeds.

No, too mushy. She needed something with more cover.

Maybe she'd have to dig a hole.

Just get this over with. Somebody was going to find Arty, and she'd have to cook up some story about why she wasn't with him. Shouldn't be too hard, but who needed the trouble?

Trouble is for losers, her mother had told her. Trouble was something you didn't need to keep. There was always a way out of trouble, and money was usually the quickest way. If you had plenty of it, you might not be able to keep trouble from kicking you, but you could make sure the foot didn't stay in where the sun don't shine.

Speaking of where the sun don't shine, there it was. The spot. An actual hole in the hill. More of a bowl-shaped impression, like a dent on a car door.

But it was almost the exact size of the bundle she held, and there was plenty of dry stuff to put over it.

The location was perfect, too. This was not a place people would come by casually. It was not on any trail and there was nothing to draw foot traffic. She didn't even give it a second thought. This was the spot.

In ten minutes the stuff was hidden. She took a step back and made sure she could identify the place. Like in that movie with Morgan Freeman, where he gets out of prison and finds a rock the other prisoner had put money under.

Then it was time to move to the next part of the whole plan. It was unfolding to her, step by step.

•••

The muted light of Franco's Bar & Grill was just what Rocky needed. No one could see her face clearly when the lights were low.

In the booth, Geena said, "You really do need to see Swami T."

"Oh please," Rocky said.

"Really."

"Is Swami T any relation to Mr. T?"

"Now you're being silly."

"I think it's silly to pay a guy two hundred bucks to listen to him talk like Apu Nahasapeemapetilon."

"Who?"

"You know, the guy that owns the Quickie Mart on *The Simpsons.*"

"You are so Western. So either-or. *Resistant.* That's the word."

"Geena, the guy is bilking you and everybody else. He's sitting around in a lotus position, spouting clichés the way Paris Hilton spews text messages. You really believe what some twenty-year-old says about the universe?"

"He was enlightened from a very young age."

"That claptrap on his website? Who verifies those things?"

"You have to have faith. If you want to be enlightened you—"

"Babe, my ex-boyfriend smashed my car and set fire to my clothes. I got enough enlightenment to last me a long time. I see things. Maybe that's my problem."

A young server, a model boy wanting Hollywood stardom, came to the table. He smiled perfectly white piano keys at them and asked what they'd like to drink.

Rocky watched Geena flash her pearlies right back at him. Never one to turn away from a flirtatious smile, Geena. Got her into a boat-load of trouble that she never seemed to learn from. Not even Swami T could educate her. Fat lot of good he must be. If there was a swami union, Rocky would report him.

Geena ordered a microbrew of some kind. Rocky opened her mouth with the word *Cuervo* poised on her tongue. She rolled it around a second, then thought of Boyd and his alcohol-stale breath and swollen eyes.

"A 7UP," Rocky said.

Model boy said he'd be right back.

"We'll be right here," Geena said.

"Smooth," Rocky said. "You learn that from Swami Whatsisname?"

"You need some of his wisdom now," Geena said.

Rocky looked at her and wondered how they'd become such good friends in the first place. Geena Melinda Carter, blond and blue-eyed, as if yanked from the beach at Santa Monica. In fact, she was from Providence, Rhode Island.

And Roxanne Julie Towne, red of hair, much to her mother's chagrin. Mom loved Julie Christie in *Doctor Zhivago* and gave her daughter that middle name probably in the hopes that her hair would become golden. In fact, it was like bricks. So was her personality, Rocky was often told.

Another thing: Julie Christie never had the left side of her face mauled by a dog. Never had deep blue scars embedded in her skin. Never drew the stares of little kids wondering why half her face looked stapled.

"Thing is," Rocky said, "I would love it if one of these guys just once had the bead on something, you know?"

"But you've got to give it a chance. You never do."

"How much of a chance?"

The server came back with the beer and 7UP on a round tray. He placed a couple of square white napkins on the table, then the drinks on the napkins. "Can I bring you anything off the menu?" he said.

"Are you on the menu?" Geena said.

The Ken doll-look-alike blinked. "Not at the moment. Can I tell you about our specials?"

"That's okay," Geena said. "You can come back later."

The server smiled weakly, then walked away.

"Gay," Geena said. "Wouldn't you know it? Aren't there any straight guys left in this stupid town?"

"I know of one," Rocky said. "One I'd like to forget." She took a sip of her bubbly. "Now good, old reliable 7UP. You know what you're going to get. With men it's a crapshoot. You don't know what you're getting with men or swamis named T or even Jesus Christ himself."

"I like Jesus," Geena said.

"Yeah, you and my brother both."

"Arty? I thought he was all skeptical."

Rocky knocked back more sugar water, then said, "He was. He got religion. Spun his head right around."

"I don't think Jesus is supposed to do that," Geena said.

"Do what?"

"Spin your head around." Geena giggled. "Like in that movie about the devil."

"The Exorcist."

"That's the one. Eww."

"You know what I mean," Rocky said. "I'm happy for him and all, but I just don't want him to be getting scammed. There's lots of ways the church can get money out of you if they scream *Jesus* enough."

"Is there anything you actually believe in?"

Rocky smiled. She held her half-filled glass up to the bar lights. Reds and yellows refracted through the glass. For a second it looked beautiful and fresh and clean. It made her think of fulfilled promises, like the time she was seven and her dad said they would all go to Magic Mountain and they did. At night, the colors were magic indeed, because they were all together in one place, happy. The last time she could remember them being happy.

Before that dog mauled her face. Before her father stopped looking at her with dancing eyes, like he once had.

When she thought of that—thought of her *after* Dad—the colors in the glass changed, too. They became ordinary and dull. Nothing but old bar lights hitting soda. She thought that unless something changed, and soon, these would be the kind of colors she would see from now on. No more promises, no more magic.

"Hey," Geena said. "You all right?"

Rocky lowered the glass and put her head on her left hand and her left elbow on the tabletop.

"You left us there for a second," Geena said. "Where'd you go?"

"To the center of the universe," Rocky said. "The seat of all knowing. The power of the third eye. The secret of existence."

"Oh yeah? And that is?"

"Friends don't let friends go nuts," she said. And found, to her surprise, that she was crying.

"Hey, hey," Geena said. "What is it?"

• • •

Perfect.

It had all gone down without a single hitch. The sun was heading for the hills in the west and Liz had still seen no one.

Arty's little canyon was perfect, the jewels' hiding place was perfect, and now there was one last item to make this ... what? The perfect crime?

No, she hadn't committed anything. Arty's death was not premeditated. And he'd brought it on himself, really. He'd gone off the deep end even though he knew she was not one to boss around.

He'd contributed to his death by forgetting that.

Liz was back near Arty's body now. She couldn't look at him. If she did, she thought she might throw up. She couldn't afford that.

She had to concentrate. She was so close.

One more thing to do.

She got on her hands and knees.

Make this a good one, she told herself. One time only, a little bit of pain, then all the rest gain. The old Arty would have understood. He would even have gone along because there was maybe a million, maybe more, at stake. Tax free.

Yes, the old Arty would have understood, though maybe not completely. Nobody could figure her out completely, and that was the way she knew it had to be. Ever since Jackson, ever since the night Miller Jones had tried to touch her.

Make this good, she repeated to her herself, then slammed her head into the rock.

• • •

"Mac, you home?"

Mac blinked awake. He must have dozed off for a few minutes there.

"Mac?"

It was Pastor Jon.

"Come on in," Mac said. He felt like it would take him ten minutes to get out of his chair.

His pastor came in, dressed in off-Sunday casual. Today it was black jeans and a Boston College sweatshirt. Pastor Jon was a fifty-three-year-old African-American who tossed away a pro baseball career to go to seminary. He was the same height as Mac, six foot two, and they matched shoulders pretty much. But Jon still looked like he could stretch a double into a triple. Mac's head and leg wounds were better fitted for strolling through a garden.

"I saw that water spot in the ceiling," Pastor Jon said, "and with the rains coming, I—you okay?"

"Just one of my things," Mac said.

"Has it passed?"

"Pretty much." Mac started to stand up. Pastor Jon gently pushed him back to the chair. "You just hang on there, take it easy. Can I get you something?"

"Not anymore," Mac said. "My PO came by."

"Again? What's with him?"

"Hell if I—I mean, I don't know. Sorry. Man! What a mouth I've still got."

"My friend," Pastor Jon said, "give yourself some time."

"I don't have time." Mac shot to his feet. "I've got to get better. I can't mess up anymore. If I mess up, I go back. Slezak wants me to go back. I'll never see my daughter again."

"Easy," Pastor Jon said.

"I've been trying to get hold of Arty. He's not answering his phone."

"He was going hiking today."

"What?"

"I talked to him this morning. He said he and his wife were going out to the canyon."

"Would have thought he'd take his phone," Mac said.

"I can get somebody else to look at the ceiling."

"No, I'll do it."

"You don't have to—"

"I do have to," Mac said. "It's my end of the bargain."

"Mac—"

"I need to keep my word. It's something I have to start doing again."

"Don't try to be Cool Papa Bell."

Mac looked at him. "You want to tell me what you're talking about?"

"Cool Papa Bell, he was one of the great players in the old Negro Leagues. Fastest man in baseball. Satchel Paige said Cool Papa could turn the lights out and be in bed before the room got dark."

"Okay . . ."

"So growing in grace isn't like Cool Papa Bell going to bed. Takes time. Don't try and get it all at once."

"Then how about I try to stretch a single into a double?" Mac said.

3:36 p.m.

Ted Gillespie did not like being fat. Hated it, in fact. Hated the thirty-pound bag of lard that was his stomach, that he carried around with him like a toddler in a Snugli. Fat, creeping up on him for a decade, adding to itself like landfill.

The day he turned forty, a month ago, brought the hatred home, home being the little apartment in the old building at the edge of Topanga. It was the only thing he could afford. It had been eight months since he'd been canned from the insurance company, which was now outsourcing all of its IT.

Some birthday. No wife, no family, no job.

And when he stepped out of the shower that morning he got a good look at his gut in the mirror and it was an alive thing. An alien had found its host in his puffy body.

A body that, many moons ago, played a pretty mean first base for Pierce, the local community college, which was the full extent of his education.

He wondered what his life would have been like if he had married Nora. Why hadn't he? She was willing. She was smart and selfless and great around people.

So what was it?

He knew. He thought he could do better in the looks department. He thought a woman with a "Hollywood face," complete with blond locks—Nora's hair was raven—was what he wanted, what he could land if he waited around long enough.

That plan didn't exactly work out. Ted eventually gave up his gym membership and poured himself into his professional life, put on the pounds, and tried serial dating.

Then he stepped out of that shower on his fortieth birthday to realize that he wasn't the pretty good-looking athlete of twenty years ago, but an out-of-work, out-of-money IT guy.

But it was the fat that got to him the most.

Which is why Ted Gillespie was walking vigorously through the late afternoon in Pack Canyon's back country, trying to work up a good sweat.

He wore a green double-X T-shirt with Chuck Norris on the front. It showed Chuck in a Ranger's hat and the caption said, "Only Chuck Norris can prevent forest fires."

Ted loved Chuck Norris. Loved the *Walker, Texas Ranger* series. There was a guy who was in shape and could kick the living snot out of bad guys. If he could be anyone in another life, Ted would pick Chuck Norris.

Because Chuck Norris is so fast he can run around the world and hit himself in the back of the head. Chuck Norris can slam a revolving door. Chuck Norris can ...

Ted stopped. Thought he heard something. A distant voice, somebody calling.

He was at a turning point on the path, about to go around some of the larger boulders. Somebody had sprayed an ugly graffito on the face. Black paint, indecipherable letters.

If Chuck Norris ever found that guy ...

"Help ..."

A voice, all right. A real cry.

Ted started to jog. The voice was coming from around the bend.

When he got to the other side, he saw a woman. She was on the path about fifty yards from him. She had a gash on her head and walked like she was drunk.

"Help me," she said. "Please!"

3:38 p.m.

"What do I do now, Geena?"

Geena looked at Rocky in amazement. "You're asking *me*?"

"Surprised?" Rocky leaned back on the futon in Geena's apartment.

"Well, yeah, sort of." Geena sat on the ottoman which, like the rest of the place, was done up in Indian folk-art colors. "I mean, you're always Miss I-Know-Everything-That's-Going-On."

"Well, right now I know squat. I know less than squat. I could go on *Jeopardy!* with squat and lose."

Geena laughed, putting her hand in front of her mouth.

"So tell me, if Swami P is so — "

"T."

"What?"

"It's Swami T."

"I don't care! If you have any answers, give. Be brutally honest with me."

Geena blinked a couple of times. "Oh Rock, I can't."

"Why not?"

"I don't know. I'm embarrassed."

"All right," Rocky said. "I'll be you. Listen to yourself. 'Rocky, you've gone off the rails. You drink too much, and you settle for guys like Boyd. You never try to sing like you want to. You're afraid ...'"

Fresh tears choked off her words.

Geena slid off the ottoman, got on her knees, and put her arms around Rocky. "That's what we'll do," Geena said. "We're gonna get you singing again. Who needs a man when you've got a voice like an angel?"

"Come on ..."

"No. This I insist on. You've got to go for it."

"Geena — "

"If you don't, then I'm going to start singing. Around you. All the time. And you've heard me sing. It's not pretty. It's not even cute."

Rocky smiled, wiped her eyes. "You've got a point there, Geena."

"And you thought Swami T didn't give me any insight. Now, what's the place you wanted to sing in?"

"Huh?"

"There was a place you told me about once, in Hollywood, a lounge place. It had something to do with food. Potatoes or something."

"The Mashed Potato?"

"That's it! That's the place. You were going to audition there."

"Yeah. They have open auditions. I just got busy."

"You're not busy now. Call them."

"Geena—"

"Now. Swami T says you have to take action right away when you want something. It gets the universal ball rolling. So get your phone and—"

"Geena—"

"Or I will."

Rocky got her phone.

3:41 p.m.

"You're hurt," Ted said. "Here, sit." He took her arm and guided her to a patch of weeds. His mind calculated all sorts of things as he did this.

I am helping somebody, he thought, really helping somebody. How long had it been since he could say that? But this was more than getting somebody's desktop to function again. More than installing some new system across a network.

This was someone in physical trouble, out in the wild. If you could consider the back of Pack Canyon wild. It was where they used to shoot Westerns in the old black-and-white TV days. Ted knew that much.

Cowboys rescued ladies in distress on television shows. He was doing it for real.

What a moment this was. And the woman was nice looking. What had happened here? I wonder if I'll see her again after this, he thought.

I have to show her I know what to do here. Take command of the situation.

"I'm calling for help," Ted said, whipping out his cell.

"My husband …"

Husband! Ted squeezed the phone. *Just my luck. The good ones are always taken. All right, you're still here, impress her anyway.* "What about your husband?" Ted said.

"Down … there." She waved her hand. "I think he's dead."

A chill ran the length of Ted's sweaty body. Now this was serious. No more thinking about her and you or any other absurd fantasy of being some cowboy.

Take command.

"Wait here," he said, surprised and pleased with his authoritative tone. His father used to tell him you had to lead, follow, or get out of the way. Ted had spent most of his career doing the last two. When he tried to lead, it ended in disaster. He was not a lead dog.

Right now he was.

He walked toward where she had pointed. As he did, he punched 911. He told dispatch, in a firm but calm voice—he was in control now, all would be well—where they were and that someone was injured and possibly dead.

Finishing the call, he found himself looking down a steep dropoff at the still body below.

He paused and thought about waiting for help to arrive. But he had come this far. He was at least doing something. This time he wasn't going to blow it. "Fat, fired, and forty" was not going to be his epitaph.

Edging down the rocks slowly, almost stumbling once, Ted kept eyeing the body for movement. Nothing. The poor guy had to be dead. The woman's husband. Tragic. He was participating in a real, honest-to-goodness tragedy here.

At least it was out of the ordinary. That alone made this an experience worth having. He felt alive in a strange and exhilarating way.

The blonde woman with the head gash was so vulnerable. If he could find a way to comfort her …

He didn't get too close to the body. This was a crime scene. He'd seen enough TV to know you don't mess with a crime scene. You don't touch anything. You don't want the cops chewing your rear because you blundered all over the evidence. He did look for a sign of breathing or movement. There was none. The sun had baked the blood around the man's head into a dark gel.

He backed away, almost retracing his exact steps. Started up the hill.

She'll need me, he thought. She'll need someone to tell her everything will work out, to just stay calm.

He was glad he'd dropped three pounds over the last two months. What he lacked, he always knew, was motivation. She could be his motivation.

He couldn't help himself. He didn't want to think of her the way he was thinking of her, not yet anyway, but he just couldn't help himself.

She wasn't exactly beautiful, not in a movie-star way, but she had this kind of hot quality that just poured out of her. Even with that ugly gash on her head. Maybe because of it.

"They'll be here soon, I know it," Ted said.

The girl said nothing, just nodded. Her eyes looked dazed.

They both sat on the ground, the sun dropping fast now. It would be dusk soon, then dark. Ted pictured them sitting by a fire all through the night. Maybe she'd put her head on his chest and he'd hold her and comfort her.

"Can you tell me your name?" he asked.

She looked at him. Her eyes were blue, like a Kansas sky. "Liz," she said.

"I'm Ted," he said. "Ted Gillespie. I'll stay right with you until they come."

"My husband …" She left a lilt on the end, like she was asking a question.

"I'm afraid that ..." How do you break this kind of news?

"Afraid what? Tell me."

"I'm so sorry."

"Tell me!"

"You've got to be strong," he said. This is just what Walker, Texas Ranger, would have told her. "Your husband, he's ..." He found he couldn't complete the thought.

But the expression on her face told him he didn't have to.

"And now we've got to take care of you," Ted said. "Got to make sure you get better."

She said nothing. Looked like she was in shock.

Now what? Where was the script? Ted felt like a crab out of water, clacking blindly around the deck. Maybe if he kept talking—

"I just happened to be walking, see, and maybe it's one of those things that's meant to be. For me to get you help. I don't know how things happen or why things happen," — *If there's a God, help me now!* — "but things do happen, and there's a reason. I'm just glad to be here to help."

She still said nothing. She was holding her knees now and resting her head on top of them.

"I'm a computer guy," he said. "Used to work for AIG, Blue Cross, some other big companies. I'm on my own now. Always wanted to start up my own consulting group. You?"

He felt stupid trying to draw her out like this. But he had to do something. Sitting in silence wasn't acceptable. Whenever he did that, he had the feeling people were watching him, judging him.

"I can't talk now," she said.

Idiot! "That's okay. That's really okay. I didn't mean—"

"I know. Thank you. Just thank you for being here."

So silence it was, but he didn't feel judged at all. She was grateful.

He was grateful, too. There *was* a God.

● ● ●

Why wasn't Arty answering or returning her calls?

Rocky snapped her phone shut and breathed a small curse. She needed money, and Arty had always been good for a loan, because she always paid him back. She always managed to find more work. She always scraped by.

Sure, there were plenty of lean times. Like now. The past year had been the worst so far. But Arty was always there to help. Even though they hadn't been as close in recent years, Arty was the rock of the family.

Older by two years, Arty had been her protector when they were kids. If he ever heard anybody making fun of her face, he went after the kid like the Tasmanian Devil in those cartoons.

It didn't matter if the kid was older. She remembered when one eighth grader, a big kid who played on the flag football team at Arty's school, called her "freak face." It was summer and she and Arty were walking back from the park. Arty was teaching her how to play softball. She must have been ten at the time.

It was a hot day, and they stopped at the 7-Eleven. Arty bought them both Slurpees. As they were walking out, the big kid came in with a skinny friend and almost bumped into them.

The big kid said, "Watch it," and then threw in a word Rocky thought only applied to a mean woman. But the kid had called Arty that.

Arty said, "You watch it."

The big kid looked down and sneered, then looked at Rocky. "You and freak face better get out of here," he said.

At which point Arty shoved his Slurpee into the kid's face. Before the kid could even sputter, Arty was all over him, getting him in a headlock, pulling him to the ground, pummeling him with both hands.

The skinny kid just stood there, like he was watching two dogs fight and was afraid to get bit.

The man behind the counter shouted something that sounded like, "You stop that!" and ran around to pull Arty off. Arty wouldn't be pulled. He kept the fists flying. Another man, who had been browsing the magazine rack, came over to help. The two men finally subdued Arty.

The big kid was crying. "You're dead!" he said through sobs.

But Rocky couldn't remember ever seeing the kid again.

She did remember Arty walking her home and not saying anything about it, except that the kid shouldn't have told him to watch it. What he didn't say but that she knew to be true, was that he had done it for her.

She wished they'd been closer these last few years, but there was that woman in the way. The one he was blind about.

Liz. Elizabeth. Little Southern Belle. The way she'd squeak her voice, as if she could twist any man around her little finger. It drove Rocky crazy.

Liz, the woman who had come between her and Arty.

Jealousy was probably a factor, too. Rocky hated to admit it, but she felt it and it was strong.

Geena came back in with hot tea. "You know what I feel like?" she asked.

Rocky said, "Tell me."

"I feel lucky."

"Lucky?"

"Yes."

"As in going out and buying lottery tickets?"

Geena looked dead serious. "Aligned with the right spheres," she said. "And if you stick close to me, it could rub off. We'll go to the Mashed Potato, and you'll get lucky."

Rocky picked up a teacup. "You want to my philosophy of luck? It's all random. Arbitrary. It's like Darwin said."

"The evolution guy?"

"It's all a roll of the dice," Rocky said. "Mutations happen by pure chance. You get dealt a hand, and you can't draw any more cards."

"But we have the power to change our lives," Geena said. "Through visualization and—"

"You think visualization changes anything? You think the woman on the freeway who gets taken out by a drunk driver could have changed that by putting a different picture in her mind?"

Geena said nothing.

Rocky shook her head. "Random," she said and raised her cup. "Cheers."

5:17 p.m.

"Are you feeling well enough to give us a statement?" the young deputy sheriff asked. He was tall and lanky. His uniform hung loose on his frame.

"I don't know," Liz said. She held her head, now with a large bandage on it. The medics were just pulling out of the small lot at the entrance to Pack Park. They had her sitting on a hard bench, and her head was absolutely splitting.

She really didn't know if she could talk.

But she was glad this guy, this hiker, happened along. A lucky break, really. He would make a nice witness to her distress. He seemed just the sort of guy you'd want at a time like this.

He was a bit pudgy, hair thinning, didn't have a wedding band. He wasn't going to be dating any models. And judging from the way he talked, a little too eager to please. He was definitely of the malleable variety of male. A doofus.

Liz knew all about that kind. When she'd first arrived in LA, she found one early on. Went hunting for just the right one and found the hunting grounds—Beverly Hills, to be exact—teeming with possibilities.

Her head really hurt, though. The things you have to do.

The doofus—What was his name? Ted?—talked in the way doofuses do. A little too fast, a little too much. She filed that information away. Maybe he'd do other things for her.

"Maybe you should talk to her tomorrow," Ted said to the deputy. He had refused to leave her side. Liz got the impression the deputy was annoyed.

"If I can just get a few facts out of the way," the deputy said. Liz thought he looked a little like Christian Bale. Not bad.

"I don't think—" Ted started to say.

"It's all right," Liz said. "Let's just get it over with."

The deputy had a clipboard box with a form on top and was ready to write. There was ample illumination from a light post near the bench.

"Can you just tell me, briefly, what happened to you and your husband?" he asked.

"We were hiking," Liz said. "And we fell. Really, I was falling and Arty tried to . . ." Liz put a sob in her throat.

"Just take your time, ma'am."

Ma'am? She didn't like being called that. Not one bit. *Ma'am* was what you called the old frump in the checkout line, rifling through her coupons.

"How did you fall?" the deputy asked.

"I don't know. I wasn't watching where I was going. I was being kind of reckless. I don't know why. I was just happy to be outside on a hike with my husband. He was always so serious about things. Always so serious . . ."

She choked her words off again.

"Is this necessary?" Ted said.

"Please, sir," the deputy said. "If she doesn't want to go on—"

"No," Liz said. "I have to. For Arty. You have to know what kind of man he was. I slipped over the edge and he reached for me. I reached for him and grabbed his shirt. But he wasn't balanced, I guess, and he went down. Over me."

She cleared her throat.

"You're doing good," Ted said.

Liz nodded. "I went after him. I hit my head and blacked out, I guess. Oh Arty!"

She put her head in her hands.

"Let me," Ted said. "Take my statement now."

The deputy paused, nodded.

"I was hiking along and enjoying myself when I heard this woman, Ms. Towne, call for help. I saw her on the trail and saw she was hurt and called 911. I had her sit and wait and went to see about the guy. I climbed down and saw he was dead. I just can't tell you how strong she's trying to be."

"I can see that," the deputy said.

"I want to be with Arty," Liz said. "We can't leave him there."

"No, ma'am. They're sending a team to get him. We'll take it from here."

Liz jumped up from the bench and started walking back toward the hills.

"Ma'am?" the deputy said.

Liz cried, "Arty!"

6:42 p.m.

Mac thought he'd take a chance and catch Arty at home. He had left three voice mails but still wasn't getting a call back.

Maybe there was something wrong with the phone.

Or maybe there was something wrong at the house.

It was no secret to anyone at church that Arty's wife was not exactly down with his Christianity. She'd shown up with him at a couple of Sunday afternoon potlucks and was nice enough. But she was obviously strained.

He tried to talk to her once over a piece of Mrs. Axelrod's lemon cake. His impression was that she didn't want anybody to get too close to her. He thought at the time she might just be shy.

But according to Arty, it wasn't shyness at all. She had a resistance, Arty called it, and he asked Mac to pray for her.

He prayed for her now, as he drove his pickup around the curves of Circle Road, passing the little white church on his right.

He thought about the first time he met Arty.

Mac and Pastor Jon were fixing a flooded bathroom on a hot afternoon. It was a Saturday, and the place needed cleanup before the service the following morning. They'd rented a snake and were cleaning out some mean things in the depths of the porcelain abyss.

"Does this mess remind you of anything?" Pastor Jon had asked.

Mac laughed. "My past life?"

"Exactly," Jon said. "How ugly sin is, and how Jesus cleans us out. But not like this. Not on hands and knees with a lot of hard work. With Jesus, it's instantaneous."

Jon liked to use everyday events and items in his sermon illustrations. Mac figured he was trying a new one out.

"The Bible says God looks at us as righteous when he sees us through Jesus," Jon said. "The fancy name for it is *imputed righteousness*. It's like an accounting. The books are cleared when you're in Christ."

Mac picked up a crescent wrench. "How about this?" he said. "Can you make up a Bible illustration with a crescent wrench?"

"The love of God grips you," Jon said. "And turns you around."

"Man, you're quick," Mac said. "Were you this quick when you were playing ball?"

Jon was about to answer when they heard a knock.

There was a guy standing at the open door, and he said, "Is there a minister around?"

That was how Mac first got to know Arty Towne.

Later, Mac would realize Jesus *had* performed a miracle in that bathroom. Only it had nothing to do with a backed-up toilet.

It had to do with regenerating another sinner.

Turned out Arty Towne was a guy full of questions. What good is religion when there's so much suffering? Why did Jesus have to die? How can we know the Bible is true? Why are there so many nutty Christians?

He also talked about making money. He made a lot of it, but in some kind of way he was starting to question. He wasn't specific about it, but it was there just the same.

Pastor Jon let him ask all he wanted, and the three of them sat inside the church for four hours, talking, reading the Bible.

A little after five, Arty Towne received Christ in the Pack Canyon Community Church.

Since then, Arty and Mac had become close. An unlikely pair. Arthur Towne, with a university education and a great job and a wife. And Daniel Patrick MacDonald, high-school dropout, wounded vet, ex-con.

The only thing they shared was a Savior, but that was enough to start. Along the way, they found they both loved good Mexican food and the Los Angeles Dodgers. Mac told Arty that while he was in the joint, listening to the voice of Vin Scully on the radio on hot summer evenings kept him sane.

Arty told Mac that radio sportscaster Vin Scully's voice was etched like audio gold into his childhood memories, because of the '88 Kirk Gibson homer in Game One of the World Series. They laughed and reminisced about that. They'd both seen that game on TV.

Gibson, limping to the plate, barely able to move, Dodgers down a run in the bottom of the ninth. Eckersley on the mound. The most feared reliever in baseball. Two outs, a man on. Gibson fights the count to three and two.

And then the shot heard round the world.

Mac remembered Scully saying, *In a year that has been so improbable, the impossible has happened.* For a time after that, Mac thought everything in his life would be okay. If the Dodgers could beat the A's and Eckersley in the ninth, an out-of-whack vet could get his act together against the curves and sliders life was throwing at him.

Arty told Mac he remembered those words from Scully, too, and that they made him want to go out and conquer the world. Made him think anything was possible if you believed enough.

Their friendship was forged out of Jesus, baseball, and good eats. How could you get more American than that? Mac thought it made perfect sense. The amazing part for Mac was that Arty turned to *him* for Bible teaching. In the three months since Arty became a Christian, they'd been through almost the whole New Testament together.

The lights were out at Arty's place when Mac pulled into the driveway. There were no streetlights in this part of the canyon. The night seemed extra dark. LA haze in the sky obscured the stars. He went to the door and knocked.

No answer.

Sure. They could be anywhere. Movie. Dinner.

But for some reason, Mac didn't think so.

For some reason, he thought somebody was in trouble.

Headlights broke through the darkness.

● ● ●

Who is that? Rocky thought. And why is he standing in front of Arty's house?

She checked the number. 871. And she knew it was Feather Lane—a street name she always found strange. But this was Pack Canyon. They did things differently here, and she didn't much like it.

A few weeks ago, there'd been a shooting. The *Daily News* ran it on the front page. A biker shot another biker at a biker bar. It was Wild West time.

The guy looked like trouble, whoever he was. Broad shoulders and a hard expression as he squinted into the lights.

She thought about backing up and driving away. She didn't like Pack Canyon. She thought maybe she'd come back another time. But she had come all this way, and it was just one guy, and maybe he was a friend of Arty's or something.

If she needed to give him a swift kick, she would.

She stopped the car but kept the engine idling. She got out and stood behind the door.

"Is Arty home?" she said.

The guy started down the steps. He wore blue jeans, a white T-shirt, and black jacket. He wasn't bad looking, either. But then, neither was Boyd. *Just get that thought out of your mind right now, Roxanne, you idiot.*

"No," the guy said. "I've been trying to reach him."

She felt better when he said that. His voice was at least friendly. Still, she was ready to jump in the car and gun it if she had to.

"You're a friend of Arty's?" she asked.

"A good friend," he said. He was at the door now. "Daniel Mac-Donald. People call me Mac."

"Oh yeah, Arty mentioned you," Rocky said. "I'm his sister."

"Rocky? Glad to know you." He stuck out his hand. "I was wondering when we'd meet."

"Uh-huh." She shook his hand. "So any idea where he might be?"

"No," Mac said. "I've left a couple messages for him. Maybe he's out with Liz."

"Great."

"Nothing wrong with that, is there?"

"Nice meeting you," Rocky said. She started to get back in the car.

Mac said, "Don't you want to wait?"

"Maybe I'll come back in a while."

"I was thinking of grabbing a burrito, if you want to wait with somebody."

She was hungry, and a burrito sounded good. Any kind of Mexican food sounded good. But she only had two dollars on her. And she wasn't exactly ready to socialize with a stranger.

"Thanks anyway," she said.

He said, "Are you sure? It's about time we got to know each other. Arty's sister and his bud. Besides which, I'm buying."

She hesitated, another refusal on her tongue. But it stayed there. Arty's friend. Maybe he was right. Maybe it was time to get close to her brother again. This was a start.

Besides, she noticed her stomach was playing mariachi music. "You talked me into it."

7:03 p.m.

Liz made herself cry over her husband's body, even though it was in a zipped-up coroner's bag. She got the tears flowing as it was shoved into the back of a van, where it would be sent downtown.

So they said. They seemed as unconcerned about it as if it were a sack of laundry. She guessed that must be the way it is when you handle a lot of dead bodies. Just another day at the office.

Arty didn't deserve that. She'd grant him that much. It made it a little easier to cry.

They were still near the parking lot, she and this guy named Ted, and the detective from the LA County Sheriff's office. A woman named Moss. She wore a brown suit with a white blouse, and she had a six-point star on the left side of her belt. She was about forty-five years old. Wheat-colored hair with tight curls that looked like they did push-ups. She was throwing around a little too much authority to suit Liz.

"Once more, Mrs. Towne," Detective Moss said. "And this will be all for tonight."

"I hope so," Ted Gillespie said.

Moss turned to him. "I believe a deputy took your statement. Is that correct, Sir?"

"Yeah—"

"Then we'll be in touch. Thanks for all you've done."

"I'll stay."

"I'd prefer to speak with Mrs. Towne alone for just a moment, if you don't mind."

Ted glanced at Liz. He had a lost-puppy look. "But somebody needs to take her home," he said.

"I can drive," Liz said.

"We'll take care of it," Moss said. "Thanks again."

Ted shuffled his feet but didn't move in any direction. Then he said to Liz, "Can I check on you tomorrow?"

"No need," Liz said.

"But I want to."

"Thank you. I need a few days."

"Of course."

"Thank you, Mr. Gillespie." Moss gently pushed his arm and got him started off toward his car. He didn't move very fast. Like a dinghy against the current. Resistant.

"Good thing he came along when he did," Moss said.

"Yes, it was," Liz said.

"Now you were saying that as you were falling, you grabbed your husband's shirt?" Moss had a little notebook to jot things down in.

"That's right," Liz said. She didn't need to try to sound tired. She was. But she gave it an extra sigh anyway. She wanted to get home, be alone, regroup. Think things through. She had plans to make.

"And what, you went backward and your husband went over you?"

"Something like that."

Moss scribbled. "If you can just tell me, to the best of your recollection, how he fell."

"Why is this necessary?" Liz said. "He fell and died. Isn't that enough?"

"It's just so I can give a full report," Moss said.

"Can we finish this right now and be done with it?"

"Would you rather do this at your house?"

Liz shook her head. "Here is all I remember. I grabbed Arty by the shirt as he was reaching out for me. Then I felt myself go backward. Arty went right over me. Then I remember falling. And I hit my head, and I think I blacked out for a minute."

Moss nodded, wrote.

"When I came to, I saw Arty there, and he wasn't moving. I guess I knew he was dead, but I didn't want to give up. So I got back up the hill and started for the entrance."

Moss stopped. "You didn't have a cell phone with you?"

Cell phone. She'd forgotten all about it.

"No, no ..." Liz said. "Please, can I go home now?"

"You left your cell phone at home, or in the car?"

Liz rubbed the sides of her head. "I don't remember. We just didn't have it. We were hiking."

"Of course."

"I want to go now."

"Yes," Moss said. "There really shouldn't be any need for you to relive this further. I'm very sorry for your loss, Mrs. Towne."

The detective patted Liz's arm. Liz forced a smile and nodded. She walked slowly to her car. She felt like Moss was watching her as she did. Two eyes boring into her back. Or was it just the feeling that something was behind her? Trouble, gaining.

Keep moving.

7:38 p.m.

El Toro was a great little hole-in-the-wall Mexican place in Chatsworth. Mac had many a meal here with Arty. It was the most honest Mexican food in the valley, they agreed. Maybe the city, which was saying something.

He and Rocky got a table near the window looking out at Topanga Canyon Boulevard. That was another honest thing about the place. No pretenses on the view. You came for the food and watched the cars go by.

A waitress asked if they wanted something to drink, and Rocky looked at Mac as if asking permission.

"Have whatever you want," he said.

"I'll have a Corona and a shot of Cuervo," Rocky said.

Mac ordered a Coke.

The place was about three-quarters full. Traditional Mexican music played in the background, and the smell of hot tortilla chips mingled with the thick scent of steaming carnitas sizzling on a serving pan at the table next to them.

It was a smell Mac associated with friendship. He could see the family resemblance in Rocky. She had Arty-like lines in the face. Except for the scars.

He thought then that he deserved those scars more than she did.

"Arty says you're a singer," he said.

"That was nice of him," Rocky said. "Maybe when somebody actually pays me to sing, I will think so." She'd find out on Monday if that would happen. Under Geena's watchful eye, she'd called the Mashed Potato Lounge, and they said she could come in then. The thought of it made her stomach clench.

"He says you're great," Mac said.

"Diana Krall is a great singer," she said. "Keely Smith is a great singer."

"Keely who?"

Rocky sat up, the way someone does when a subject they love is the topic of conversation. "Keely Smith was married to Louis Prima. Big in the fifties and sixties. Did a lot of great songs with him. She was gone for a while but made a comeback. I love the way she can shape words."

"Shape words?"

"That's the art of it. Words make sounds. You can clank 'em or you can turn 'em into music."

"I never thought of it that way," Mac said. "I always used words like a club. To get my way."

"And now?"

He sat back in his chair. "In the interest of full disclosure, as they say, I'm on parole." He watched carefully to see what her expression would be. She didn't look shocked. He appreciated that.

"Want to know what I did time for?" Mac said.

"If you want to tell me," Rocky said.

"Robbery."

"And you paid your debt to society?"

"Not quite," he said. "Parole is sort of like a waiting period. I have to keep my nose clean and do what my parole officer tells me to do. I can't get into any trouble."

"Have you been in any trouble?"

"What's your definition of *trouble*?" Mac said.

"I got lots of definitions of —"

The waitress appeared with chips and salsa, a Coke, and a bottle of Corona with a lime wedge sticking out of the top. And a shot glass with tequila.

Mac watched as Rocky licked the webbing between her thumb and forefinger, then shook a little salt on it. She licked the salt, threw down the shot, then bit into the lime. She chased it with a swig of beer.

"You've done that before," Mac said.

"And you?"

"Tequila and I don't get along. I was in San Diego once, in a park. I had a full bottle. About sixty seconds later I remember it being half-empty. That's all I remember. Next day I woke up and I was in Mazatlan."

He took a sip of Coke and remembered the other time he had gone on a tequila ride, that one ending up worse. That one ending up with him in prison.

He didn't go into that. Instead, he told Rocky the story of meeting Arty at the church. He started to go into Arty's conversion but saw only a cold expression on her face.

"I'm sure Arty's told you all about that," Mac said.

"He tried once," Rocky said. "I stopped him."

"How come?"

She shrugged. "It's good for him, fine. I don't need to hear about it."

"Don't be too hard on him. He's got the *can't help its*."

"The whats?"

"Can't help its," Mac said. "Pastor Jon put it that way once. In the Bible, there's the book of Acts. It tells all about Christians right at the start. It was a Jewish thing at first, and the leaders in Jerusalem didn't like the story being told."

"No?"

"They took Peter and John in and told 'em, 'Look, dudes, no more preaching Jesus. Got that?' But they said, 'We have to obey God. We can't help preaching what we've seen and heard.' That's the *can't help its.*"

Rocky bit a corner off a tortilla chip. "I've got a friend who has that, only it's for a swami."

"Swami?"

"That's what he calls himself," she said, then leaned forward and whispered, "only I bet if you look real close, he's probably a former insurance salesman from Schenectady."

Mac laughed. It felt good. He realized he hadn't laughed in a long time.

He liked her. Maybe it was the fact that she wasn't putting up a false front. If you had scars deep enough outside or in, trying to fool people was stupid and useless. Scars made you honest, in a way. Forced truth on you.

Like the terms of a lifelong parole, he thought.

7:54 p.m.

Ted unlocked the door and slipped into his apartment.

He hated his apartment. It was near gang territory. At night he could hear the thumping of the cars as they played their music. He could hear the screams of drunken people. High people. Every now and then, he heard a gunshot.

This is your life. This is as good as it's going to get.

But then he thought of her. Liz. He pictured her in the apartment with him, telling him how much she appreciated what he had done for her.

He looked at the old chair with the frayed arms by his sliding glass door and saw her in it. She was dressed casually but provocatively. She was perfectly comfortable being in his presence. She was over the initial grief of losing her husband, and now she was ready to get on with her life.

And she was here. With him.

He would have cleaned the place up, of course. The two days of clothing he had piled by the TV would be long gone. He would have aired the place out and sprayed some freshener. And he would dust, naturally.

Oh yes, everything would be ready.

But then what? Would he even know what to do? What would be his next move?

Who was he kidding? *Dude, you're a computer geek.*

Yes, a geek who has been handed an opportunity. What are you going to do about it?

He peeled off his T-shirt, which was crusty with dried sweat. He threw it violently against the wall and watched it fall.

No. He wasn't going to let this opportunity slip away. Not this time.

Next step, next step.

That book. Where was that book? He went to his bedroom and opened the closet. He had several stacks of books in there because he hadn't gotten around to buying more bookcases. He got on his knees and searched the spines. All the diet books were in one spot, sports books in another. He passed over Michael Jordan's biography and a book on being a champion by Bruce Jenner.

Where was that one book, the one his mom had given him a couple of birthdays ago in an obvious attempt to get him out of the doldrums?

There it was. Blue cover. *How to Have Confidence.*

He grabbed it. Glad he'd remembered it. He hadn't read it yet, partly out of pride. No guy in his thirties wants his mom giving him self-help books. Especially not a mom who took most of his confidence away when he was in high school. Especially when he discovered Hendrix. He wanted to listen to Hendrix, and she said, "No Hendrix, no way. You'll get on drugs. Not as long as you live here will you listen to Hendrix."

So confidence had he none.

Ted took the book with him to the kitchen and opened the refrigerator. The half-empty jug of V8 was still there.

He took down a glass from the cupboard and poured himself some juice. Then he took the glass and the book to the chair where he'd imagined her being. He put the glass on the side table and sat in the chair and opened the book to the table of contents.

He scanned it and found the chapter heading "How to Create a Great Impression on Others."

Ted Gillespie took a long sip of V8 and turned to that chapter.

This was the start of a new life.

8:06 p.m.

He was right about the burrito. It was one of the best Rocky had ever had. A perfect blend of beef, beans, and spices. A tortilla wrap of fresh and precise consistency. A jazz ensemble of taste.

She started to relax a little. "You asked about my singing," she said. "So what are you into?"

He looked for a moment as if the question pained him, and she immediately wanted to take it back. She felt she might have opened a door he wanted to keep shut and that her intrusion breached an unspoken agreement between them.

But then he blinked and, with a sheepish smile, said, "Flowers."

"You're kidding."

"Why should I kid?"

"I just ... oops." She wanted to hide. Another breach! *Don't yap so much!*

"I know," he said. "Ex-cons and crocuses."

He was putting her at ease, ignoring her clumsiness. But the revelation was still surprising. "You plant crocuses?"

"You like gardening?"

"I want to like it," she said. "I haven't had much of a chance."

"I'm pretty new at it," he said.

"Why crocuses?"

"I just like saying it. *Crocus.* It sounds like a Roman emperor, doesn't it?"

She laughed. "Aren't those hard to grow out here?"

"I'm hardheaded," he said. "It's an early spring flower, and there's a shady part behind my shack. I'm hoping. I chilled the bulbs in the crisper of my refrigerator. I guess it'll be a miracle if they grow, huh?"

There was an innocence about the way he said it. A parolee who liked flowers. He was a mix of strength, hard edges, and a kind of raw transparency. The combo hit her like a wave crashing, threatening to knock her over.

Don't, she told herself. Do not start to feel.

She kept telling herself that through the rest of the meal. When they were finally finished, ready to go see Arty, she almost sang a song of relief.

8:53 p.m.

Alone, but not.

There was evidence of Arty everywhere. Even the place smelled like Arty, that Old Spice he used. Cologne and deodorant.

Liz hadn't counted on that one. To smell him.

Even to miss him a little.

She would have to get rid of all evidence of him, to keep from falling into carelessness. But not too soon. No, she'd have to play it right for the neighbors, for the law, for his friends.

She could play it frosty. She learned that from Mama. Oh, how she had learned from Mama.

She learned her history from Mama. They were survivor stock. Hardscrabble, not to be trifled with. Her grandfather, Gus Turner, from Arjay, Kentucky. A coal miner like his father before him.

He met Grandmother Carrie at a church social. Not that Gus was a churchgoing man. He decidedly wasn't, but he wanted to nab somebody "pure," Mama said, and show Carrie the way of the world.

Which he did, taking Carrie from her church and family and town and moving to Jackson, Mississippi, in 1954, the year Mama was born.

By then Gus had decided that working underground was only for those who wanted to die young. So he got into a new line, the pawn business.

Which was good to him. Helped him pay for booze.

The Turner women, Mama said, always seemed to draw the boozers. It was a genetic trait, she said, like blue eyes and the ability to do math.

The booze he paid for seemed to fuel his increasing rages over what he called the "tar baby problem." Mama didn't quite know what he meant, except that each night her daddy got to yelling at the TV news louder and louder.

He started to stay away nights. Carrie, who by this time was drinking as much as her husband, tended to just fall asleep. When Mama's daddy came home, he wouldn't say exactly where he'd been. But Mama got the idea he met with other men about the "problem."

Then one night he didn't come home at all.

Mama never did find out where he went. He could have died, for all she knew. But later she heard some talk in town and got the idea that her daddy had to go away.

Had to go away because a black man was shot in the back of the head while sitting in his car. A man who had been part of a boycott of local white merchants.

They never could prove Liz's granddaddy did it, but Mama said a gun went missing from the pawn shop and was never recovered.

Grandma Carrie was left to carry on the business. She did for a few years, but eventually her mind broke. That's the way Mama put it. Her mind *broke*. She was hospitalized one night, screaming about Satan trying to rip her clothes off and get to her.

That broken mind, like Humpty Dumpty, never got put back together again.

Mama was only seventeen when she took over the store. A couple of "smoothies" (she called them) tried to buy her out, but she refused. She was a Turner. Hardscrabble, and you didn't want to mess with them.

She would make it work.

And she did. She learned. She met the right people, though they were the wrong people to the law.

One of them, Old Dane Lowery, was what Mama called a "fence." Liz thought that was funny when she was little, but Old Dane got to be kind of a grandfather to her.

He was around a lot more than her real father, Lester Summerville.

Convicted rapist and local drunk, Lester Summerville.

"One thing," Mama used to say to Liz, after Lester had gone to prison and Liz asked about her father. "One thing I wish'd happened.

I might could have forgiven him everything, even that. I wish'd he'd've given me a ring. You know, a diamond ring. They're supposed to do that. Give you a ring. That brings good luck. I always wish I got me a ring. I got you though, and I'm glad of that."

A knock at the door, and Liz snapped back to the present. She almost wished she didn't have to be here. Wished she could go back and start all over and find somebody else, not Arty.

The knock again. Who could it be at this hour?

She stayed in the chair. Then another knock. And a voice. "Arty? You home?"

It was Arty's friend.

He knocked again. "Liz? You there?"

She had to answer. If he got snoopy and looked in a window, he'd see her. Or hear her moving around.

"Who's there?" she said.

"Hey, Liz. It's Mac. I'm with Rocky."

Rocky?

"Is Arty okay?" Mac said.

Liz got up and put herself in mind of all that had happened and all that was at stake. She reminded herself she had been here before. With Mama and the police. She had done it then, and she could do it now, and no one was going to guess what was really going on. No one would ever guess.

She smoothed her blouse and walked to the door, paused, rubbed her eyes hard, then opened it.

• • •

"Liz, what's wrong?" Mac said. He saw her red eyes, her face knotted in anguish. And the large bandage on her forehead.

"Arty!" Liz cried and fell into Mac's arms. She sobbed into his chest.

He held her, glancing at Rocky, who looked almost angry. He shook his head at her, slowly. To Liz he whispered, "What is it, now? You can tell me."

"It's horrible!" Liz's voice was muffled.

"Is he hurt?"

Liz's face came up from his chest, cheeks wet. "Dear God, Mac. He's dead."

For a long moment, no one moved. Then Rocky started pushing Liz away from Mac, gently but firmly.

"What happened?" Rocky demanded.

Mac saw fear in Liz's eyes.

"Easy," Mac said, putting his hand on Rocky's arm. "Liz, can you tell us?"

Liz fell to her knees, dissolving into tears.

"Where is he?" Rocky said.

Mac put his hand up to Rocky, silencing her. Then he knelt and helped Liz to her feet. She was shaking and seemed so small. He held her again, stroking her hair. "Liz, we have to know what happened. Where is he? Can you tell us?"

Still sobbing, Liz nodded.

"Please, do your best to tell us. Come on, let's sit down."

He helped her to the living room and into a chair, the news starting to sink in. Arty, dead? He swallowed hard. Both of the women in the room with him now seemed to be in shock. Liz for obvious reasons, Rocky out of some kind of frustration, or something else as yet unidentified.

Mac was now the one who had to comfort them. He uttered a silent prayer for wisdom.

"Get some Kleenex," Mac told Rocky. She went but seemed to be moving slowly. With attitude. Strange.

Liz whispered, "She doesn't like me."

"Let's talk about what happened to Arty."

"It was an accident," Liz said. "We were hiking. There's a place ... he fell." She stopped, taking in a labored breath. Her forehead furrowed, as if all the tension of the moment was focused there, seeking release.

"How long ago was this?" Mac said.

"This afternoon."

Rocky said, "I want to hear this." She was back in the room and put a box of tissues on the coffee table.

"Why don't you have a seat?" Mac said, hoping Rocky would get the message from his tone that she should sit down and shut up. She didn't sit.

"I fell, too," Liz said. "It was horrible."

"What happened exactly?" Mac said.

"Don't make me tell," Liz said. "Please. It was an accident. A man came along, he called 911. The police came, paramedics. I just got home a little while ago." Liz sat up and grabbed Mac's wrist. "What am I going to do, Mac? I'm all alone!"

"No, no, you have us," Mac said.

Rocky said nothing.

"We'll be right here to help you," Mac said.

Liz shook her head. "I can't believe it. I can't. It's a nightmare. I can't face it ..."

"All right, listen," Mac said, "let's get you to bed. You need to sleep—"

"I can't possibly ..."

"We're not finished yet," Rocky said. "Did the police question you?"

Mac turned on her, tossing fury from his eyes.

"No," Liz said. "It was a sheriff's detective."

"Pack Canyon would be a county matter," Mac said.

"You have the name of the detective?" Rocky asked.

"Let's just take it easy here," Mac said.

"Look, who are you anyway?" Rocky said. "You're not family. Who asked you to run things?"

"He *is* family," Liz said. "More than you."

"Arty's my *brother*," Rocky said.

"He's my *husband*!"

"Okay," Mac said. "This is hard right now. Liz, you need to rest. Have you got anything you can take?"

"Let's look," Rocky said.

Liz's eyes flashed. "You have no business going through my things!" She got up and ran from the room, slammed a door.

Mac looked at Rocky. She appeared about to say something. Her lips twitched.

"What about you?" Mac said. "You all right?"

Rocky shook her head.

"You need to get some rest, too," he said.

"There's something going on here," Rocky said.

"Rocky—"

"I'm going to find out what."

"Maybe you need to go home."

"You telling me what to do?"

"I'm just making a suggestion," Mac said.

"Keep your suggestions to yourself."

"Look, you don't have—"

She turned away from him.

Mac said, "I didn't mean to come on so hard. But until we find out what's happened, we need to be real easy around Liz. She's vulnerable."

"Oh yes," Rocky said, without facing him. "So, so vulnerable."

10:43 p.m.

No way he was going to get some sleep.

Not tonight. Not lying on top of the bed, staring at the ceiling, every synapse in his brain firing away.

There were big, bright letters on the ceiling. They spelled out, *This is your life, Ted Gillespie.*

And there was a movie screen on the ceiling. It showed the same scene over and over again.

A blond woman, calling for help, coming toward him. He saw himself in the movie. He looked a lot better in the movie than he did in the mirror. The woman threw herself into his arms.

This is your life, Ted Gillespie.
He smiled in the darkness. He liked movies.

11:16 p.m.

Something going on, Rocky had said.

Mac rubbed his eyes and looked at the wall. The only sound now was the *tick tick tick* of the Elvis wall clock. One of Arty's treasured possessions. Elvis's legs were the pendulum. It was 1950s Elvis, not Vegas Elvis. Not even the Elvis of *Kissin' Cousins*.

Real, revolutionary Elvis. Mac's mom had been so totally into Elvis. She used to tell him all about seeing him in 1956 when she was just fourteen and her girlfriend got her into the Mississippi–Alabama Fair and Dairy Show.

"So, so crazy," his mother said with a faraway look. "I was *there*. I saw it happening. It was … amazing."

She played Elvis around the house all the time. Mac got the idea that she wished she didn't live in Newark, but back in Alabama or in Las Vegas with an Elvis impersonator.

Not that any of that mattered now.

What mattered was Liz. Finally in bed, hopefully asleep.

Definitely alone.

She would need a lot of care now, and she had no one close to her. Arty's father wasn't in the best of health. And clearly Arty's sister wasn't ready to come alongside.

Mac didn't know much about Liz's family. Arty never really told him about it. Neither had Liz. She was from the South somewhere. The only impression Mac had about her background was that it probably wasn't real nice.

A little of that seemed to apply to Rocky, too.

What was her deal, anyway? Arty had mentioned her a few times. Said they weren't as close as they used to be. Hoped maybe they could talk more. He also said she was talented and capable and sort of independent. A chip-on-the-shoulder kind.

Lost. That was the last word he remembered Arty saying about her.

It occurred to Mac that both Liz and Rocky were lost in very much the same way.

Should he stay? He could sleep on the sofa and be here in the morning, when the shock would renew itself all over again, a poke in a fresh wound. She might need someone most of all then. And it wasn't like he had anyone to go home to.

He wondered if he'd ever get married again. If he was even capable of it with the episodes and all. If the rages would ever be healed, the way Pastor Jon said they could be.

He wondered if he'd ever get to see his daughter again. See her graduate from high school. Meet her boyfriends —

"You're still here."

Liz was standing there, in the living room, dark blue robe around her, eyes bleary.

Mac stood. "Why aren't you sleeping?"

"Couldn't," she said and shuffled to a chair. She pushed some hair aside and over her ear. "Can we talk?"

"Sure," Mac said. "That's why I'm here."

"You were Arty's best friend in the world."

"One of them," Mac said.

"No, I think his best friend. After he started going to church, it was you he looked up to."

Mac thought about that. They certainly had spent a lot of time together. It made Mac feel good that Arty thought that highly of him.

"I think he would have wanted you to keep after me," Liz said.

"After?"

She nodded and wiped her eyes with her middle fingers.

"I think you need to get back to bed," Mac said. "In the morning —"

"No. Please. I want to talk. To you. Now."

Mac thought he saw desperation in her tired eyes.

"I need to talk about what's happening inside me," she said.

"Of course." Mac sat in the chair next to hers. *This is why you are here tonight, boy. Don't blow it.*

He suddenly felt nervous. A little shaky. This could be one of those life-altering moments. Except his tongue felt like a tree sloth. His brain mushy. He silently said a *help me, help me, help me* prayer and waited for Liz to talk.

She took in a long breath and let it out, making a whooshing sound. Gathering her courage, Mac thought. Gutsy.

"I just can't believe he's not here," she said. "Can you tell me, please, why God would take him away like this? When we still had so much to say to each other?"

Great, Mac thought. Cut right to the biggie. The mystery of why God allows bad things to happen to good people. He hadn't come near to figuring that one out himself.

"I know he's with the Lord," Mac said. "I know that. That's what the Bible says. So you have to know that, too. Bad things do happen to us, but it's all in God's hands. Nothing happens that he doesn't know about."

She shook her head. "Arty would say that, and I didn't understand. But I wanted to, Mac. That's why we went hiking today. I told him I wanted to go to his favorite spot and have him tell me all about God. I was ready, Mac, to drink it in. And now ..."

Her voice receded like a wave off a rock. Mac felt if he didn't catch her now, she herself might slip into a darker despair. *Help me.*

"And now you need to keep on going," Mac said. "We'll keep on the way Arty would have wanted it. We'll be family together."

She pasted a slight smile on her face, the way sad people do sometimes to fight against grief. "That's nice, Mac. That's very nice. No wonder Arty liked you so much. Did he ever talk about me?"

"'Course he did," Mac said. "He loved you."

"You can be honest with me. He was frustrated with me sometimes, wasn't he?"

"What married couple doesn't have frustrations? Believe me, you're talking to an expert here."

"You were married before, right?"

Mac nodded.

"A daughter, right?" she asked.

He nodded again.

"Ever get to see her?"

He shook his head.

"See," Liz said, "I don't think that's fair. Why would God ..." She stopped, looking at his face. "What would he say, Mac?"

"Arty?"

"What was the bottom line?"

"Bottom line," said Mac, "was he wanted you to be happy, and he thought you weren't. Because he wasn't happy till he surrendered to God."

"That's what I wanted to do," she said. "That's what I was moving toward, but I fought him about it. Now it's too late."

"It's not too late."

"Can you help me? Can you make me understand?"

"I can try," Mac said.

"Do," she said.

He'd never done it before, made someone *understand*. Where did you even start? He could only think of one place.

"Prison makes you take a long look," he said. "Some guys keep looking to the outside, what they're gonna do when they get out. The jobs they're gonna pull. Or some of 'em think they'll be able to go straight, but they end up not. But I was looking at what I was, and it took me a long time to figure it out. It wasn't until Pastor Jon came that I started to get it."

"Pastor Jon came to see you?"

"He does prison ministry. I could sit in my cell every night, or one night a week I could get out if I went to Bible study. So I went to Bible study. Just to kill time. I thought I'd be hearing some namby-pamby, but that's not what I got."

"No?"

"Pastor Jon's not like that at all. He looked us in the eyes and opened his Bible and said, 'The heart is wicked, man. It's an ugly rock sitting there.' And I knew that was true about me. There was no way I couldn't know it. He told us that no heart can be changed unless God does it. And the only way he does it is through Jesus. He told us how Jesus got to a bad dude named Saul. He was blinded by light one day, and Jesus spoke to him, and when Saul got his sight back, he was changed. I mean, how could you not be? And I thought, I want to be changed like that."

"I want that, too," Liz said. "I want my heart changed. I want what you have. What Arty had. Can I have that?"

"Yes."

"Tell me how. Please tell me how. Because I thought God made that decision for you, and you were stuck wherever that was."

"I've never heard that," Mac said. "I only know that God wants everyone to be saved and that's why Jesus came. I mean, it says right there in the Bible that Jesus died for the sins of the whole world."

"What if you're not good enough to be saved?"

Mac shook his head. "That's not it. Not it at all. Nobody's good enough. It's a choice you make, to take Christ or not. Anybody can take him if they want to. So that's the thing. Do you want him?"

"I think so."

"It's freedom," Mac said. "It's the only thing that gives you real freedom. But you have to be willing to give up the old life."

"Old life?"

Mac nodded. "You have to give up your life for his." Was he making sense? Was he doing it right?

A sudden fear twisted around his heart. *What was that all about?* Then he realized he was afraid for her. For her soul, for her soul for eternity.

Mac grabbed her hand.

11:59

Rocky Towne, covered with Geena's knitted afghan, head propped on the arm of the sofa, looked out the window at the moon. It was a crescent over Los Angeles. Not full, not whole. Sliced. Like her.

The moon became a blur. She wiped her eyes with the back of her hand. "Arty," she whispered. "I wish I could see you one more time. One more ..."

Sunday

8:35 a.m.

Rocky woke up crying.

In the dream, she and Arty were kids again and playing at the park. The park was by their house. They used to play there all the time. Arty would push her on the swings and then twirl her on the roundabout.

When Arty was doing that, she felt safe. Happy, too, because he loved her. Even though they fought sometimes, she never doubted his love. Not because he said it, but because of what he did.

In the dream, Arty was on the slide and was about to come down to the sand, where Rocky was waiting.

But he hesitated. He was looking at her. His face was sad. He was crying. She asked him what the matter was. He didn't answer but slid down. When he got to the end, he went into the sand and disappeared.

The Rocky in the dream cried out.

The Rocky on the sofa in Geena's apartment felt herself shaken awake.

"Hey, hey," Geena was saying.

Rocky put her face on Geena's leg until the tears stopped.

Geena stroked her hair. You had to hand it to her, Rocky thought. She was a little flighty, yes. Sometimes the two sides of Geena's brain were like a couple of hummingbirds looking for nectar. They'd pause at a thought every now and then, wings beating wildly, then be off to another flower or guru or movement or cause. Always wanting to drink in life, experience it, and most of all take flight.

But say what you would about Geena Carter, Rocky loved her like a sister because she had a heart the size of Texas. And she'd come to Rocky at just the right time.

Five years ago, Rocky was singing, as she often did, in an isolated stretch of Griffith Park. It was her favorite spot in LA, between two hillsides in a crook with trees, rock, ice plants, and grass. It took a bit of getting to, but that was the point. Not a lot of foot traffic. And you could see people coming. If she had to stop singing she could before any sound reached other ears.

It was her private lounge. There she sang show tunes and jazz favorites and big band. Those were the songs she liked. Upbeat. They were the songs that reached the deepest part of her heart.

In her spot in Griffith Park, she could let them all out in glorious solitude.

One cool fall day, Rocky had gone there straight from a scene out of a bad soap opera. Only unfortunately, it was a scene from real life, *her* real life. Jeremy was his name. Jeremy of the silver tongue, of the *I love you for you who are.* That Jeremy. Six months they'd been together. One harried afternoon he'd made love to her, then asked her to please leave quickly, he had to get to an appointment. When she took too long he got mad, and then she found out why. There was a leggy blonde knocking on his door.

Funny thing was—if *funny* was even the right word—the blonde didn't even seem to care. She waltzed in without so much as a second look. Jeremy gave a shrug, as if to say, *That's life in the big city.*

So Rocky, driving, then running almost blindly, went to her spot in the park and raged into the hillside, cried her tears into it, and screamed the name of Jeremy attached to all sorts of cathartic epithets and animal sounds.

When her rage was spent, she sang The Andrews Sisters. "Boogie Woogie Bugle Boy" to be exact. Their most famous song. If that couldn't lift your spirits, you had none.

She practiced it once, then went for it again. She must have been really into it because when she got to the part where the voice did this bugle riff, just before "eight to the bar," she noticed a woman just standing there, smiling.

"Keep going!" the woman said. "This is way cool."

Rocky was too surprised to reply. Where had she come from? Was she some sort of urban wood nymph, sent to municipal parks to spy on innocent citizens? Just what did she think she was doing, invading like this?

Rocky was about to be angry when, without warning, she burst again into tears. Ashamed, all she could do was turn her back.

The woman came to her like an old friend and said, "Whoever he is, he isn't worth it."

Which brought Rocky up as short as a sparrow flying into a sliding glass door.

She said her name was Geena, and she loved whatever that song was. It turned out she had no idea who The Andrews Sisters were, and just talking about them took Rocky out of the dark clouds of Jeremy and into the sunshine of Geena Carter.

The sunshine that was now, once more, comforting her in her time of need.

9:58 a.m.

"Arty was so special," Liz was saying. "So very special."

The little church was packed, almost like they knew she would be there. Like they knew something important was going to be happening that morning. It was a little creepy. All those eyes on her. Those anxious, expectant eyes.

But she felt she was in total control. Like the way some comedians are when they're clicking on a Vegas stage. Or when some really good lawyer has a jury eating out of his hand. That's what Liz knew she had going on. It took over all the other feelings, covered them up, just the way Mama said they could be.

"You all knew him, you knew how special he was," she said, then paused as several heads nodded. She heard sniffles and saw one older woman dabbing her eyes with a handkerchief.

These are alien beings, Liz thought, though she recognized some of the faces. Arty had brought people over to the house, and she'd gone with him to a few church things. But mostly his church life was separate, which was the way she wanted it.

"I wasn't going to say anything today. I wasn't going to come here.

I'm still kind of in shock. But I'm here because I feel that Arty would want me to be here. That the Lord wants me to be here."

She paused and looked to the side. Pastor Jon and Mac were sitting next to each other, nodding encouragement. This was a big deal for them. God was moving, oh yes.

Somebody said, "Amen."

"You all know about the accident." She paused, turning her head to each side of the church. They could see the Band-Aid on her forehead that way. "I have so much grief in my heart right now. But I know what to do about it. I know because Arty told me, and Pastor Jon and Mac. You see, I came here this morning so I could be baptized and give my life totally to God, forever and ever. And—"

She was stopped by the applause and people shouting, "Amen!" and "Praise God!" Beatific expressions popped out all over.

Liz closed her eyes. She made it look like she might weep in a moment. The applause died down. The two hundred or so people in the little A-frame church went silent again.

"I want to give my life to the Lord Jesus," Liz said. "I want to be made clean from the sins I've committed."

More *Amens.*

"Pastor asked me if I wanted to say a few words. All I want to say is, you were Arty's family, and I hope I can be part of that, too."

An older woman stood up in the middle of the congregation and said, "Yes, you can, girl! God be praised!"

Several others echoed the sentiment. Liz smiled and looked to Pastor Jon. He came to her, put his arm around her shoulder, faced forward.

"You know me," he said. "I don't always stick to the plans. I think we ought to stop right now and just have Liz here go into the waters of baptism and everybody celebrate. That'll be our church service for today. How's that sound to you?"

From the response, it sounded like everybody was as pleased as could be. Almost before she knew what was happening, Liz felt herself being led by a couple of the ladies toward a side door. They said something supportive, but she barely heard. She was overtaken by a sense of dread.

Waters of baptism? What happened to a person who went in without really believing? It wasn't that she thought God would reach down with a bolt of lightning. But what if the water burned like it did when holy water hit the Devil?

She almost bolted. Thought about running, getting away. She could explain later. But then she was in a small cubicle with a robe, and they were waiting for her to put it on and go get wet.

She could hear Pastor Jon talking to the congregation as she undressed.

"... what we can do for her," he was saying. "Be there, be ready with some meals, make sure she feels the support. And remember to give praise to God because we know Arty is with the Lord even now, and his wife, and all of us, will see him again."

See him again? Ice crystals formed on her spine. What if that was true? When she was little, she believed in ghosts for a while. It freaked her out that apparitions could be watching her in the shower. They haunted you.

Would Arty do that to her? What if she *did* see him again in some afterlife? What if he haunted her dreams? Was a disembodied head floating above her at night?

Ridiculous. You die, you become the stuff they sprinkle on gardens. You are one with the earth. Literally.

She never believed in that afterlife stuff, because she couldn't believe that the white-haired man who shouted at her in church as a kid was going anywhere after he died, let alone heaven.

For some reason, that old pastor had singled her out. Hated her, she was sure. Mama wanted her to get some Sunday schooling and dropped her off at the nearest church. She didn't want to go, but that was what Mama wanted for her daughter, and Mama had a way of getting people to do what she wanted.

So off Liz went to the Sunday school in the hot, white building that had one window air conditioner. It didn't much work, and everybody sweated. Even the teacher, a plump old woman whose name Liz couldn't remember. The teacher whose face always looked like it carried three days of rain.

Liz went twice to that Sunday school. The second time, the plump lady wasn't there. A tall, skinny man in a suit stood in for her. Liz thought later he looked like Abraham Lincoln, if the president had a sour stomach and lived till he was seventy.

He came to give the kiddies a lesson about being good. He said you had to be, because when you died all your sins were going to be announced all over the sky for everyone who ever lived to hear about them.

She thought she heard him say it this way: "You're gonna all have to give a count of yourself to God."

Liz wondered how a person could count herself.

As he droned on about good and bad and sin, he kept looking at *her*. Making eye contact with *her*, even though there were fifteen, twenty kids in the room.

It made her a little mad. Because she was bored and didn't want to be there in the first place. She didn't want to be sitting there in the heat getting the beady eye from a scarecrow with white straw for hair.

When Sunday school was over, she was going to be the first out the door, but he stood there and told her to wait.

She didn't want to wait. She tried to get out the door, but he grabbed her by the front of her dress. The other kids laughed. The scarecrow shooed them out and slammed the door.

It sounded like a gunshot.

Liz writhed in his grip.

"Stop it!" Scarecrow shouted.

His voice went through her like a cold spear. It froze her in place, her heart beating hard to keep her breathing.

Scarecrow's grip was strong and he pulled her, then pushed her down onto a chair. He bent over her and said, "Now you listen to me, young lady. In this room and this church you will not bring your willful defiance."

She had no idea what that meant, only that it was bad. She remembered what her friend Emily said once, that dogs can't understand your words but they sure can understand your tone. Emily looked at her own dog, Ruffles, and started saying, "Bad dog, yes, you're a bad dog, yes, you are," in a high, friendly voice, and the dog wagged its tail.

Well, Scarecrow's tone was the exact opposite, and Liz wasn't wagging anything.

"You need to get some things straight," he went on. His voice wheezed a little when he spoke, like there was a little pipe organ in his throat, and his words were the wind blowing across the pipes. "It does not matter how young you are or how old you are. By your fruit you will be known."

What was he talking about? She didn't have any fruit. She and Mama didn't have an orchard or even a berry plant.

"I will tell you this," Scarecrow said. "They that are not the elect will produce nothing but wickedness, but that is God's decree for his glory. So, you see, you cannot fool God. And you cannot fool me."

He bent over her even further, looking now less like a Scarecrow and more like a fire-breathing snake. With fangs.

Which is why she kicked him.

It was fear, pure fear, she would tell Mama later. But she knew then that wasn't the whole truth. She knew she kicked him because she hated him and wanted to hurt him.

She ran all the way home. When Mama found out what happened, she told Liz to say put and got in their old Ford Escort and took off.

When she came back, she told Liz she'd never have to go back to Sunday school again. Later, when Liz was walking in town with Mama, they saw the scarecrow coming out of Franklin's Hardware. He turned his back at once and walked fast away from them.

Much later, Liz learned that his name was Mr. Zeleny and that he had a daughter who had "fallen into sin" and had never come back.

As Liz finished putting on the baptismal robe now, she wondered if people really could fall so far they never came back. She wondered if that was about to happen to her. She was going to be dunked in a big box of water. Maybe she'd just sink in and not come out.

No. You can get through this. And quit thinking Arty can see you from beyond the grave. Don't get all creeped out now.

Just then she thought she really *did* have a choice. Right this second. She could come clean or go through with the phony baptism. Tell the truth about what happened or go down the line with the lie.

Whatever she chose, though, there was one thing certain: There'd be no turning back.

10:02 a.m.

Here is a Geena bonus, Rocky thought. Geena made the finest cup of coffee in the city. You can have your Starbucks and your Coffee Bean, your store-bought Seattle's Best or any brand of your choosing. Geena had a way of grinding organic beans just right and making her own blends that beat them all.

Rocky sipped the warm comfort by Geena's front window, which looked out over a back alley and up to the tops of the slender palms that made the LA skyline what it was. Something inspirational there, the doggedness of them. The way they stayed, swayed, shed but never broke.

She knew she'd need to be the same in the weeks ahead.

Was she being unfair to Liz? True, they'd never really liked each other. But how much of that animosity was Rocky's feeling that Arty was being taken away from her? How much of it was pure selfishness?

They had been so close, growing up. Arty had his friends, but he always made time for his little sister, especially after their mother died and Dad became a walking zombie. The loss of Mom hit Rocky hard. Mom was the affectionate one, the one with the smiles and touches.

Her father was never one for hugs. Maybe at one time, before Mom was gone, he might have been. Not that he wasn't a good provider, but he'd built a wall of cold stone, and any attempt to scale it was met with retreat and reinforcements. Anger could flare when she pushed for his attention.

Rocky didn't need therapy to know why she drifted toward men like Boyd Martin and stayed with them much too long.

In those awful months after Mom's death, it was Arty who made sure school lunches were prepared, clothes washed, the house taken care of. Yes, Aunt Cheryl was around a lot, too, but she didn't live with them. And no one could get her father's stone wall to come down. If anything, it got higher.

Arty was her protector, all the way through high school. It was Arty who took her to museums and the beach. And the movies. *Forrest Gump* and *Jurassic Park*. He wouldn't let her see *Pulp Fiction*, though. It was not as cool as everyone said, he told her, and even though she begged him, he wouldn't budge.

Later, when she finally saw it, she knew he was right.

No one knew her or cared about her the way Arty did.

Then came the day when he wanted her to meet the new girl in his life. The one he said he was sure he'd marry. He broke the news to her the way someone might announce a death in the family or the loss of a pet. And that's the way it hit her, like bad news.

She hated herself for that and told herself she would do everything she could to welcome her.

Arty chose a high-end restaurant in Beverly Hills. Clearly wanting to impress both of the main women in his life. Clearly wanting to blow a week's salary.

Rocky had to admit she went in with a bad attitude. She really didn't want to make friends with this intruder. And as much as she told herself that Arty deserved happiness, she could not get rid of the childish petulance fizzing inside her like Alka-Seltzer.

Arty and Liz were already seated at a booth under a softly lit painting in the contemporary style.

Rocky never forgot seeing Liz for the first time. Big, blue eyes with a gold nimbus around the pupils. Light blond hair that could have been dyed. There were no highlights.

"This is Liz Summerville," Arty said.

Liz smiled and slid out of the booth so she could hug Rocky. "It's so nice to meet you." She had the faintest wisp of a southern accent. The kind of voice that could drive men wild.

As could the rest of her. Rocky had to admit Arty had picked one good-looking package.

In fact, in every way, Liz Summerville seemed right for Arty. He clearly was taken with her, in more than a superficial way. Arty was never one for dating a lot of women. He wanted stability. And deserved it.

But could this woman give it to him? As hard as she tried not to, Rocky kept studying Liz all through the meal. Interpreting every gesture, analyzing every nuance of voice. Everything Liz did fell on the positive side of the ledger, at least objectively.

But there was just something a little too perfect about Liz's riffs. They flowed out in shy simplicity, but somehow seemed cunning.

Rocky tried to tell herself to relax, but she was trained, after all, to ferret out deception, both subtle and overt. Still, she had almost convinced herself that Liz was what she appeared, until the talk turned to Liz's background.

Rocky brought it up quite innocently, though it might have sounded like a job interview question. "Tell us about your growing up," she asked, using the word *us* without really thinking about it.

It was then that something happened in Liz Summerville's eyes. A slight shifting of the temperature, a delicate but discernable drop.

The change signaled that this was an area Liz did not want explored. And that Rocky had breached some unspoken agreement in even suggesting it.

Arty answered the question. "She had kind of a hard life back there, and that's why she's out here, to start all over again. Let's talk about something else."

They tried. Liz's voice and look returned to normal, but whenever her eyes met Rocky's, from that moment to today, there was a flash of granite in them.

Geena came to the window and sat with Rocky, holding her own cup of coffee. "You can stay here as long as you want," she said.

Rocky nodded.

"Is there anything I can help you with?" Geena said. "Arrangements, anything like that?"

"There's one thing I have to do, and I'm dreading it."

"What's that?"

Rocky looked at the mountains. "I have to call my dad."

10:14 a.m.

"Because of your good confession of faith," Pastor Jon said, "I baptize you in the name of the Father, the Son, and the Holy Spirit."

He gently guided her hand to her nose. She squeezed her nose and took a breath, and he lowered her into the water.

For half a second, she wondered if he'd let her up. This was their revenge. Death by baptism.

No noise under the water. Panic. Not fear of being held under and of drowning. No, it was like she was being baptized into fate. Not faith, which she didn't have. She had made the choice now, and it was irrevocable. Pastor Jon had called baptism a pledge, the pledge of a good conscience toward God.

She was making another pledge, a pledge to herself. To see this whole thing through to the end.

I can't breathe.

Someone was in the water with her.

No.

Yes.

Not Pastor Jon's hands. Some other set of hands.

What was this?

I have to scream!

Then she was coming up out of the water. Rivulets streaming down her face and hair. She was alive. And she heard applause. The people in the church were clapping for her.

All of them.

She knew she was supposed to smile, so she did.

"Praise the Lord, Sister," Pastor Jon said.

"Amen," Liz said.

10:20 p.m.

"How you doing, Pop?"

"Roxanne?"

"One and only."

"What time is it?"

"I wake you?"

"I was dozing. Why you calling?"

Is it that shocking to you, Father? Your only daughter calling you on the phone? How about a nice, "How've you been?" *A little bit of,* "I'm sorry I've been so distant over the years."

"Pop, I've got some bad—"

"You need money or something?"

"No—"

"That guy you're shacked up with have any money?"

"Listen to me, will you?" *For a change?*

"What is it?"

"Arty ..." The words stuck.

"What about Arty?"

"He was hiking ..."

"He's hurt?"

She swallowed once, hard. "He died, Pop. Arty died."

She heard a muffled gasp, like someone had punched him in the stomach.

"Pop, are you—?"

"Don't talk. Don't say anything."

She waited. She kept waiting. She thought she heard a sob. "Pop, you need me to come down?"

"No. When can I see him?"

"I don't know. Liz'll be handling all that."

"I have to talk to her."

Like you don't have to talk to me?

"Pop—"

The connection dropped.

He dropped her! So he could call Liz!

Geena came into the living room. "How'd it go?"

"Not real good."

"Tell me, did you think it would go good?"

"No. It never does."

"But see, that's the thing." Geena sat on the arm of the chair. She looked down. "You have to get it vibrating in your head, before it happens in reality."

"Oh, yeah?"

Geena nodded.

"Well then," Rocky said, "why don't you vibrate me some tequila? You have any?"

Geena shook her head.

Rocky got up. "Then I'll go get some."

"Want me to come with?" Geena said.

"No thanks. Too much positive thinking makes me grouchy."

Rocky took the stairs down to the parking area. She looked at the cracks in the asphalt. Everything was crumbling in LA these days. Infrastructure becoming obsolete. Life running down. She was caught in a vortex, and—

Boyd was leaning against her car, smiling.

"Hey, babe," he said.

She stopped, as if hitting an electric fence.

"We need to talk," he said.

"I don't think so."

"We kind of left things up in the air." He pushed off from the car and took a step toward her.

"Just stay where you are," Rocky said. "We didn't leave anything up in the air."

"We have to talk this out."

"You smashed my car window and burned my clothes."

"Oh, that," he said. "I was drunk, okay? You know how I get."

"Yeah, I know exactly how you get."

He put his hands out and took another step. "I was mad, okay?"

"Stop, Boyd."

"Let's go get a drink and talk about it."

"A drink? That's the whole thing that got us into trouble."

"We can drink together, we can make love together, we can work out anything."

"I don't want to."

"I want to."

"So?"

"Come here," he said, gesturing.

"Boyd, please, just go."

He put his arms down. "You don't really want me to."

"I really do."

"You can't," he said.

"Why can't I?"

"Because you need me," he said.

Rocky shook her head.

"Don't treat me like this," he said.

"Treat *you?*"

"I'm not about to be dumped by you. Your prospects aren't real good, if you know what I mean."

Rocky was not surprised by the epithet that blasted out of her mouth.

Boyd's face darkened. "You shouldn't have called me that."

"Go away," she said. "Now."

"You should not have said that to me."

"Stay away from me, or I'll get a restraining order."

"That ain't gonna help you, babe."

"Or worse."

He smiled and shook his head. "You like to play tough, but you're not. Don't even try. I'll be around."

He pointed his stupid finger at her. For a second, she thought he'd make a move. But one thing he wasn't was dumb. In broad daylight, in an apartment complex parking lot. He wouldn't do it that way.

No, he'd wait for his moment.

"We'll be in touch," he said and walked away whistling.

10:45 a.m.

Later, after wet-haired hugs and smiles, Liz made desperate eyes at Mac, a look he interpreted as, *Take me away from here!*

So he did. She took his arm and he walked her to the far end of the parking lot, running a little interference on the way.

She needs to get home, Mrs. Axelrod.

Thanks for the offer of the meatloaf, Mrs. Mayhew.

Yes, I'll let you know how she's doing.

All the way to the car, Liz clung to him. Then she turned and gave him a hug, thanking him. She held on.

Then she pulled back and looked at him. "What if I'm bad?" she said.

"What?" Mac said. He gave her a disarming chuckle. "You're not bad."

"What if I am? What will happen to me?"

"No, listen, you're in Christ. You are a new creation."

"What if I'm not?"

"But you are. That's what the Bible says. It's a promise."

She almost said something more but then turned and got into her car.

She's going to need you. She's going to need all the help she can get. Think you can manage that without messing up, Bud?

As Liz drove away, Mac felt, well, scared. That was it. Like he was responsible for her now. The way they used to say in China or some-place, that if you save a life, you have to take care of 'em for the rest of your days.

A guy who grows up on the streets of Oakland isn't supposed to be scared of anything. But then you join the Marines at nineteen and before you can say *John Wayne* you're being shipped off to Saudi Arabia.

Saudi Arabia! What kind of place is that? You arrive in Khobar, and your feet have barely touched sand when you hear an air-raid siren.

You start running around with your buds, looking for shelter, and then you're told, "Dudes, that's the Muslim call to prayer."

Yes, what kind of place is it when you're told you can't show the palms of your hands or the soles of your feet to native Saudis? Or you can't wear white underwear because they believe Paradise is white? How would they know the color of your underwear anyway?

You can't give the "okay" sign with your fingers or point or talk to Saudi men about the women in their family.

It must be what it's like on Mercury. Sand everywhere, heat like you've never experienced. Drinking water all the time. Your "chocolate chip" uniform scratchy and heavy and hot. Not to mention your chemical suit and gas mask.

And when a *shamal*, a sandstorm, blows, fuggetaboutit. How can anybody live here?

You want to fight, but it's all about waiting. You clean latrines and take barrels of human waste to a pit, where you get to pour in diesel fuel and mix it all up, then light it on fire.

Funny, but the recruiter never told you about that particular aspect of military life.

Oh, and there's drilling. Every day, drilling and training and singing out the metronomic cadence:

> *If I die in a combat zone*
> *Box me up and ship me home!*
> *Pin my medals on my chest,*
> *Tell my mom I done my best!*

And then. Finally. It comes.

G-Day, the ground offensive to liberate Kuwait.

And it was that day in Saudi Arabia when Mac knew fear. It tasted like a mouthful of nails. In his guts, just below the stomach, all the wires got tangled and crackly, shooting sparks into his groin and down his legs.

No, the Oakland streets were never like that.

On the morning of February 24, they got ready to cross from

Saudi Arabia into Kuwait. Mac was part of the team that sent out the MICLIC, line charges for clearing the minefields. After they exploded the mines, plow tanks followed, clearing a path for the Army's Tiger Brigade and the Marine Second Division.

Mac's division.

Traversing two hundred yards of hell.

Still, the Marines advanced, right into the teeth of mortar and rifle. Where was the air support? Twenty minutes of pure bloodletting passed before the Cobra helicopters arrived and started spraying the hills with machine-gun fire.

The advance got easier after that.

Up to the first of the bunkers. What they found blew Mac away. Iraqi soldiers, his first sight of them, huddling in the dirt and refusing to come out. The elite guard of Saddam Hussein? No. Dirty, wide-eyed men curled up and frightened as babies in a thunderstorm. Mac learned later the Iraqi soldiers had been taught that U.S. Marines all had to kill one of their own family in order to join up.

No wonder they were scared.

Mac looked on them with a mixture of scorn and pity. One of the soldiers couldn't have been more than fifteen. A couple were over fifty. The proud Iraqi army.

The kid was crying and wouldn't move. When they started tying his hands, his eyes opened in primal fear and he screamed, "I love you! I love you!" in fractured English, over and over again.

For a moment Mac wondered if he was in a nightmare, if this was all a crazy, cosmic joke being played by an evil god. What were they all doing here? What were human beings like this fighting over?

Was it worth it for a kid like this to throw his life away for some dictator who was lower than scum? Who would kill you for a wrong thought or careless word?

Mac heard his name being called. He was standing on the edge of the bunker.

Before he could take a step, the explosion came, and his world snapped to black.

He woke up screaming in a hospital. His head was on fire. Someone quickly administered a sedative and put him back under. The next time he came to, he was on a plane.

That was the last he saw of the Middle East.

For the next three years, trying to get help from the VA, Mac realized he was unfit for most work. Officially, he had a penetrating craniocerebral injury. What it meant was hot metal in the brain. They didn't get it all out. What he got was pain that flared randomly. What wasn't random was what followed the pain — rage. Until, in a perverse twist, his rages started to *precede* the pain. When that happened, Mac would find himself lashing out at the first thing in his path: man, machine, or animal.

He thought several times of killing himself.

For some reason, he never did. He wondered about that, why he hadn't gone through with it. Then he met Athena, and Aurora had come along. For a short time there, a blessed window, he'd lost those thoughts.

But the window slammed shut and the jobs dried up. Because of his own choices, bad ones. Lots of bad ones. But none as bad as the night he went into that liquor store with a gun in his jacket.

The night everything shattered, like glass under a boot.

11:20 a.m.

As soon as Liz came through the door, she had the feeling she wasn't alone. There was somebody in the house. She had to stop a moment and really listen. It took a full minute to assure herself that she was the only one there. She was attuned to sound and could tell when people were in her vicinity.

It was that skill she developed as a kid. From getting picked on a lot. Like that time after school when three of them were hiding behind a tractor, armed with dirt clods. She knew the bullies were there without seeing them. She ran away fast. Only one clod got her, on the leg.

Just to make sure she was really alone, Liz checked the house. The rooms were empty. The sound of the ticking Elvis clock was the only thing she heard.

No. Somebody was here.

"Shut up," she said out loud. Talking to herself. *You've got to get over this. It's like you're paranoid or something.*

Stress. That's what it is.

She went to the pantry and reached back behind the flour and pancake mix for the hidden bottle of Jim Beam. Arty went all pure with the Christian thing. Didn't want any alcohol in the house and stopped drinking when they went out.

Well, her act of defiance was back there behind Aunt Jemima, and now she really needed it. She poured herself a jolt in a regular drinking glass and knocked it back neat. The way she'd seen the men in the bars of Jackson do it.

The way the NASCAR, gun-show, Confederate-flag-wearing Mississippians did it. The way the proto-punks did it at the club W. C. Don's, which stood for "We Can't Decide on a Name" and where the local rock scene, such as it was, pretty much became a bunch of drunk kids at three a.m.

Knocked it back the way the Rankin County boys did it, to display their redneck bona fides to the uppity set in Jackson proper.

Liz could beat them all. She had and she would again.

The drink warmed her throat, then her nose. She poured herself another, brought the glass to the living room and set it on a table. She sat and let the warmth take over. Now it was just a waiting game.

She would have to pick the right time. Decide when to go get the stones. Then figure how to get out of town without suspicion. Without a lot of questions being asked.

She heard a car pull up in front. She went to the window and peeked out. Who was it? From the passenger side emerged that old woman with a cane from church. Coming around to help her was a man almost as old, in a rumpled brown suit and red tie.

Church people.

She practically ran into the kitchen and hid the booze. She opened the drawer that held some restaurant mints, unwrapped one and popped it in her mouth. She did not want anyone to think the church's newest convert was a drunk or something.

They knocked at the door. Liz pushed her hair back over her ears and went to open it.

"Praise the Lord this day," the old woman said.

What was her name? Axelrod. That was it. She was wearing a hat with a lacy brim, the same dull yellow color as her dress.

"You ran out before I had a chance to talk to you," Mrs. Axelrod said. "Mr. Dean and I would love to come in and visit awhile. Is this a good—"

"Actually," Liz said, "I was about to—"

"That's just fine, dear." And the woman breezed right in. The man behind her seemed to understand Liz's consternation. He smiled sheepishly but didn't make any apology as he stepped inside.

Now what? Liz couldn't very well be rude. She had just been baptized and raised to new life, so they said. All right, she told herself. Endure for a little while. There's a great reward waiting at the end. And not one of those heavenly things people keep hoping for. Her reward was in the here and now—cold, hard merchandise, worth a couple of million, at least.

"Are you all right?" Mrs. Axelrod said.

Liz brought herself back to the moment. "Oh. Yes."

"If you don't mind my saying so, you look a bit shaken."

"I—"

"Don't think anything of it. You've been through tremendous lows and highs in a matter of hours. May I sit?"

Before Liz could say a word, the woman sat.

"I, um, suppose I should offer you something," Liz said.

"Oh, that's all right," Mrs. Axelrod said. "We won't be here long."

"Nothing for me," Mr. Dean said.

Liz smiled and sat opposite Mrs. Axelrod. The man stood behind the old woman. Like a queen's attendant.

"I wanted to tell you what a joy it was to see you baptized today," the queen said.

"Thank you," Liz said. *Keep the voice quiet and reverent. Just agree with everything and then they'll go home.*

"You know," Mrs. Axelrod said, "my late husband, Elmer, and I founded the church. We had a vision for God's work here in the west end of the San Fernando Valley. When we first came to Los Angeles, we attended the Church of the Open Door."

"Oh?" Liz said, trying to sound interested.

"Dr. McGee was pastor then. Oh, what a lovely man. You must listen to *Thru the Bible* on the radio. You must begin your education now."

"Oh?"

"Bible study and prayer, you see, especially as you are new in the faith. It's a vulnerable time. I remember when I received the Lord ..."

No.

"... It was in a little country church in Texas ..."

No, please, no. The old man was smiling and nodding, like he'd heard this a hundred times before and loved it each time. Liz breathed in and out steadily, waiting for the drone to die out.

"... came forward at the invitation ..."

Liz watched the swing of Elvis's legs on the clock on the wall. Liz thought he'd conk out before Mrs. Axelrod finished.

"... not a bed of roses after that, by any means."

Four minutes.

Five minutes.

Elvis swayed. Mr. Dean nodded. Liz listened.

Finally, mercifully, Mrs. Axelrod seemed to be finishing. She said, "The point is that sin is real, and Satan walketh about as a roaring lion, seeking whom he may devour."

How did we get to Satan?

"But we, your church family, are here for you to lean on in good times and bad. We will pray for you and with you."

No, anything but that!

"Thank you so much, Mrs. Axelrod."

"Our prayer warrior," Mr. Dean said. "When she prays, she gets results. Storming the throne room."

What did that mean?

"You can go to bed every night, knowing God will be watching over you," Mrs. Axelrod said. "Every little moment."

Now that was a curse if there ever was one.

Without warning, Mrs. Edie Axelrod reached for the glass of Jim Beam that Liz had left on the table. And smelled it.

"Ah, my dear," she said.

Idiot! Me and her!

"Alcohol will kill your soul," Mrs. Axelrod said. Liz tried to make herself seem attentive, but all she wanted was to get this chattering church lady off her case.

This was the price of her deception, she knew. She had to make like the good little convert.

"I know that you've come from a very different place," Mrs. Axelrod said. "But now that you are a new creation, it is time to put away the old and take on the new."

And turn into you? Liz nodded.

"You see, my brother died of alcoholism," Mrs. A shook her head sadly. "Oh, he was such a handsome young man. You would have thought so. We called him the pride of Sandusky. He was valedictorian of his high school class and ..."

Please, oh please, stop.

"... off to the University of Michigan, and he got in with a fraternity and that's where he started to drink. I remember a time ..."

Am I capable of killing her?

"... called our father from Chicago, from a hospital, and we had to go pick him up ..."

Yes. I am capable of killing. Oh, yes.

"... did not accept the Lord as his Savior and died that winter. That, my dear, is all alcohol will bring you. Now you have the power of God inside you ..."

Scary thought. No. Not that.

"... so I want you to come to Bible study tonight."

"Excuse me?" Liz said.

"Our weekly Bible study at the church. Tonight. Led by Pastor Jon. It's the only way to grow, dear."

"Tonight? I was going to—"

Mrs. Axelrod put her hand on Liz's arm and bore into her with a look. "My dear, I know people. I know when they are running from something. Or to something. Now I'm not going to let you go until you promise to come to Bible study tonight. You're a babe in the woods, and there are wolves out there, and they carry bottles of whiskey."

Liz had to make this stop. Now. Or she would scream.

"Fine," Liz said, her insides crying out for the drink she could not have.

That's when Mrs. Axelrod finally stood up. Or made a move to stand up. Mr. Dean helped her make it all the way.

"Come here, dear," Mrs. Axelrod said, opening her arms. Liz obediently let the woman pull her to her bosom. Mrs. Axelrod's dress seemed drenched in perfume.

Which gave Liz a headache that lasted long after they left.

But what lasted even longer was the thought of lions. Liz kept thinking of devilish-looking lions, wanting to eat her up.

She even thought, for a brief moment, that the whole day was a dream. A crazy dream, and she was going just a little bit crazy herself.

No. Just stress.

She went back to the bourbon. Then she locked the front door with the dead bolt. If anybody came knocking, she'd ignore them this time.

She'd ignore every bad thought, too. She was going to keep moving now, devil lions or no.

2:33 p.m.

Rocky looked at herself in the mirror on Geena's closet door. She wanted to see Keely Smith looking back at her. At least a mental image of Keely. She wanted that confidence and assurance to melt into her, make her believe in her singing, if just for a moment.

But it was just Rocky Towne staring back at her from the glass.

Geena came in. "There you are."

"Here I am," Rocky said.

"Whatcha doing?"

"Trying to go through the looking glass."

"Cool. If you make it, let me know." Geena went to her nightstand and grabbed a book.

"I don't think I can do it," Rocky said.

"You can always try a rabbit hole," Geena said.

"No, I mean the audition. Tomorrow."

Geena stopped and looked at her across the bed.

"Too many things are happening at once," Rocky said.

"But that's why you should go." Geena tossed the book on the bed and came to her. "Listen to me, I know. I'm the one who always has to get nine hundred things in my head focused down, am I right?"

"Geena—"

"I'm right, right? So you need to go for this. Even with Arty and your dad and that jerk Boyd who was never good enough for you. You need to because this is what you want, what you really want."

"It can wait."

"Wait for what? When there's no trouble in your life? Like when will that be?"

Geena had a point and had focused her mind very well to make it. It was what Rocky wanted. Had for years.

After the dog attack, maybe a year after, Rocky started to sing. She found that when she did, she got carried away from her world. When she sang, she couldn't hear the kids yelling "scar face" at her.

And her mom's albums—she had classics like Keely and Louis, Jo Stafford, Doris Day, and The Andrews Sisters—had the same, magical effect.

As long as Rocky was singing or listening to music, she was not imperfect and unsure. She could soar.

"Will you go?" Geena said.

"Behold, the new Keely Smith," Rocky said.

7:42 p.m.

"Let me tell you a story," Pastor Jon said.

Liz and Mac and the others at the Bible study sat in folding chairs. They were in what the church called its fellowship hall. Liz thought the walls had eyes. All looking at her to see if she'd give herself away.

She fought back at the eyes. She would not crack. *Stare all you want to.*

"There was a famous preacher named Torrey," Pastor Jon said, "who was preaching in his Chicago church one night, and he saw a large, flashily dressed man, the kind they used to call a *sport*. A gambler. Someone used to fast living. That's what my grandma used to call it. Fast living."

He was holding his Bible in one hand and gesturing with the other.

"So as Torrey was preaching, he kept noticing this man's eyes just boring into him. He had the look of a man intent on something. Well, they used to have inquiry rooms, rooms where people could come after the preaching to learn the ways of the Lord. Torrey was in the inquiry room when one of his deacons brought this man back."

Pastor Jon paused. He looked almost like he'd been there. "This big sport was groaning, and he said to Torrey, 'I don't know what's come over me. I never felt this way in all my life.' Torrey asked him a question or two, and it turned out this man's mother ran a gambling house in Omaha. And the man had come to Chicago and was walking down the street, and he happened by a street-corner preacher."

Liz had heard a few of those back home. They always freaked her out.

"Torrey used to train laypeople to stand out on the sidewalks and start preaching and teaching the Word of God. It just so happened that the man doing the preaching was someone the sport knew. A man who once lived the high life, just like the sport. After listening awhile, the sport went on his way, heading for a gambling den. But something had taken hold of him. Something that kept dragging him back to the open-air meeting. From there, he was invited to Torrey's church, and that's when all this happened."

Pastor Jon took a dramatic breath.

"The man said to Torrey, 'I don't know what's the matter with me.' And Torrey said, 'I'll tell you what's the matter with you. You are under the conviction of sin. The Holy Spirit has got hold of you. Will you take Christ as your Savior right now?' And the man fell on his knees and started crying. He was led to Christ by Torrey, and when he left that night he was changed forever."

That, Liz thought, is about the scariest story I have ever heard.

Monday

9:23 a.m.

Liz found the life insurance policy in the blue vinyl folder in the study, where Arty kept important papers. Passports, birth certificates, a record of accounts.

The life insurance payout was five hundred thousand dollars.

Half a million.

Tax free.

Her head went light. She'd never been stupid enough to play the lottery, but this felt like winning it.

Arty's death benefit, plus those rocks.

Maybe she should forget about the gems. Too hot to handle. Take the half a mil and—

No, that wasn't enough. Not these days. Not to put her into the life she deserved. Those stones would put her over.

But what if she got caught with them?

She wasn't going to get caught. She knew exactly what to do with them. In the world she came from, finding a fence was a no-brainer. It would be like going back to her roots.

Don't get jumpy about the life insurance, she told herself. Don't seem anxious. It's just sitting there. Grieve a while, then put in the claim.

It wouldn't be that hard to grieve. She had really liked Arty at one time. Maybe even loved him. If she was capable of love.

There was a photo on the desk of the two of them. It was taken on their honeymoon. Arty looked happy.

She looked, she thought now, like one of those fishermen standing by their record-breaking Marlin.

She had landed Arty. Skillfully. Hooked him and reeled him in.

She met him at a party in Hollywood. She was living in a studio apartment in the hills north of Franklin Avenue and working for a themed catering firm. Reel Parties, Inc., which specialized in dressing their people up as movie stars by decade.

On the night she met Arty, she was working a forties film-noir theme. The host of the party had asked specifically for a Burt Lancaster and a Veronica Lake.

Liz was no Burt. That honor fell to a curly-headed acting student. But Toby Gray, owner and operator of Reel Parties, said she was definitely his Veronica Lake.

"Who's Veronica Lake?" she asked Toby in his office, four hours before the party.

Toby rolled his eyes, pulled out a big book, and plopped it on his desk. He flipped some pages and showed her a page with a glossy lobby card reprint from a movie called *This Gun for Hire*. He pointed at the blonde. Then he flipped to one called *The Blue Dahlia*, pointing out the same blonde. On the opposite page was a black-and-white photo with the caption "Veronica Lake."

"She had a peek-a-boo bang," Toby said. "Her hair fell over one eye. Drove men crazy."

Liz studied the picture. That drove men crazy? Well then, why not? Her hair was long enough.

Toby, former hairdresser and makeup artist for the studios, did all the costumes and styles for his crew. He was known to run with some shady LA characters, but Liz did not mind that in the slightest. He seemed, in fact, very much like her in many ways.

They could make themselves anything they wanted on the outside and hide the inside as they saw fit.

Toby set to work. A curling iron here and a little tease there, and Liz *was* Veronica Lake. From his vast store of costumes, Toby selected a dress that might have been last worn in a nightclub in the 1940s.

"You could have totally gone to Ciro's in this," Toby said. "That was the place to be seen. No doubt Veronica did many a night there."

As she looked in the mirror, she asked, "Is Veronica Lake still alive?"

Toby didn't answer. Liz turned on him. "Well?"

"Oh no," he said. "And she was only fifty when she died."

"How?"

"She was an alcoholic, dear. And mentally ill. Paranoid."

For some reason that made her skin cold. It lasted only a moment, but it was almost enough to make her want to be Burt Lancaster.

At the party she served puff pastries and forties-style hors d'oeuvres to the guests, most of whom knew who she was. They'd laugh and say, "Veronica Lake, huh?"

It was the square-jawed guy in a black fedora who changed it up. "Femme fatale, huh?" he said, nabbing a cheese chunk from her tray.

"I'm sorry?" Liz said.

"Classic femme fatale," he said. "In film noir."

She didn't want to appear stupid, so she nodded and smiled.

He went on. "Like Barbara Stanwyck in *Double Indemnity*. Or Ann Savage in *Detour*. You know, the woman the guy gets involved with and then regrets it?"

"Of course," she said.

"See, sometimes the girl kills the guy," he said. "You didn't put poison in the cheese now, did you?"

He smiled.

Liz felt those cold hands again. She quickly smiled the chill away. She bent her head forward and let her hair fall completely over her right eye. She did a little lip pout and turned. She let her caboose sway rhythmically as she walked away.

The rest was up to him.

It was close to eleven when he approached and asked if she'd like to meet for coffee in the morning.

"I don't know anything about you," she said.

"And I don't know anything about *you*," he said, "which is the whole reason for coffee."

"How about a teaser trailer?" she said. *Good line.*

"My name is Arty Towne, and I'm VP of marketing for a start-up called RumbleTV. We're developing video content for cell phones."

"Video content?"

"You know that cell phone you carry around in your purse?"

"I don't have a cell phone," she said.

"You will. Right now, people think all they do is place and receive calls. But there's going to be little screens on them soon enough, and we are going to be there to put things on those screens."

"You mean like little TV shows?"

"That's exactly it. And sports highlights. And news. So when you're standing in line at Starbucks, you can watch a little TV while you wait. Tell me that's not cool."

"I won't tell you that."

"Then tell me about you. I've done my teaser."

"I'm new in town."

"You've got a little bit of that charming southern accent."

Which she had worked so hard to get rid of. "Just a bit."

"Nashville, I'd say."

"Pretty good," she said. "You'll have to wait till tomorrow for the answer."

Now, looking at the insurance policy in her hands, Liz felt that same chill she felt when Toby mentioned the death of Veronica Lake. And when Arty mentioned the femme fatale. The woman the guy got mixed up with in the movies. Then ended up dead.

This time the cold hands did not release her.

She dropped the policy to the floor.

She stepped back and looked at it. Then she sucked in a big gulp of air and said, "I will, I will, I will."

Her phone rang.

"I will, I—"

Rang again. She closed her eyes, took a deep breath, and answered.

It was that detective. Moss.

"Have I caught you at a bad time?" Moss said.

Caught you.

"No, no, it's fine," Liz said.

"Good. Just wanted to let you know there will be an autopsy in the next day or two, and then we can release your husband to you."

Autopsy?

"You'll want to make arrangements," Moss said.

What was she looking for?

"I'm surprised," Liz said. "Why an autopsy?"

"It's procedure. Nothing to—"

"His body is going to be cut open?"

"Probably not. This is just to determine the exact cause of death—"

"He fell off a cliff!"

"Yes, as I say, just procedure, and an external exam is probably all there'll be. I just wanted you—"

"This is so hard—"

"—to be aware—"

"Thank you for calling. I have to be alone now."

"Of course."

Liz hung up. Moss was after something. Suspected something.

Autopsy? What would that show other than . . .

Scratches to Arty's face. She'd scratched his face. She remembered that now. A little detail she didn't give to Detective Moss. They'd find out it was fingernail marks. . .

The thought popped into her mind that she should just stop, stop now, not push this any further, because it could only end up bad. Very bad. *Stop now and tell them . . .*

But the money, the money.

No stopping now. All the way. You can deal with this. You have money now, you can deal with anything.

Keep moving.

But where? Where to turn for *this* problem?

And then she knew.

10:25 a.m.

Mac's hand was actually shaking. He couldn't believe it. He never trembled like this, not even in the joint. Not even approaching a desert bunker.

Butterflies in the stomach maybe, but his hands stayed steady. That's why they gave him the MICLIC duty. Steady nerves and hands.

But not now. Sitting in the guest room Pastor Jon rented to him, holding his phone, trying to punch the numbers. He had to do the number three times to get it right.

"Bedford-Mulrooney," the woman's voice answered.

"May I speak to Athena, please?" Mac said.

"May I tell her who's calling?"

No, because if you do, she might not take the call.

"Mr. MacDonald," he said.

"One moment," she said.

Classical music came on. It made him think of people in tuxedos sitting in a concert hall, like he'd seen on TV. He had never been to a real concert hall in his life.

It was some sort of nice melody with strings. He at least knew this was strings. Violins and cellos and ... whatever else strings were. A pleasant—

Cut off. Then, "Daniel?"

"Hey, Athena."

"How did you get this number?"

"I ... what do you mean? I knew you were working there."

"You did? I can't remember."

"How are you, anyway?"

"Busy."

"Well, it's good to be busy, I guess. If you're working."

"Of course I'm working."

"I didn't mean—"

"Why are you calling me, Daniel?"

The shakes got worse. A bead of sweat formed in the middle of the base of his hand, the one holding the phone. The bead rolled downward to his wrist, where it stalled.

"I wanted to know how you were doing," Mac said. "And how Aurora is."

"She's just fine," Athena said with clipped authority. As if cutting off an errant stem in a garden with one crisp snap of the shears.

"I mean, what's she into these days?"

"Daniel, is there any purpose to this?"

"I just want to know how she's doing, that's all. Is that so bad?"

"It might be."

"What do you mean by that?"

Long pause. Then Athena said, "I'd rather we not do this anymore."

"Do what?"

"Have contact."

The bead of sweat trickled on, tickling his arm, then dissipated. It was there, then it wasn't.

"Please don't say that," Mac said. "I want to see her again."

"I thought we decided—"

"You decided—"

"—it was best all around. Listen, Daniel, you need to know something. I'm going to get married, and it's best to transition out of the past."

"Transition out?" Mac said, "Like I'm some account you want to get rid of?"

"I didn't say that."

"I'm her father."

"Daniel," Athena said in her parental tone, "you aren't. Aurora is going to have only one father, and she's already bonding with Tony."

"Tony? He mafia or something?"

"Daniel, I have to go."

"Wait. Are you saying I can't see Aurora? Ever?"

"Don't you think that's best?"

"What if I don't think that's best?"

"It is, Daniel. She's at a very vulnerable stage—"

"Does she ever ask about me?"

"This isn't doing us any good," Athena said. "I would like you to honor my request that you don't contact us anymore."

"I don't think I can do that."

"I don't want to have to take steps."

"What steps?"

"I don't know, whatever the law—"

"I'm her father. I have rights."

"You waived those when you went in, remember? You signed off—"

"I can go back and try to get them."

"Please don't," Athena said. "I have to go."

"Wait—"

She didn't. The line went dead.

No classical music. Only silence.

Mac put the phone down, barely aware of the action. He didn't so much walk as drift toward the back door. He knew at some level of consciousness he was moving. But he also felt trapped, almost as if he were back in prison. It was a terrible and familiar feeling, one he would often get upon waking in his cell. A relentless despondency would form just below the ribs, where all the nerves came together in a knot, then spread upward, filling his thoughts.

Then he was outside and facing the hill behind the church. Studded with rocks, flowing down to the edges of what Mac hoped someday would be a flower garden, the hill now looked like the dead end of the world. Or a giant's grave.

Mac sat on the back steps and looked at the dirt and rocks, seeing and not seeing.

11:15 a.m.

"Don't be nervous, don't be nervous," Geena said.

"You're making me more nervous," Rocky said.

"Get in touch with your bliss," Geena said.

"Please be quiet—"

"Just try it!"

Rocky stopped and faced her. They were on Hollywood Boulevard, outside the Mashed Potato Lounge. "Geena, I love you, but I am not going to touch my bliss, center my spirit, or walk the Navajo way. I don't want to find any bliss, all right? My brother is dead, my father hates me, and my ex-boyfriend is psycho, and all I want to do is kick a baby seal, okay?"

"Rocky . . ."

"And I have to sing for a guy. I have one shot to get this gig, and I have to sing Cole Porter and look like I'm enjoying it. So don't talk to me about bliss right now."

Geena looked at her feet.

"Oh gee," Rocky said, and hugged her friend. "Let's just get this over with."

The only good feeling Rocky had about this was that she and Geena were about the same build. And Geena had one good dress for this occasion. Red, lacy, with spaghetti straps and a sweetheart neckline. Retro-looking. Sequin accents.

Luck. A little of it. Maybe it would rub off for the audition.

The manager of the lounge was a short, florid man with Moe Howard hair and a Sicilian accent. "Hey, you made it," he said. The lounge was done up in fifties nightclub style, with tables and a small stage area. Not very big, but some of the best jazz in the city was played here.

She was aware he was studying her face. And frowning. "I'm Ermano Militi," the man said.

"Roxanne Towne."

He glanced at Geena.

"My name's Geena. I'm just here for support."

"You sing?" he asked.

"No."

"You ever try?"

Geena shook her head. Militi winked at her. "You should," he said. He looked at Rocky. "So you got nice pipes?"

Rocky swallowed. "That's why I'm here."

"You got some music?"

She handed him a sheet. He looked at it. " 'Anything Goes.' Lenny?"

A black man in his forties came over from the bar. Militi handed him the sheet, and Lenny took it to the piano. Militi took Geena's arm and walked her to a table with a couple of chairs. They sat.

"You're on," he said to Rocky.

She was more nervous than she thought she'd be. This audition felt like the last audition on earth, her final shot.

Make it like Keely, she told herself. Like Peggy Lee.

She nodded at Lenny, who started playing.

Rocky leaned against the piano and sang.

> *In olden days a glimpse of stocking*
> *Was looked on as something shocking.*
> *Now heaven knows,*
> *Anything goes!*

A little rough. Rocky gave a quick look at the audience, such as it was. Militi's face was stoic, Geena's encouraging.

> *Good authors too who once knew better words*
> *Now only use four letter words*
> *Writing prose,*
> *Anything goes!*

And then she was into it. Feeling it. Shaping it, she thought. *This is one thing I can do.*

> *The world has gone mad today*
> *And good's bad today*
> *And black's white today*
> *And day's night today*
> *When most guys today*
> *That women prize today*
> *Are just silly gigolos.*

Take it home now.

> *So though I'm not a great romancer*
> *I know that I'm bound to answer*
> *When you propose,*
> *Anything goes!*

Lenny gave a little flourish at the end. Then the place was dead silent. Not that Rocky expected applause.

But the applause came. Geena clapped heartily and shouted, "Yes!"

Good old Geena.

Ermano Militi nodded a couple of times. He appeared to be studying her.

"You were right about the pipes," he said. "You got good ones. Good style."

Good isn't good enough, though, is it?

"I got your card," Militi said. "I'll call you."

What did she expect? To get the job right then?

Yes.

Outside, Geena said, "You nailed it."

"Sure."

"You'll get this thing."

"There's probably a hundred others who are up for it."

"They got nothing," Geena said. "You got the magic. You have to believe it. You can make your own reality, did you know that?"

Rocky found herself wanting to believe it. Who knew? She'd never talked to this Swami guy. Maybe he had something right.

"You think I can make this happen just by believing it?" Rocky said.

Geena perked up. "Yes!"

"So what do I do, just close my eyes and wish?"

"Yes!"

"Like it's my birthday and I have a cake?"

"You have to really believe it," Geena said. "If you don't believe it, the flow doesn't work."

Rocky closed her eyes. I want this, she told herself. I want, want, want this. I want something to go right for a change, be positive, vibrate, here I go, I want, want, want this.

She waited for something to click in her brain, an answer, a feeling, anything.

What she got was a big silent nothing.

She opened her eyes.

"Well?" Geena said. "How do you feel?"

"Like the biggest idiot in the world," Rocky said.

12:47 p.m.

When Mac walked through the door, the woman at the reception desk smiled and said, "May I help you?" and he thought, If anyone could really help me, I'd like to know. I'd really like to know who that person is.

"Can I see Mr. Newberry?" Mac said.

Her smile began to wane. She was about twenty-five and had short dark hair and a sharp chin. The chin reminded Mac of a prison guard he ran afoul of a couple times in the joint. What was it about the Department of Corrections anyway?

"Do you have an appointment?" she said.

"I used to be a client."

"Oh. Your name?"

"Daniel MacDonald."

"One moment."

She picked up a phone, and Mac looked around the office. Newberry had come a long way since his days as a public defender. Now he had a receptionist, a ficus tree, a framed painting of Lady Justice on the wall, and classical music piped in from hidden speakers.

He heard the receptionist say that a Mr. MacDonald was here who says he's a former client. She paused and listened, looked at Mac, said *Daniel* MacDonald, listened again, and looked at Mac again. Then she said, "All right," and put the phone back.

"He'll be right out, Mr. MacDonald."

"Thanks."

They looked at each other. Said nothing.

The phone rang and the receptionist answered. "Mr. Newberry's office, may I help you?"

She was good with the offer of help, that was for sure. Maybe it was a good sign. Maybe the legal system would work in his favor for a change.

Yeah, and maybe the pope would do handsprings on *Oprah*.

The interior door opened and Michael Newberry entered. He was thicker than the last time Mac saw him, six years ago. His hair was still black but he was styling it in a sleeker style now. It almost glistened under the lights.

"Mr. MacDonald." Newberry extended his hand.

"Howdy."

"Been a long time."

"Yeah."

"You're out."

"Yep."

"Good. That's good."

"Yeah," Mac said, "it's good to be out."

Newberry took a breath and nodded. "How much you end up doing?"

"A nickel."

"That's right," Newberry said. "So it worked out."

Yeah, the deal had worked out. Mac copped to robbery. They dropped the firearm count, which could have gotten him another ten years. He got five instead, and Newberry got rid of a file.

"How you getting on?" Newberry asked. He did not offer to have Mac step into his office.

"That's sort of why I'm here," Mac said.

Newberry nodded.

"Can we talk?" Mac said.

Newberry looked at his watch. "I have someone coming in —" He looked at Mac. "I've got a couple of minutes."

He led Mac into the office. It had several stacks of files on the floor, tucked up against the walls. Newberry's desk was cluttered in a workmanlike way.

They sat.

"Looks like you're doing pretty well," Mac said.

"A little here, a little there," Newberry said.

"Just doing criminal?"

"Mostly. You got something come up?"

"I'm being hassled by my PO. I don't know why, but he's got a jones for making my life miserable."

"What's he doing?"

"I know he's got a right to search, but all the time? Pushing me? He wants me to snap."

"Why would he do that?"

"No idea."

"No witnesses to anything, I presume." Newberry tapped his fingertips together.

"No."

Newberry pursed his lips, said nothing.

"So what can I do?" Mac said.

"You want the truth? Not much. You take it until you're termed out."

"That's it? That's all?"

"Reality."

Mac swallowed. It felt like a rock going down. "Can't I sue or something?"

"For what?"

"Harassment."

With a sigh, Newberry said, "Look, you know what it's like for a felon. You got a search condition, you waived your Fourth Amendment rights. He can stop you, search you, search your place, whenever he wants. And he can be a real jerk about it, too. Not supposed to be, but there you go."

"Can't I get an injunction or something?"

Newberry shook his head. "Only thing you can do is 602 him."

"What's a 602?"

"It's a form from the Department of Corrections for prisoners and parolees to file a complaint."

"I have to send it to the people who employ this guy?"

"It's called administrative appeal, and you can't go to court unless you do this first, and even after you do it your chances in court are about the same as you and me playing first base for the Dodgers."

Mac thought about it a moment. "I have to do something. Let's go for it."

"You can get the form online."

"Can you file it for me?"

"You want to hire me?"

"I guess, I thought ..." What had he thought? That his old PD would rep him for free?

Newberry said, "You working?"

"I got a little thing with a church. Not much luck anywhere else. When I apply, I have to check the felony box, and that's that."

Newberry nodded. "They say they want to help guys get back into society, then they do everything to make it impossible. Including random searches. Doesn't make sense to me."

"I got a couple hundred I can give you," Mac said.

"It's not really something—"

"I can get more."

"I'm not going to be able to help you with this one, I'm afraid."

Mac laughed. "What if I got you two thousand dollars?"

"Are you kidding?"

"Of course," Mac said. "Where'm I gonna get two grand?"

"I really wish there was something—"

"My daughter," Mac said.

"Right, right. How is she?"

"I don't know. I need a court order to see her. I'm trying to keep my nose clean, but this Slezak keeps rubbing mud in my face. So I have to file a—"

"I don't do family law."

"—I need help."

"I can give you a referral," Newberry said.

"Yeah?" Mac said. "To a lawyer who'll charge me two grand?"

"Daniel, we do have to make a living."

"Oh sure, yes, you all have to make a living," Mac said. "You all have to sit back with wives and families and ..." He stopped himself. "I'm sorry."

Newberry nodded. "Hang in there," he said.

2:15 p.m.

"My dear, you look fabulous!" Toby Gray came out from behind his mess of a desk, arms out, and pulled Liz in for a hug. Then he pushed her outward, holding her shoulders, looking at her. "You know my standing offer. Anytime you want to come back."

"Thanks," Liz said. Toby himself looked fabulous. Thick black hair in a fifties pompadour, his chosen look ever since she first met him. His thin body held clothes well, and Toby knew how to dress. He was one of the few men she knew who could wear pastels and make them seem dangerous and sexy. To other men ... of a certain kind. Toby was thoroughly and openly gay.

"Now then, you simply must tell me the story of your life since you stopped being Veronica Lake."

"You remembered."

"Remember! Dear, every new recruit, I show them this." He went to the floor-to-ceiling bookcase, which was completely stuffed with movie books and Hollywood biographies, and pulled down a large photo album. He shoved some papers on his desk so he could lay the album down. He opened the cover.

There was an eight-by-ten color photo of Liz as Veronica Lake on the first page.

"*This* is what I show them, my sweet. You are the cover girl. The glam shot. The one that hooks 'em."

Hooks 'em. Yes, she and Toby were very much alike indeed.

That's why she was here.

"I'm in trouble, Toby."

He closed the photo album. "That sounds serious."

"It is."

Toby went to the office door, closed it. Then he guided Liz into a wooden chair, the kind a lawyer might have used in the 1950s, and had her sit. He parked himself on the edge of his desk and said, "Tell Uncle Toby what's wrong."

"I don't know where to start," Liz said.

"The beginning, dear."

Liz smiled. "That would be here. The Veronica Lake party, the first time I went out."

"It is emblazoned on my mind like Apollo's chariot. A magical night."

"The night I met Arty, my husband."

"Ah, yes. The whiz kid businessman who convinced you to abandon me."

"He's dead, Toby."

Toby put his right index finger on his lips. "I'm sorry."

"It's complicated," Liz said. "An accident. We were hiking, I got mad, he fell — "

"Fell?"

"Off a small cliff. Enough to hit his head on the rocks."

"I'm sorry, dear." Toby touched her arm.

"It was an accident. A terrible accident. But there are some questions, a sheriff's detective with questions."

Toby nodded. "They tend to do that, don't they? Horrible people. Tell me, do the questions have any basis? And before you answer, please remember it's Uncle Toby here."

"Barely," Liz said. "I don't want to go into it, please. The thing is, they are going to do an autopsy, and I need to have them . . ."

"Not find anything?"

Liz nodded.

Toby put his hand on her cheek. "You knew the right person to come to," he said.

"Can you really do it?"

He put his right hand on his chest, fingers spread. "Dear, this is *Toby*. Already the cogs and wheels are spinning in my well-connected head. Now, the county morgue, that's a good thing. That's going to work for us. The place is absolutely nuts. However ..."

"Yes?"

"It's not going to come without cost. We have to spread some money around."

"I have money."

"That's good enough for me. You let me take it from here. I forgot your married name."

"Towne. Husband, Arthur."

"And he died when?"

"Saturday."

"Wow. Not long."

"Is that good or bad?"

"Probably good. Call me here tonight, but use a pay phone. And sweetie ..."

"Yes?"

"Try not to worry, okay? Remember. This is *Toby*."

8:05 p.m.

Rocky tried not to yell into the phone. "I want to have a say in this."

Liz's voice, coming back at her, was cool and measured. "Rocky, I know what Arty's wishes were, and he did not want to have a big deal made over his death."

"He talked about death to you?"

"Oh, we did talk about it."

"It was the topic of conversation how many times?"

"Rocky, why are you talking to me this way?"

All right, pull back, Rocky told herself. Maybe Liz, for all her standoffishness, was really grieving. Give her some slack, but don't let her run all over things.

"Look, Liz, I just want to make sure the family is involved."

"You will be. I'm going to get with Pastor Jon and talk about it."

"But why rush it? Why does it have to be Wednesday?"

"I need closure, Rocky. And all his friends are right here."

Rocky sighed. "Where's the funeral going to be?"

"I have to talk to Pastor Jon."

"I'll talk to Pastor Jon, too, then."

"Please, Rocky, I'm really hurting here. I don't want anything to come between us, especially now."

Right.

"Arty wouldn't have wanted that," Liz said.

"I just thought in planning this whole thing, we could — "

"Pastor will handle everything. And I promise to keep you in the loop."

"Well, thanks, I — "

"I prayed this morning that God would bring us all closer together."

"You did what?"

"Rocky, yesterday I accepted the Lord Jesus as my Savior. Just like Arty wanted me to. It's a feeling like starting all over again. I'd like that to be true for us. For us to be sisters."

That thought went down like a dry cracker. Rocky started to think maybe she was being a jerk. That wouldn't be too much of a stretch.

Arty wanted them to like each other. Rocky wanted to but just couldn't.

Then, when Arty got religion, he thought that might make things better. As if he could be the center that pulled two opposites together.

Didn't quite work that way.

I'm sorry, Arty. Really sorry.

"And now," Liz said, "I just want to live right and make Arty proud of me. I know he's with the Lord now, and I want him ..." Her voice trailed off into what sounded like tears.

"Okay," Rocky said.

She heard a sniff.

"Sorry I was a little short with you," Rocky said. "Now's not the time."

"Thank you, Rocky. I know the Lord is going to work this all out for both of us."

Fat chance.

After the phone conversation, Rocky followed the Eastern music into the kitchen. Geena was doing some interpretive dance, barefoot.

"Join me?" Geena said, swaying like a flag in a stiff breeze.

"I'll pass," Rocky said. "You have any Milanos?" A bag of cookies and an old movie on TV were just the ticket.

"I don't think so," Geena said. She danced over to a cupboard and flung it open. "I have some saltines."

Just my luck, Rocky thought. And the only old movie was on TCM, some 1940s navy movie. It looked like a comedy. The info display said it was *Bring on the Girls* starring somebody named Sonny Tufts.

Who?

Oh, and Veronica Lake. Fine. Rocky always liked Veronica Lake. She had that hairdo.

Maybe this wouldn't be such a bad way to kill some time. "Hey, Geena," Rocky called. "Do you at least have some Cheez Whiz?"

8:32 p.m.

Tomorrow, Liz thought. Tomorrow, I'll go get the sacks.

Don't be seen. Figure out your story first.

You went out to the canyon to pray. Pray over where Arty had fallen. You went out there to spend some time alone with God.

She shivered. The house wasn't cold. She had the heat on.

But she was cold. Even after the drink. The bottle of Beam was half full. Well, go for it. Whatever.

It would help her sleep. She hadn't slept too well last night.

Of course you didn't, just some nerves. Relax.

Mama, don't worry, I'm going to relax. And then I'll come see you. I'll come...

The phone rang. Liz almost jumped out of the chair.

Should I answer?

It rang again.

Better answer. If I don't answer, somebody might want to stop on by.

"Hello."

"Liz, it's Mac."

"Oh hi, Mac."

"How you doing?"

"Fine."

"You sure?"

"Yes. Just tired."

"You had a big day yesterday."

"Yes, I did."

"I wanted to read you something," Mac said. "A little encouragement."

"Why?"

"Well, you kind of seemed upset in the parking lot."

"Oh, that. I was just ... overwhelmed."

"I know. I know just how you felt."

"You do?

"Do you have a Bible?"

"Arty has one."

"Can you get it?"

"Now?"

"Now," he said. "I want you to read something with me."

If she had to, she had to. She put the phone down, got up, and went to the bedroom. Arty actually had three Bibles. That annoyed her. Why not just one big one and be done with it?

He kept one on his bedside table, and it was still there. Red leatherette cover. She reached for it and then stopped. Like her hand would burn if she touched it.

Crazy, she thought. Don't give it that power.

She picked up the Bible. Nothing happened to her hands. She went back to the phone.

"Got it," she said.

"Okay," Mac said. "Open it to about the middle, and look at the top for the book of Psalms."

"Psalms?"

"It'll be printed at the top of the page."

She lay the Bible on her lap and opened it. It freaked her out a little. Like something might pop out at her. Like a hand grabbing her throat.

Only pages. "I see Proverbs," she said.

"Flip a little to your left, and you'll find Psalms."

She did. There it was, just like he said.

"Okay," she said.

"Now follow the numbers till you get to Psalm 51."

She did, and dark memories of Sunday school floated back. That was the last time she had looked in a Bible.

She flipped to the Psalm numbered 51. "I'm there," she said.

"Now look for the verse numbered 17."

Liz ran her finger down the page and stopped on 17. "Okay."

"You see it?" Mac said.

"Yes."

"It says, 'The sacrifices of God are a broken spirit; a broken and contrite heart, O God, you will not despise.' "

"What's that mean?"

"What it means," Mac said, "is that you showed a brokenness of spirit yesterday, and that is what God wants. He is going to heal you and hold you up always."

Liz shuddered.

"So you just go to bed with this Scripture in your mind," Mac said. "Good night."

"'Night."

Liz hung up the phone and closed her eyes. *Just gather yourself, take it easy, day by day. Everything will flow.*

She looked down at the open Bible. Her eyes fell on some words. *For I know my transgressions, and my sin is always before me. Against you, you only, have I sinned and done what is evil in your sight, so that you are proved right when you speak and justified when you judge.*

Liz almost screamed. She pushed the Bible off her lap. It fell to the floor, pages down. Liz just stared at it, like it could, at any moment, turn over and crawl back at her.

Tuesday

9:23 a.m.

"Thanks for seeing me, Mrs. Towne," Detective Moss said. Thanks? Liz was tired and didn't want to do this. Not now, not ever. Why couldn't they just leave her alone? It was over.

Funeral tomorrow. That was all they needed to know.

But the woman detective had this bulldog look about her. Arrogant. Even with all her surface politeness. She stood at the door like she had a right to be here.

You can do this, Liz told herself, then said, "Can we make this fast? I have so many things I have to see to."

"Of course. Inside or out?"

"Oh, would you mind out here?" Liz said. "The house is a mess."

"I'm sure you're awfully worn out," Moss said.

Liz motioned to a couple of white plastic patio chairs, coated with a thin veneer of dust. That was one thing you could count on in Pack Canyon. Dust and dirt and everything muddy when it rained.

They sat. The detective held nothing in her hands. It was just like she wanted to have a friendly conversation. But Liz knew about those. She knew how cops and sheriffs talked to you when they wanted something, like when they tried to get her to rat out her own mother.

You had to be careful with the law. They were silver-tongued snakes.

"I just want to say again how sorry I am for your loss."

"Thank you."

"Is your head all right?"

Liz had put a fresh Band-Aid on her forehead five minutes earlier. It actually hurt, but she said, "Fine."

"Good, good. You need to take care of yourself now. Anything you need?"

"I've got some good people looking out for me."

"Oh? Family?"

"Sort of. My church."

"Ah. What church is that?"

"The community church. Just up the road."

"Little white one? Across from the market?"

Liz nodded.

"Your husband, he was an active member of that church, wasn't he?"

How did she know that? She'd been talking to people. "That's right."

"You didn't attend with him?"

"No, not then. Now I do. I mean, now I'm a member."

"I hope that didn't cause any friction in the marriage. It sometimes does."

"Not really," Liz said. "But anyway, that's all taken care of now."

"Taken care of?"

"Arty was leading me to God. I went to church yesterday. Because I knew that's what Arty would want me to do. And I accepted Jesus as my Lord and Savior."

Moss did not saying anything. Her face was impassive. Then she nodded. "Religion is quite a comfort at times like this, isn't it?"

"Is there anything else you need to know?"

"Oh, just a couple of things. Just to wrap things up, you know, get the old file off the desk."

"You have a file?"

"Every accidental death requires some attention. Oh, yes, and I got a call from the coroner's office. They already released your husband's body to a mortuary."

"Yes?"

"Things are moving very quickly."

"Did they find anything?"

"Like what?" Moss said.

Playing possum, this one was. "Wasn't there supposed to be an autopsy?"

"Right," Moss said. "There was. That was fast, too. I got the verbal on it. Accidental death. I'm very sorry, again."

Liz tried not to look relieved. Toby had apparently come through.

"I would like to ask you just one more thing, if I may," Moss said. "When you were out hiking with your husband, did you see anyone else out there?"

"No. It was pretty quiet."

"Didn't hear anything?"

"Like what?"

"Odd sounds. Sounds that shouldn't be in nature."

"Not that I remember."

The detective knew about the biker body. Liz was sure of that now. They had found the man and wanted to see if she knew anything. Liz felt her pulse pounding in her neck and was sure Moss could see it, like little fists popping out under her skin. She took a breath and composed herself.

"So you didn't see or hear anything out of the ordinary?" Moss said.

"No. Nothing. I was on a nice hike with my husband who is —" Liz put a little catch in her throat, then lowered her head.

"I'm sorry, Mrs. Towne. I know how fresh this is. I promise I won't be much longer."

You'd better not be, or I'll be calling your superiors. "Go ahead."

"Well, it's the strangest thing. Really, a terrible coincidence. Not very far from where your husband fell, we found a corpse."

"A corpse?"

"Yes."

"How awful. Who was it?"

"We're looking into that. It was a man on a motorcycle. I wonder how he got there. That's why I wanted to know if you heard anything. It was a Harley, so it would have been hard to miss."

Liz shook her head. "It was as quiet as always out there."

"It's just very strange. It could have just been a guy out for a ride, he got a little careless and went over off the path. It's happened to some kids on bicycles around here. But never something fatal."

"I can hardly believe it."

"Oh, and there was one other thing. His motorcycle had a couple of saddlebags on it that were empty. Not that that means anything, of course, but it's just so doggone strange. You never know, you know? You stay in a job long enough."

Liz nodded. A hot, dry wind blew across her face. It felt like the fever she had when she was twelve that sent her to the hospital. She remembered almost fainting because of it. But later she thought it made her stronger, because she never got that sick again. She refused to.

"I'm sorry, Detective. We didn't see or hear anything. It was just supposed to be a nice walk. That's ... all ..."

"I understand. Thanks for your time."

"No problem," Liz said. Sweet relief. But she kept herself from showing it and stood up.

Moss stood and started for the steps, paused, turned around. "Just one other thing. Do you have Arty's cell phone?"

"What?" Liz said.

"Do you have it in the house?"

"Um, I don't know. Maybe it's at his office."

"Oh," Moss said. "Was he still working at, what was it?"

"RumbleTV."

"That's it. Do you have the address?"

Liz rubbed her right eye with the heel of her hand. "No, he hadn't been there for a while. I'm just so upset. Do you mind?"

"No, of course not," Moss said. "I'm sorry to have disturbed you so soon."

Meaning what? You'll disturb me later?

At the foot of the stairs, Moss turned. "You'll look for that cell phone, won't you?"

"But why?"

"I don't know exactly. I just like to clean things up."

I'll bet you do, Liz thought.

10:35 a.m.

How do you not look conspicuous?

Mac wasn't any good at this, sneaking around. And he felt dirty. Was this deception? Would Jesus approve?

He had to get it right this time. Quit letting God down. Stick to the true.

He was parked in his pickup across from the school. He had a map of California open on the steering wheel, but he was not studying the map. He was looking across at the school yard, looking for his daughter.

Was this like a lie? To pretend to be studying a map? It was a dodge, in case someone thought a battered Chevy pickup with a guy behind the wheel just sitting there didn't look right.

He was even ready to tell a cop or security guard that he was on his way to Ojai and wondered what the right way was.

And that would be a lie.

The children were out playing kickball. This was supposed to be Aurora's school, at least it was the last time he'd ever gotten any useful information from his ex-wife. This was the school she had picked for their daughter to attend.

Of course, all he knew about Aurora was that she had red hair. And right now he didn't see any girl that fit that description.

A teacher or an aide, a woman, came to the chain-link fence and looked directly at him.

He quickly turned his eyes to the map, even moved it a little as if studying.

Lord, help me. If this is wrong, I won't to do it. But I need to see her. Can you at least let me see her?

The woman was still there. She looked back at the kids, then at Mac.

Headache coming.

He was almost watching himself now as he crumpled the map in his hands. Made it into a wadded ball and threw it against the windshield.

It ricocheted off the glass, hit the passenger seat, rolled harmlessly to the floor.

God.

Please.

He fired up the truck and drove on.

10:48 a.m.

"Hi," Rocky said into the phone. "Is Mr. Militi in?"

"Who's calling?"

"Roxanne Towne."

"Just a second."

Rocky looked at Geena, who was smiling and holding up crossed fingers. "Go ahead and vibrate if you want to," Rocky told her. "If you want to spin like a top, I won't stop you. Remember the Tasmanian Devil on—"

"This is Ermano."

"Oh, hi, Mr. Militi. This is Roxanne Towne."

"Yes?"

"I was just wondering—"

"Oh, yes! Yesterday. Here in the lounge. You want to know, I know."

"Yes—"

"You got good pipes, you do."

"Thank you—"

"And that's my job, you know. Pipes. You got 'em."

"Thanks, I—"

"You got some style, too. Maybe not as distinct yet. But you keep working."

"I will work my heart out, Mr. Militi."

"You do that, and sometime down the road, eh?"

Her heart fell to the pit of her stomach. "I can bring them in for you. I do a whole Cole Porter slate—"

"I just don't think it's the right fit for the club at this moment in time."

"Right fit?"

"You know, being around as you are, each club's got a personality ..."

Yeah, like yours is the Mafia, she thought. Then she told herself it was unfair. It was her face. Too distracting for the customers.

"So I want to wish you all the luck in the world, kid," Militi said. "Truly."

Before she could say another word, the connection cut.

Geena said, "Not good, huh?"

"Chalk up another victory for the singing career," Rocky said.

"Rocky —"

"No, it's time I got it through my head that I am not going to make it in public. Better to sing in the shower because nobody can see me in the shower."

"Come on," Geena said.

"I'll go back to the apartment today. Get whatever's left and put it in the car and go find my own place."

"Stay here with me," Geena said.

"I don't want to bring you anymore bad luck."

"You haven't brought me any bad luck, and anyway —"

"Thanks for trying." Rocky put her phone in her purse and started to leave.

"I'll go with you," Geena said.

"No," Rocky said. "I want to be alone right now."

"Where are you going?"

"I don't know. I thought maybe I'd go to the park and scream at people as they walk by."

Geena blinked.

"I'm kidding, cutie," Rocky said. "Half kidding, anyway."

"Don't get drunk."

She left Geena smiling at the door.

Rocky did go to the park, five blocks from Geena's. The day wasn't so bad. A little cloudy. They said it was supposed to rain later in the week.

Just not tomorrow, she hoped. Tomorrow when Arty's rushed funeral would be held. She wanted it to be good for Arty, for his memory.

And she kept wondering about Liz's conversion story.

Very, very convenient.

But what if it was true? *What are you missing out on, Rocky Towne? Is there some sort of spiritual brass ring out there? Need to grab it?*

She found a bench by the fountain and watched some kids playing on the slides. A little girl in a red jacket was being helped up the steps by her mother, who sat the girl at the top of the slide.

Rocky remembered her dream of Arty sliding down and disappearing.

The little girl on the slide, she was maybe three years old, whined. But her mother took her hand and said, "Hold on to me. I'm right here."

The girl stopped whining. She took a breath and then she went. She screamed on the way down, a joyful scream. When she got off, she had a big smile on her face.

"Again," she said.

It must be nice to have somebody right there, Rocky thought. To hold your hand on the way down.

She noticed a boy staring at her. Short black hair, like a brush. Six or seven years old.

"Hi," Rocky said.

"What happened to your face?" the boy said.

Direct little fellow. "A dog bit me when I was a girl."

"Did it hurt?"

"Yeah."

"Does it still hurt?"

"No."

"Not ever?"

"Maybe a little sometimes."

The boy didn't say anything.

"What's your name?" Rocky said.

"Andrew," he said.

"My name's Rocky."

"Rocky?"

She nodded.

"Is that a girl's name?" Andrew said.

"Sometimes."

"Okay. Bye."

The boy turned and ran toward the slides. She kind of admired that. You say what you want, then get out. Ask your question, then go on about your business.

Good luck there, Andrew, she thought. I hope you have some good times. Somebody should in this life.

1:52 p.m.

Replacing a fuse for Mr. Hecht, Mac thought, People sometimes kidnap their own children.

He shook his head, almost as if trying to jostle the idea from his mind.

But it stuck.

Just take your own child and—

"Stupid," he said.

"How's that?" Mr. Hecht said. He was sitting in a lawn chair, reading the newspaper. Another one of the old church members, Mr. Hecht was. His wife had died a year ago.

"Sorry," Mac said. "Just mumbling." The new fuse in, Mac shut the box. He tried to shut his mind off the same way.

But he couldn't stop the thought of running, getting away from this place, from Slezak and the courts and the rules. Taking Aurora with him.

Of course, he couldn't. Not that he wasn't capable. There was still larceny in his soul, he was sure of that. This whole new-creation business was slow on God's part. Especially with the material Mac had handed over to him.

Stop thinking about yourself, stupid. Help Liz and Arty's sister get through this time.

"Can I run my washing machine now?" Mr. Hecht said.

"Sure can," Mac said.

"And watch TV?"

"Yep."

"I dunno," Mr. Hecht said. "Maybe I'd be better off watching the washing machine. Not much worth it on television. Only that reality stuff, what do they call it?"

"Reality shows, I think."

"Why'd I want to watch those?" Mr. Hecht asked. "I got enough reality as it is."

You and me both, Sir, Mac thought. More than enough.

3:33 p.m.

Ted did one more crunch. His stomach was burning, but he felt no pain.

He was too busy thinking of her.

Resting now, in his apartment with the water-stained ceiling, Ted did his confidence-building exercises.

The book had said you have to self-talk it into being. That was the start.

You can be anything you think you are, if you say it to yourself and give yourself enough feeling.

The subconscious, the book said, can't distinguish between a real event and an imaginary one that is vividly imagined.

So even though he was alone in an apartment in a lousy neighborhood, sweating through his T-shirt, for a moment Ted was on the prow of a ship, the woman of his dreams under his arm.

The woman. The only one he wanted.

"I am confident," Ted said.

Wednesday

11:10 a.m.

Rocky stood apart from the small crowd starting to gather at the grave site. They were at a far corner of the cemetery. It ended at chain-link fence. On the other side of the fence were the dry brush and rocks of Pack Canyon.

The cemetery was a carpet of green grass dotted with markers. The sky was more forbidding than yesterday. Cloudy and cold.

She turned her back on the mourners and looked at the marker at her feet. A woman's name, *Erin Gerber*. With the dates 1984–2001.

Beloved daughter, the marker read. *She gave laughter and joy and memories forever.*

Seventeen years old. What memories was that enough time for? No one should die at seventeen.

Rocky had time for memories, and they flooded her head. Memories of the two girls from her high school who died on prom night. Drinking with their boyfriends in the back of a van. Making out one moment, smashed to death the next.

One of them, Billie Harper, was a secret friend. Secret because she was on the "A List" and couldn't be seen consorting with an outsider like Rocky. But she did go out of her way to be nice in English Lit, where they found out they both hated George Eliot and loved Jane Austen.

Billie, who was going to be one of the golden ones. Her life literally came to a crashing and sudden end.

Now Billie was under a grave marker. Just like this Erin. Just like they all would be.

But Arty believed a marker wasn't the end. What had happened to make him believe that? He had tried to explain it to her one night. It sounded too mystical, too much like one of Geena's fads. But then, Arty wasn't like Geena. He was the smart one in the family.

Was he singing with the angels now? Was that what his religion taught him?

A slap of breeze hit her cheeks. She sensed someone looking at her and turned.

He was leaning on the hood of a car at the access road. Expressionless.

The coldness inside her now was not from the wind. It came from his gaze.

He did not move. She would have to go to him.

He would never come to her.

11:12 a.m.

Mac put his arm around Liz. "You doing okay?"

She nodded. She wore sunglasses and was zipped up in a black jacket.

"You need anything, like water?" Mac said.

Liz shook her head.

"Try to think of this as a graduation," Mac said.

Liz looked at him.

"Arty graduated early," Mac said. "That's all."

She shuddered a little under his arm. He wasn't doing a very good job here. That's why he wasn't a pastor. Pastor Jon, now there was a man who knew the right things to say at a time like this.

They were standing by the small table with a red cloth over it. On top of the table was the urn with Arty's ashes. Mac wondered about that. But he figured Liz must have known Arty's wishes better than anyone.

Mac looked across the grass and saw Rocky. She was walking toward the cars parked along the interior road.

He should go to her next. Make sure she was doing all right.

11:13 a.m.

"Hello, Pop," Rocky said.

"Roxanne." He didn't even nod. He was dressed in an ill-fitting sport jacket and thick blue tie. The knot on the tie was the size of a fist. His curly hair, once a vibrant brown, was almost completely white now, and thinning.

She hadn't seen him since last Christmas. He seemed to have aged five more years in that time.

"How are you?" Rocky said.

"Can't complain," he said. "Except a little."

"A little about what?"

"Nothing."

"Not nothing. What is it?"

"Bodies break down," he said. "Even when you used to have a good one."

"What's happened, Pop?"

"Nothing."

"Don't keep saying that. What's the prob—"

"I'm not here to talk about medical conditions," he said. With his final-authority, end-of-this-part-of-the-conversation voice. "I'm here for Arty."

Not for me, though. Right?

Her father said, "You working?"

"Yes," she said. "But—"

"How much?"

"How much what?"

"Have you been working?"

She looked at the sky, the steel-colored clouds hovering. "Off and on, like always."

"Still nothing steady."

"I'm a freelancer, it's—"

"Not stable."

"It's work, okay? I get paid."

"When you work."

She shook her head, wanting to run screaming through the cemetery, screaming at the ghosts that they were the lucky ones. They didn't have to put up with anymore of life. They didn't have to hear how their fathers never thought they could do anything worthwhile and feel lower than dirt—

"You still living with that guy?" her father said.

"Not one for the small talk, are you, Pop?"

"What's the point?"

A long moment passed. A sullen silence woven from too many disappointments, too many lost years. Rocky felt like they should touch, at least. Maybe not embrace, but at least put a hand around the shoulder or something. She'd even take shaking hands.

Then her father said, "Well, I guess we better get over there." And he started walking toward the grave site.

11:25 a.m.

"If the world were to look in on us at this moment," Pastor Jon was saying, "people might say, 'They have come to say their final good-byes to someone they love.' They would only be partially correct. It is true that we have come to express our love and share our loss, but the good-byes are not final."

Liz thought, *I hope this does not go on too long. Can't they just be done with it?*

On a table, Arty's urn was sitting, waiting to be lowered in a hole. At least that had worked out. A fast cremation, a fast ceremony.

Once the urn was buried, she could get on with it. Endure the little gathering they'd have back at the church. Everyone would eat and talk about Arty and comfort her, and she'd be grinding her teeth on the inside. But she could take it. It was a small price to pay for the payoff to come.

In truth she did feel a little sorry for Arty. He was a good man who had gone a little off the beam with religion. It had affected his lifestyle. Even more, it had affected hers.

Well, he died because of it. An accident. She hadn't wanted him to die. But now it was the best thing all around.

"At the heart of the Christian faith is the truth of eternal life," Pastor Jon said. "This eternal life is not an abstract idea, not a work of fiction, not a superstition passed down through the ages. It is a fact that has been taught throughout the Bible. Jesus taught it on many occasions. Jesus said, 'I am the resurrection and the life. He who believes in me will live, even though he dies.'"

Never die? Liz thought. *That's kind of scary.*

"Jesus, when speaking with the disciples before he went to the cross, said, 'Do not let your hearts be troubled. Trust in God; trust also in me. In my Father's house are many rooms; if it were not so, I would have told you. I am going there to prepare a place for you. And if I go and prepare a place for you, I will come back and take you to be with me that you also may be where I am.'"

Why do people believe this?

"The Bible tells us that to be absent from the body is to be present with the Lord. That is where Arty is right now. He is with his Savior, awaiting that joyous time when all of us, his church family, will join him in our eternal dwelling place."

Can Arty read my thoughts? Talk about scary. Maybe there was such a thing as ghosts. But they have no power. She would not let them have any power. No one would ever have power over her.

"Now," Pastor Jon said, "we'll take a few moments for those who'd like to say something about Arty's life."

Liz had forgotten about this part. Pastor Jon had gone over all the particulars with her the night before. Including this deal about letting people talk.

Things were going to go on a lot longer than she'd hoped.

11:31 a.m.

Mac said, "Arty was about the closest friend I had. He was there for me when it counted. Even though we didn't know each other that long, he was like a brother to me."

Tears pressed against his eyes. He took a deep breath.

"I haven't had a real good time of it in the last few years, and it's only because of church and Pastor Jon that I haven't done something real stupid, like put my head through a plate-glass window. But there was this one time I felt like I was going to do it, and the only guy I could get hold of was Arty."

Warm tears beginning now.

"He came right over, even though it was late at night, and he sat with me and started telling me stories. He was a real storyteller, Arty was. He started telling me about this doctor at UCLA who was doing some genetic experiments with animals. He went on and on, and I started to listen. It was really fascinating."

Mac paused, took a breath, continued. "I mean, all the things this doctor had to do to fight the administration and the press and even his other colleagues. And Arty goes on and on, and then finally describes the big breakthrough the guy had, when he was able to cross a dog with a chicken, and got pooched eggs."

A moment of silence, then people started to laugh. As did Mac, wiping his eyes. It was a moment Arty would have liked. He was that kind of guy.

11:38 a.m.

"I don't have a whole lot of funny stories," Rocky said when it was her turn to speak. "Arty liked to laugh, I know that. He used to make me laugh when we were kids. He used to help me, too. I guess Arty was just like that. A helper."

Keeping her eyes on Liz, Rocky said, "He would have done anything for anybody. I guess that's what we're trying to say here. And that he shouldn't have died. It was too soon."

The face of Liz Towne, hidden behind dark glasses, was expressionless.

"He was the most loyal person I knew," Rocky said. "If he was for you, you knew you could count on him. I just can't imagine anyone who knew him not liking him or not trusting him or wanting to play him false."

Liz looked away.

"I know that Arty felt like he found a family with all of you." This time Rocky looked at her father. He was already looking away.

Her heart dropped. She closed her eyes. "That's all I really have to say," she said and melted back into the small crowd, on the opposite side from her father and Liz.

11:40 a.m.

"Thank you so much, everyone," Liz said. Her voice was shaking. "You were family to Arty. And now you're family to me. I am so touched that you all came out today."

All except you, Rocky. I don't like at all the way you're looking at me.

"Arty was close to the earth, I guess you could say. He loved the outdoors. He loved being in Pack Canyon, where you could still find some undeveloped land, right here in Los Angeles, to hike around in. Now as his ashes go to be with the earth, I know that his soul has gone to be with the Lord. That's the most comforting thing of all. I just praise God."

12:09 p.m.

Mac stood right by Liz's side as she greeted folks. First in line was Pastor Jon.

"Thank you for a lovely service," Liz said to him. She held out her hand, but he put his arms around her and gave her a bear hug.

"You just lean on us now," he said.

"I will," she said. "Of course I will. You and Mac."

"That's right." Pastor Jon held her a moment in his strong arms, then moved to minister to some other members of his flock.

Mac whispered, "You're doing fine."

"Thanks," Liz said.

Then Mac saw Mrs. Axelrod step up, along with Mr. Dean. Mac gave Liz's arm an encouraging squeeze.

"Brave girl," Mrs. Axelrod said. "Come here." She opened her arms like a grand dame and almost smothered Liz.

Mac saw the look in Mrs. Axelrod's eyes, a portent of long-windedness. He patted Mrs. Axelrod's arm and said, "We'll be along to the church in just a bit."

"What? Oh. Yes." Mrs. Axelrod smiled at them both and turned around. Mr. Dean nodded, said nothing, followed after her.

A man Mac recognized from town but not church stepped over. He looked like a young college professor.

"Mrs. Towne, I know this is a hard time for you," he said.

"Yes," Liz said. To Mac she sounded dead tired.

"I do most of the reporting for our little Pack Canyon paper."

"Paper?"

"The *Herald*. We have a Web site now, but we still churn out the ol' dead trees." He smiled. His teeth were a bit yellow.

"Oh, yeah," Mac said. "I read the *Herald*. My name's Mac-Donald."

"Brady," the reporter said. "Mike Brady. I wanted to run a story about your husband, Mrs. Towne."

"Story?" Liz said.

"Yes. I wonder if you could tell me about anything you found out there in the canyon."

Mac sensed Liz stiffen next to him. "Maybe now's not the time," he said.

"I just would like to get the facts—"

"Maybe another time, Mike. We're at a funeral here."

"But my story won't be—"

"Please," Liz said. "Please just leave me alone."

She practically ran toward her car.

1:13 p.m.

The world has gone mad today, And good's bad today, And black's white today...

The lyrics kept coming back around in Rocky's head. Was Cole Porter some sort of prophet?

She remembered something Arty said to her, just a few weeks ago. "Everybody's going crazy today," he said. "No one knows what to believe."

That was right. Good was called bad, black called white.

It really was gone mad today.

Here she was at Arty's church, among the people all eating and doing their best to comfort Liz Towne. Were they all mad? All of them, for believing in a good God?

Didn't they know about just plain bad luck?

"I appreciated what you said about Arty."

Mac had come up behind her.

"Thanks," Rocky said. "You were probably about his best friend."

"One of them, I think."

"Can I ask you something about him?"

"Sure."

An older woman holding a paper plate with a triangular sandwich and glob of potato salad bumped Rocky's elbow.

"Oh, excuse me," the woman said. She looked at Rocky, gave her the familiar facial once-over, then added, "You are Arthur's sister."

"Yes," Rocky said.

"This is Mrs. Axelrod," Mac said to Rocky. "A member of the church."

"Mr. Axelrod and I started this church," she said.

Rocky smiled, nodded, and wondered how much more smiling and nodding she would have to do before this was all over.

"Are you thinking of joining?" Mrs. Axelrod said.

"I don't actually live around here," Rocky said.

"Pack Canyon is the last frontier community in all of Los Angeles County," she said, "the last honest community."

7:35 p.m.

Finally, they were gone. The whole chattering mess of them.

A small group of the women from church had left Liz with all sorts of food at the house. A couple of casseroles and a meatloaf. Tossed green salad and a bottle of Newman's Own Ranch Dressing. A pie.

One thing you could say for the folks at the church, they knew how to feed you if your husband died.

And they knew how to hang around offering all sorts of doe-eyed sentiments to make her feel better, when all she wanted was to stop faking gratitude and be left alone.

Liz got the hidden bottle of Jim Beam. She could use a shot.

What a production. The whole time she was afraid there might be some miracle, Arty rising from the dead or something, staring at her and shaking his head.

Forgiving her.

That would have been the worst part. She did not want forgiveness, not from Arty or any of them. Because that would mean she'd done something wrong, and there was no wrong here, only accidents and what you did with them.

The jewels. She had to start thinking about how to get them and get out of there. Away from Pack Canyon, out from under the noses of these church people.

That Mrs. Axelrod, what a hen she was! She wanted to make Liz her little egg and sit on her until she came forth as a puffy little Christian.

Forget that noise.

And that Mac. Something about him put her off. Maybe because he was street smart. It took one to know one. He could look into you and see what was going on in there. A dangerous man.

She sat in the big brown chair in front of the TV, her glass of bourbon with her. She flipped through the channels, looking for anything to take her mind off the day. She kept seeing Arty's urn in her mind. The drink was helping a little, but not much.

She settled on *Wheel of Fortune* and was into the spin when somebody knocked on the door.

Another church member, no doubt. Cleaning up the last of the duties toward the poor widow. Maybe forgot to leave her a pot roast or something.

Liz quickly downed the last of the drink, got up, went to the door and looked out the peep hole.

Now what was *he* doing here?

7:38 p.m.

Ted Gillespie tried not to think *She's hot*, but that's exactly what he thought. Even with the Band-Aid on her forehead. Even with her hair a little messy. In fact, he liked it that way, kind of loose —

She just lost her husband, jerk. And she's let you in her house. You better be a lot cooler now. One step at a time.

"I really, really hope you don't mind that I came by," Ted said. Liz Towne seemed tired but not unfriendly. "I saw about the funeral in the paper and went to the church and asked about you. I told them I'm the guy who found you, and they didn't think I was a serial killer. There was a nice lady there" — *Shut up, idiot!* — "anyway, I just wanted to see if you were okay."

Liz smiled. He thought it was shy and sweet and tired and hot all at the same time. He stood a little straighter and sucked in his gut just a little. He didn't want it to look like he was trying too hard.

"No," she said, "That's really nice of you. Want something to drink?"

"I'm fine," he said, not wanting to put her out. Not wanting to disturb her in any way. Not wanting this moment, this night, to end anytime soon.

"Come on," she said. "Then it'll seem like it's a friendly visit and not a thing you had to do."

"Oh, it's not that I had to," Ted said quickly. "I really wanted to know how you were getting along."

"Well, now you do."

"You're all right?"

"I'm all right."

"Okay," he said. That's when he realized turning down something to drink meant he might actually have to leave sooner, so he added, "if you have a soda of some kind."

"Anything special?"

"I'm sort of partial to ginger ale."

"Let me just see," she said and went to the kitchen. Ted watched her. Her clothes were tight. She fit them well.

He thought about the dead husband. Lucky guy, one who got a good one. The good ones were always taken. Always married or had a boyfriend. Your only chance, if you had a chance at all, was to catch one at just the right time. After they broke up with their boyfriend or got divorced.

Or the husband died.

Shut up.

She came back in and handed him a glass with ice clinking in it. She had one for herself. "Ginger ale it is," she said.

"Great," he said.

"Sit," she said.

He did. So did she.

"Tell me about yourself, Ted."

An opening. Don't blow it. "Oh, not much to tell." *Quit apologizing for yourself! I am confident!* "I do computer work." *Brilliant.*

"What kind?"

"Big things. System things. It's called IT. Information technology. For companies."

"You help the companies run?"

"Yeah," he said with a smile. "I guess you could put it that way."

"Sure," she said. "Without the computers, nothing gets done. Makes you the real power, right? I mean, if you ever wanted to mess them up . . ."

"I could really do a number, that's right." He took a quick gulp of ginger ale. "But I get paid to help, not mess things up." *Yeah, when I'm actually employed, that is.*

"I'll bet you do," she said, then sipped her drink.

She looked at him as she did.

His insides melted into hot goo. In a moment, he was sure he'd start babbling like a mental patient. He was going to make a fool out of himself, and part of him didn't care. The part of him that was sinking into her big, blue eyes. The part that would do anything to have this woman for his own.

The other part, the rational side, the systems-operations brain that knew when it was time to abort a program, said, "I've kept you long enough."

He stood up and almost spilled his drink. His hands were shaking.

Liz stayed in her chair a moment. Then she slowly put her glass on the table, stood up, and came to him.

She put out her hand and he took it. It was soft and warm.

"Thank you so much for coming to see me," she said. "That was very sweet of you."

Five thousand volts shot through Ted's body. She kept on holding his hand.

"If," he started to say, then stopped, then started again, "if you ever need anything ..."

"I know," she said.

7:40 p.m.

"Thanks for coming," Rocky said.

"Sure," Mac said.

They were on the outside deck of the Canyon Grind, an indie coffee place near the border between Los Angeles and Ventura counties. From here they could look down on the lights of the San Fernando Valley, a blanket of luminescent pinpricks in reds and greens and whites.

City lights seen from up high were always a comfort to Rocky. Perhaps because they were distant and didn't shine directly on her.

They kept the lights low outside on the deck. Candles on the tables. The sky was thick with clouds, so there were no stars. Rocky had insisted on buying the coffee. After all, she was the one who invited him.

"I was hoping you could tell me a little about how Arty was," Rocky said. "You know, before he died."

"Sure," he said. "I'd like to. Arty was really an amazing guy. Smart. He was teaching me about the Bible even though I've been a believer longer."

"Is that right?"

"I think he was thinking of going into the ministry, but he hadn't mentioned that to Liz yet."

"Right," Rocky said. "We wouldn't want to upset Liz."

"She was baptized. Did you know that?"

"She mentioned something about it."

"You don't sound pleased," Mac said.

"Why should I be?"

"For Liz. She needed this."

"Right."

Mac looked at her. A studying gaze she didn't like. "What have you got against her?" he asked.

"You're getting personal kind of early, aren't you, Mr. Mac-Donald?"

"Mac. And isn't that why you asked me here?"

"Excuse me?"

"To get personal. To question me. Not about Arty, but about Liz."

She wanted to get angry but couldn't. He was right. He had her pegged, but she wasn't about to let him know it.

"How well do you know her?" she asked.

"I know her even better now. Sure, she has a few rough edges, but she's changed. She's a new creation."

Rocky said nothing.

"She's going to need all the support she can get," Mac said. "I know she'd like you to be part of that."

"She tell you that?"

Mac shook his head. "I just know."

"How do you know?"

He blinked a couple of times. "I sense it," he said.

"Sense it, do you?"

"Yeah."

"Let me tell you what I sense," Rocky said. "You know what I do to make a buck?"

"Arty said some sort of insurance work."

"Investigations. I look for fraud. And I have a hero. Did you ever see the movie *Double Indemnity*?"

"I don't think so."

"It's about a smart insurance salesman who falls for the wife of a client. So he and the wife murder the husband, then the woman tries to collect on the insurance. Well, my hero is a guy played by Edward G. Robinson. He plays a guy named Keyes, who is the fraud investigator. And he says he has this little man inside. The little man tells him when something's phony. And the little man is always right."

"You have one of those, too?"

"Call it a voice. And it's talking to me. About Liz."

"That doesn't sound very — I don't know — scientific."

"How much do you know about her background?"

"Arty said it was kind of tough."

"She didn't know her father, and her mother didn't even come to the wedding. That's kind of weird, don't you think?"

"No."

"No?"

"Why don't you give her a little time?" Mac said. "Maybe if we both show her some support now, we can make a difference."

"Maybe," Rocky said. *And maybe not*, the little voice said.

Mac said, "Let's leave Liz aside for a minute. How are *you* doing?"

"Fine."

He leaned forward a little. "Was that your dad at the funeral?"

"Yes," she said.

"Everything okay between you?"

Rocky ran her thumbnail along the coffee cup, forging a line. "I don't think that's any of your concern."

"You know," Mac said, "from where I sit, I think there needs to be more concern out there, not less."

"Some people might call that sticking your nose in other people's business."

"You think that's what I want to do?"

"I don't really know what you want, and I don't care. I care about what happened to Arty."

"He died. In an accident. And his wife is hurting. I think you're hurting, too."

If she sat there much longer, this guy was going to get in way too close. "Thanks for the analysis," she said, standing.

"Don't go yet," Mac said.

She paused and considered staying. She knew she had a choice. She even knew she should stay.

But she went, quickly, and did not look back.

Thursday

8:28 a.m.

The phone woke Liz. What time was it? What business did a phone have going off this early anyway?

Why did she even have a land line? She didn't need it. She didn't need to be in touch with the outside world anymore.

No, what she needed was to be left alone. And to get the gems.

After the third ring, Liz picked up and mumbled a hello.

"Elizabeth, is that you?" A woman's voice. Who? And why was she using her full name when it wasn't even her full name? She'd been tagged Liz in the maternity ward.

"Who is this, please?"

"It's Edie Axelrod, dear."

"What? Why—"

"I didn't wake you, did I? It's ... oh my, perhaps I did ..."

"What can I do for you?" *You interfering old hen!*

"I just wanted to know if you saw the story."

"Story?"

"In the paper. In our paper, dear."

Liz tried to push the sleepy thoughts to the side and let the wakeful ones take over. Paper. Newspaper. "What paper?"

"The *Pack Canyon Herald*. Did you know I was the editor-in-chief at one time?"

"No."

"Oh yes, and I covered quite a few stories myself. I was the one who first reported on the Manson family, did you know *that*?"

"No."

"They lived at a ranch and were taking drugs all the time and—"

"Mrs. Axelrod, I will get the paper. Thank you very—"

"—getting young people to follow them—"

"—much."

Liz hung up the phone. Would she appear rude? She didn't care. All she cared about was getting that paper.

One hour later, at the Pack Canyon Market, she had it. The twelve-page paper was not what you could call major, but the people who put it out seemed to take it seriously. Maybe too seriously.

On the front page above the fold was a headlined story:

Strange Coincidence in Pack Canyon Death
By Mike Brady
Staff Reporter

Pack Canyon resident Arthur Towne, 32, died Saturday as the result of a fall off a treacherous path in the back reaches of the canyon, according to a sheriff's spokesman.

The death has rocked the community. Towne's widow, Elizabeth, attended the funeral yesterday, as did many of the congregation of Pack Canyon Community Church, where Towne was a member.

In a bizarre twist, according to the sheriff's office, an unidentified body of a male was found not far from the spot of Towne's fatal accident.

The body was located near a motorcycle in a deep cleft that is difficult to see from the main path. Motorcycles are prohibited in Pack Canyon, but this has not kept some from using the paths.

There was no identification on the body, the sheriff's spokesman says. Officials surmise that the body may have been there as long as 12 hours before its discovery.

Liz folded the paper and felt like a million eyes were on her. Each set looking to see if she would flinch or otherwise give something away.

Maybe the eyes of Detective Moss. It had to be Moss who fed this guy the story. Made sure he knew about it. Maybe put him up to questioning her at the funeral.

Moss, who wanted her to crack.

Well, they weren't going to shake her. She would simply act normal. The plan would continue. She'd keep up the illusion that life marched on, and she was the heroic grieving widow muddling through. Then she could pick her time to transition out of the community. To just get gone, as the song went.

She got a shopping cart and started down an aisle.

She wondered if she would bump into anybody who knew her. She hoped not. Just get some essentials and get out, bring the bags in so the neighbors could see her living life. Have some food in the house when the inevitable church visitors came over.

A prospect she dreaded.

It was an odd feeling. Shopping for one. No longer needing to think of what Arty liked. No more Doritos and salsa. No more Hormel chili. Frosted Mini-Wheats? Good-bye.

Yet wheeling down the breakfast aisle, she found herself stopping in front of the cereal boxes. Why? It was almost as if she'd been halted by an invisible wall. The cereal boxes themselves seemed, for a moment, to have voices. Making an eerie music from miles away.

She told herself not to go crazy. Not now, not ever. *Get out.*

"Mrs. Towne?"

She almost yelped. She turned and faced a man. He was smiling at her.

"I thought I recognized you," the man said. "I'm Bill Olson from church." He was a bit under six feet tall, mid-forties. He wore a casual blue pullover sweater and khaki slacks. Sharp but not pretentious.

"Oh," Liz said, "then we must have met on Sunday."

"There were a lot of people around," Bill said. "I didn't get a chance to talk to you. I just wanted to say how much I thought of your husband."

"Thank you."

"I hope you won't hesitate to call on any of us if you need anything."

"I'm doing fine for now, but thank you again. Everyone has been so nice."

"That's what a church is all about. We're a little community within the community. We look out for each other."

"That's a great comfort to me."

"Listen," Bill said, "I wanted to drop off some firewood that's been in my truck a couple of weeks. I was going to give it to the church, but I think maybe you can use it."

"Firewood?"

"It would mean a great deal to me, for Arty's sake, if I dropped it off."

"You don't have to—"

"I know. But I think you'll see that receiving gifts at this time will help your healing process."

She didn't want any more interaction with the people from church than necessary. Then again, a little bit was good. They had to see that she was open to their help.

"All right," she said. "That would be very nice. I'll be home in about twenty minutes."

"I'll wait," Bill said, "and follow you."

Half an hour later, Liz pulled into the driveway. Bill helped her in with the grocery bags. She put them on the counter in the kitchen. Then she offered him a soft drink. That was a good, churchy thing to do.

"No thanks," Bill said. "I'll just unload the firewood. Where do you want it? On the side of the house?"

"Yes, there's a small bin there."

"Sure," he said. "Oh, and one more thing."

"Yes?"

He reached into his pocket and pulled something out. He used his thumb on it. A curved, shiny knife blade appeared.

"I think you have something that belongs to me," he said.

10:05 a.m.

As Mac worked on Clyde Dean's garage door opener—*I can't get my car out! I need to get to the bank!*—he prayed. Prayer and work. It was a good combination.

Pastor Jon had told him about a man named Brother Lawrence. He was an obscure monk way back in time. Worked in a kitchen. But he had this idea about practicing the presence of God. Sort of like he was your partner on patrol in a battlefield.

A good idea, but hard. Mac kept wanting to do it, and he'd start off well. But then other thoughts would start crashing around in his head.

But now was the time. He'd manually opened the garage door for Mr. Dean, who happily backed out his huge, vintage Cadillac with a relieved grin.

Now it was just Mac alone with the chain of the garage-door opener and God.

He decided to pray out loud this time. Maybe that would make a difference.

"Okay, God. Here it is. I want to be able to see my daughter. Is that so wrong?"

He paused, waiting for a voice from heaven.

Nothing.

"Sorry, God, I guess I'm a little anxious here. Don't mind me."

Wait a minute. Wasn't God in the minding business? Wasn't that the whole point of prayer?

"Just make it your will, God. Your will be done. I'm all for that. From now on. No. Wait. Wait, I've got it. Something for me. Can you get Slezak off my back? Can you have him reassigned or something? I'm not asking for a car accident or anything. I'm not asking for him to go off a cliff. Of course, if it's your will. No. Wait. I'm sorry. Sorry I said that. You have the way. You can do it."

He tightened a nut with a socket wrench.

10:09 a.m.

"Please," Liz said, "I don't know what you're talking about."

The man who called himself Bill sighed. He was standing in front of her after ordering her to sit on the sofa. He twirled the knife casually in his right hand.

"Stop it," he said.

"Please —"

"Do you think I'd be here if I didn't know exactly what I was doing?" His voice was soft, each word spoken precisely.

Liz turned on a small trail of tears. She sniffed.

"You don't have to do that," Bill said almost comfortingly. "I also find it a little annoying, and I would rather not be annoyed at present."

Instinct told her to scale back. Only a little.

"Now understand this," Bill said. "You don't ever have to see me again. All I want is what's mine, and you can just hand it over to me. It will be that simple and that quick, and then I'll be on my way."

He smiled. He had crinkles at the corners of his eyes.

Liz said, "Honest, I don't know what you mean —"

"You'll have to try another —"

"Dear God, please!"

Bill held up the knife as a teacher might hold up a ruler. "Do not interrupt me again."

Liz decided she'd better be quiet. For now.

Bill's mouth twitched once before he spoke. "The facts are these: Your husband died in an accident, if it was an accident, not very far from where a colleague of mine died in an accident, if it was an accident. In his case, it was. He was careless that way. But what he was carrying with him is gone. Just gone. Some items of interest and value. "

She tried to keep her face looking innocent as she shook her head.

"So," he said, "let's see where we are. Either you know what I'm talking about, or you don't. I think you do. You give me what belongs to me, and I'll go away. We'll just forget this whole thing happened. On the other hand, you may be telling me the truth. I doubt it, but there you go."

"Please —"

"Quit saying *please*."

She looked at his close-set eyes. Sized him up, the way she would Mama's clients back home when they came in the shop.

There was a time to listen and a time to speak. A time to turn things around. Now was that time.

"I know what you want," she said.

He looked surprised. And then satisfied. "And what would that be?" he said.

"Why don't you sit down," she said.

"Why—"

She said, "Sit down and shut up."

He hesitated. For a moment, he looked like he wanted to hit her. She braced for it. But something stopped him.

She knew that something was her. She had him.

"You want those rocks, right?" she said.

"Well now, that's exactly—"

"Then do what I tell you and sit. Now."

He paused, smiled, then lowered himself into a chair. "Okay then, ladybug, I'm listening."

"I'll tell you how it's going to be. First, you tell me how you got such a nice stash."

"I don't see as I have to tell you anything."

Liz said, "You will tell me because that's the only way you're going to ever get anything. Don't bother to pose. Don't bother to threaten me. You could kill me, sure, but you would never find the diamonds and whatever else is in those sacks. You would never find them because I've hidden them, and nobody is ever going to find them except me. So don't be trying any intimidation, because I'm not going to take it."

She waited for him to respond. He just looked at her. He blinked a couple of times. "That was very good," he said. "I see that you think you are the smart one here. You know what? I like you. I almost want to ask where you've been all my life."

"Listen, you can have some of the stones."

"*Some* of them?"

"Or none of them. You choose."

He smiled again. "I really do like you."

"Yes or no?"

"And what if I say yes? How are we going to handle our little transaction?"

"We'll handle it the way I say we will."

He shook his head. "Ah, you know, I think you're going to try to cheat me. I think I'm not happy about this at all."

"I don't really care what you think or what you're happy about," Liz said. "That's the way it is."

"What if I just beat it out of you? Not that I'd take pleasure in that, but I can inflict a lot of pain. I've learned how. You'd be surprised what I've learned."

No doubt, she thought. "It won't work on me," she said.

He got to his feet. "Here I thought you were supposed to be this nice churchgoing girl, and what do I find?"

"The wrong woman."

"The woman of my dreams," he said. "Great possibilities."

Liz said nothing.

"Yes," Bill said. "Your grieving widow act is superb."

"That's enough now."

He paced a semicircle around her, nodding. "Don't think that's a bad thing, sweets. No, I admire that. I wonder what we could do together."

"You're crazy."

"Hear me out," he said. "You want to hear me out? You want to know how to get a lot more money than you ever dreamed of?"

She didn't say anything.

"Why don't you sit back and relax," Bill said. "I'll lay the whole thing out for you. You are going to like what I have to say. And if you don't, we call it quits. How's that for fair?"

10:15 a.m.

Instead of heading back to her apartment — that was going to be a real pain, dealing with the lease, because Boyd was *on* the lease, and she didn't need any more pain right now, thank you very much — Rocky drove to Pack Canyon.

She wanted to see where Arty died. Investigation, that's what she did. She wanted to start at the scene.

Who knew what she'd find?

The little voice was prompting her. She had to do something.

She took the highway and got off at Pack Canyon Road. It wound down through the hills, through the little strip of town, past the white church Arty was part of.

She wondered if Mac was there. She wondered why she wondered.

Then there was the street you turned on to go to Arty's house. What was once Arty's house. Now it was Liz's house.

Rocky felt cold just driving by.

A mile or so later she saw the sign for the turn into Pack Canyon Park. The small lot held a couple of cars, including a sheriff's cruiser.

She parked, got out, and started walking. At least she was ready for a hike. She had jeans and Nikes and a sweatshirt, courtesy of Geena.

There was a brown sign with white lettering and two arrows pointing in opposite directions. Trail One and Trail Two. Not very original but it got the job done.

So which one? She wanted to walk along where Arty had fallen but wasn't sure which way to go.

Where was Dorothy's scarecrow when you needed him? *Some people do go both ways.*

Thanks, straw man.

Life was luck, bad or good, so she decided on the right-hand path. Fifty-fifty chance.

She started walking.

She remembered how Arty liked the outdoors. Always had. She was the indoor type, and the darker the lighting the better. Maybe that was the difference between them, and when you were an outside person you found God somewhere.

She looked at the sky and the clouds and found nothing.

She walked on.

She wasn't sure where Arty had fallen, except what Mac had told her. He said the place was where Arty took him once on a hike. A place with a killer view — Mac had caught himself when he said that — that seemed on top of the world. As much as you could be on top of the world in the westernmost part of LA County.

She kept walking, expecting to see other hikers, but saw none. It was ten minutes uphill before a dirt biker pedaled by. He wore tight little bike pants and waved at her. He was coming on fast, with down-hill speed.

She stepped aside and he whizzed by, not even looking at her. If he crashes, she thought, it won't be a pretty sight.

She kept going, up and up. She came around a bend and saw a deputy sheriff standing on the trail. Wearing sunglasses, arms folded across his chest.

He looked at her as she approached.

"This must be the place," she said.

"I'm sorry?" the deputy said. He was young and in good shape. He could have been on a recruiting poster.

"The scene of the accident, as they say."

"Is there something you want, ma'am?"

"May I see it?" she said.

"See what?"

"The scene."

"There's an investigator there now, so I'm afraid not."

"I'm the sister of the man who died."

He looked at her. At least his shades were pointed her way. "I'm sorry for your loss," he said. "If you were to come back later, around—"

"Never mind."

"If you'd like to give me your—"

"No thanks."

She walked past him, on up the trail. She had no intention of wait-ing for anything. This was a big wide area and the deputy couldn't watch it all.

As soon as she couldn't see him anymore, she stopped and assessed. If she went off the path to the left, she could circle back around to where Arty had fallen, but from the other side. That wouldn't do much good, because as soon as they saw her they'd move in.

Or maybe she could find a place to watch. Then get closer and ... do what? What was she intending on doing?

She stepped off the path and started down.

10:46 a.m.

"In short," Bill said, "I'm keeping you out of a long stretch in prison and offering you the chance to make money and live free."

"Yes?" Liz said.

"Your first problem will be having to act in a way that doesn't arouse the suspicion that the cops already must have."

"So?"

"You think you can do it. You're a pretty confident woman. But sooner or later it's going to catch up. That's why you need a partner."

"I'm not interested in having a partner."

"That's the thing, you don't really have a choice."

She wanted to spit in his face right there. She could not imagine any universe where she would be partners with this guy. Then, for an awful second, she realized something—that she was very much like this man ...

"So what are you suggesting?" Liz said.

"I am suggesting that we take the rocks to Mexico. I know where to fence them down there and—"

"And what other things are you going to expect out of our little excursion?"

Bill said, "Why don't we work that out as we go along?"

"What if I want to know right now?"

"You haven't even gotten a chance to know me."

"What's your real name?"

"Don't you like Bill?"

"What's the real one?"

He looked her up and down once and smiled. "I don't think I want to get into that. You're a sweet kid. Maybe I'll tell you a little bit about why I do this."

Fine, she thought. Let him talk. The more time that went by, the more time she had to figure a way out of this.

"I used to be an accountant," he said. "'People used to tell me all the time that's what I looked like. An accountant. You know how annoying that is? Big accounting firm in Century City. Crunching numbers. Then one day I heard about a couple of guys who blew a jewelry store robbery. They got in a shootout with the police because they made dumb mistakes. That fascinated me. I started to wonder if a smart guy like me could figure out a way to make something like that work."

"And you did?"

"Oh yes, I did. And you know what? It's not that hard. All it takes is projection, planning, and research. It's what I was doing all day anyway. So I started with a little jewelry store in Torrance. Just for fun, at first. It took me two weeks to plan it. Finding out where the security cameras were located, the pattern of drive-by private security, the type of locks on the doors. I calculated the speed I would need to get in and get out, the escape route, everything. Only one thing I lacked."

Liz waited. She watched his eyes. They were almost sparkling.

"A partner. Someone to provide what I couldn't. Mainly, speed and escape. So you know what I did?"

Liz shrugged.

"I held interviews. I really did. Not in the office, of course, but in a bar in Oxnard, one I selected because I'd saved the bacon of the owner once in a financial meltdown. It was a link to a world I hadn't known before. I looked many would-be outlaws in the eyes, sized them up, and even had them show me what they could do with their equipment. Until I found the right one. Until I found Denton. He was raw and undisciplined, but he could ride a motorcycle like the devil in a hurry. I saw his potential, and I spent months working with him. I turned him into something he never would have been without me. I made him into something."

He was almost talking past her now, to an unseen audience.

"It was beautiful what we had. Four jobs in two years. Not too many, not too few. But they were all just preparation for this last job. This was the big score, as they say. And then, for some reason, he got wild and careless. It was not like him, not after the way I shaped him. Very disappointing. So now here I am. Here we are."

Liz said nothing. Waited for him to play this out.

He looked at her and said, "I also found out something about myself over these last couple of years." He took a step toward her. "I found out I can do things I never thought possible. Really mean things. I found out I can do anything I set out to do, solve any problem, take care of any people who stand in my way. And not lose a single night's sleep over it."

"You're right, Bill," she said, standing. "I am interested."

He paused and studied her face. "You wouldn't just be saying that to fool me now, would you?"

"Oh, I know I can't do that," Liz said. "And I'm not going to just roll over and give up the gems. But we can work together. On my terms."

10:53 a.m.

Rocky watched as the woman made her way up to where the deputy sheriff stood. She held a notebook. She said something to the deputy, who looked around one more time. Then the two of them walked back toward the parking lot.

Now what were they up to? Why be out here looking around at an accident scene *after* the funeral? Did they have suspicions of some kind?

She waited a couple of minutes before moving. She figured that the area where the deputy was standing was the crest where Arty fell. She'd be able to follow the sight line down. She could do a *CSI: Miami* and play David Caruso now. All she needed was designer shades and a too-cool-for-school voice.

What if it wasn't an accident? What if there had been a fight or something? Was Liz capable of cold-blooded killing?

It didn't have to be cold-blooded. What if they were arguing, and Liz just got mad? Certainly she was capable of that.

What if she killed him and then dragged his body to that spot, so it looked like he fell?

Thoughts were jumbling around as she pushed herself up on the boulder in front of her, stood, wiped her hands. She had a couple of choices. Go back the way she came and start down from the deputy's vantage point. Or try making her way across the rocky divide, going directly from point A to point B.

She chose the latter. That way, she could scan the perimeter. See if there was any sign of blood or torn clothes or any other *CSI* stuff.

She almost laughed at that but didn't, because she almost slipped. Careful now, she thought. You don't need any sprained ankles here.

Start looking.

11:01 a.m.

It all came down to choices, Liz thought.

Her first choice involved the man named Bill, standing there, considering her proposition, not even realizing what she'd chosen. Thinking fast, she'd laid out a plan mainly to stall him, but it was good enough to get him to pause. And gave her control of the situation.

She had learned how to do this from the best. From Mama.

Especially after what Mama had to do to Miller Jones.

Liz was thirteen when her mama married Jones. Her real father, Les Summerville, was doing hard time in Holman, and Mama had long before secured a divorce. That left the door open for Jones.

He had hair that smelled of cooking grease. He cooked for Robbie's, the coffee shop at the edge of town, across from the Tote-Sum convenience store where Liz bought Coca-Colas on hot summer days.

Mama started taking Liz to Robbie's, first once, then twice a week. Jones would smile at her. Liz liked him because he could crack eggs two at a time, one in each hand. And then he started coming to visit the trailer where she and Mama lived.

Miller Jones liked to laugh and even brought Mama flowers once.

Liz was glad when they got married at a little office across the county line.

Her stepfather came to live with them in the trailer. It made things a little tight, but that was just the way life was. The place started to smell different, too. Man smells. The grease, the bourbon, the sweat.

He never did give Mama a diamond ring like she wanted. Liz knew that could only mean bad luck.

And then one night Miller Jones came to Liz. It was when Mama was working late at the shop, doing the books. Liz got to watch TV and Miller Jones sat in his chair, not saying anything, pouring himself drinks from a bottle. He'd drink them right down without ice or anything.

Liz got up to go to bed and Miller Jones said, "Ain't you got a kiss for your daddy?"

She didn't want to give him one. She liked him all right, but it didn't seem like the time was right yet for kisses. Maybe later. So that's what she said.

"Maybe later."

"Come on," he said, "I'm your daddy now, and daddies get kisses from their little girls."

"I have to go pee," Liz said, and hurried to what they called the bathroom. She closed the door and did her business. Then she flushed the toilet, washed her hands, and almost ran to her bed, hoping that would be the last of it.

She drew the curtain that was her door and listened.

Miller Jones didn't say anything more.

Relieved, Liz got into her jammies and into bed and started to fall asleep.

He came in like a ghost, like he'd passed right through the curtains. He was a shadow with the light behind him. She could smell the bourbon on his breath. It was as strong as truck exhaust.

He came to the bed and sat on it.

"You like your new daddy?" he said.

"Uh-huh," Liz said. She tried to hold her breath so she wouldn't smell him.

"That's real good. I want you to like me. I want it very much." He leaned over then and she felt his weight on her as he kissed her cheek. His whiskers scratched her.

He didn't get back up.

Or move. He just breathed, loud and snorty, lying across her. His weight pressing down more and more.

"I can't ... breathe," she said.

Miller Jones said nothing.

He didn't move, she realized, because he was asleep. Asleep in that way he got when he had a lot to drink.

She put her hands on his shoulders and pushed, but he was like a sack of wet clothes.

She had to wriggle out from under him. It took her almost a whole minute, but finally she was free. Leaving Jones on top of her bed, snoring.

Liz used her feet. She pushed him and rolled him over. He clunked on the floor. And didn't wake up.

She took her blanket and pillow, went out to the couch, and fell asleep there.

Mama woke her up.

"What happened?" Mama said. There was fire in her eyes like Liz had never seen.

Liz told her mama what happened.

That night the shouting started. Liz was scared. She never knew her mama could shout that loud or say those things.

Miller Jones stumbled out of her room and Liz ran back in, covering her head with a pillow as the yelling went on and on.

In the morning, Mama had a big blue mark under her right eye. Miller Jones was off to work at Robbie's. And Mama asked her: "You know what lyin' is, baby?"

"Course," Liz said.

"What do you know about it?"

"Not supposed to do it." Liz thought she'd been caught in a lie by her mother but just didn't remember which one.

"But it's all right to lie when you have to," Mama said.

That seemed right.

"Sometimes you got to lie to help the ones you love, right?"

Liz nodded.

"You remember that, now. I'm counting on you. You need to show Mama how much you love her."

"I will Mama. I'll show you."

But she couldn't know then just how much she'd have to show. Not until the bad thing happened and the whole town yapped about it, not until then would she know.

Liz had all of it roiling in her mind as she faced the man named Bill in the house in Pack Canyon.

She had shown Mama, and now she would show her again.

Just how and when would have to be worked out.

"I don't know if I like it," Bill said, pulling Liz back to the moment. "No, I am not getting a good feeling here."

"But I am the only one who knows where the rocks are," Liz said.

"It's almost like we're stuck with—"

Someone knocked on the door.

11:02 a.m.

I shouldn't have come here, Ted thought. Shouldn't have, shouldn't have.

But he had to see her. His need was a burning inside him. He knew he was teetering on the edge. She had wrapped herself around his mind. He couldn't stop thinking about her. He knocked again. Her car was in the driveway. She was home, or was visiting somewhere and would soon be home. He was not going to leave until he saw her and gave her the package he held in his hands.

What if she told him to take a hike?

He'd cross that bridge whenever. As long as she didn't blow the bridge up, there was hope. If it blew up, went away, he didn't know what he'd do.

Maybe blow himself up with it.

11:03 a.m.

"What do you want me to do?" Liz said.

"Don't answer it," Bill said.

"But it might be somebody from the church."

"So?"

"They're dropping by to look in on me."

"You don't have to be home."

"My car is in the driveway. People know I'm home."

Another knock. Liz took a step toward the door. Bill put his hand out and stopped her.

"Just let it go," he said.

The knocking stopped. The pair stood in silence a moment, then through the lace curtains Liz saw a figure sit down on the porch bench.

"What's going on?" Bill said.

"They're waiting for me."

He looked at her, ice in his eyes. "Who is it?"

"I'm not sure."

"This is where I shine," Bill said.

"What do you mean?"

"You'll do exactly what I say. First of all, look out the curtain and see if you recognize who it is. Do that now."

Liz hesitated. Bill raised his hands in frustration, then drew his index finger across his throat. As in, *That's what'll happen if you don't do what I say.*

"All right," Liz said. "Just stay cool."

11:04 a.m.

Ted felt a wonderful sensation of fear, anticipation, and lust.

He felt alive. No matter what happened, this was worth it. He was going to go for it. He was going to go for something without thinking or pausing or being rational about it. For once in his life, he would go for it running on all cylinders, because maybe this was the last time he would have the chance to get what he really wanted.

And he really wanted *her*.

He set the small package in its plain brown wrapper on the bench next to him, crossed his legs, and looked at the front yard. He took in a deep breath of eucalyptus and dried grass.

She needed him. Like the dry grass needed water. She just didn't know it. He had saved her. She needed him then. She needed him now.

And he had to get to her before some other guy did.

You didn't get the chance to comfort a widow very often, especially one this . . . what was the word? *Hot* didn't do it, because she was more than that.

He heard the door open.

And she was there.

His pulse took off in a sprint as he stood up. "Oh, you're here."

"I thought I heard somebody knocking," she said. "I was sleeping."

"I'm sorry!"

"No, no, it's okay. Is there something you wanted?"

"I just came by to see if there was anything you needed, see if you needed anything from the store, or anything" — *stop saying* any- thing! — "or anything like that."

In his imagination he kicked himself.

"I'm fine," she said, but she seemed to hesitate. Or was he just read- ing between the lines?

She looked vulnerable.

She looked wounded.

She looked soft and warm.

"I brought you something," Ted said quickly. He picked up the package, almost dropped it, secured it with both hands.

She looked at the gift.

"It's just a little something," he said, "to kind of put a smile on your face."

He went to her. She was standing just outside the door. The door was open a crack. Ted looked at the crack as if it were the secret tunnel to a pot of gold.

"Let me show you," he said, and before she could do anything he pushed through the door.

He thought, This is too much, too fast. But he didn't stop. He couldn't back down now.

He only stopped when he saw the man standing in the middle of the hallway.

11:06 a.m.

Rocky almost fell. Again. She put her hand out to the side, flat against a large boulder. That steadied her, though she had to bend almost double to keep from diving into a cleft.

Ridiculous, she thought. Quit making like a mountain goat, will you? Just get to the other side without an accident and—

She looked down in the cleft and saw something that was not part of the natural landscape.

It wasn't exactly trash. It wasn't like a soda can or the sort of litter one usually finds in hiking locales.

What it looked like, she thought, was half a cell phone.

11:07 a.m.

Ted didn't know what to do.

He felt like a complete idiot, a moron.

Another man was in the house with her.

Wait. Liz had said she was sleeping. Was she sleeping with this guy?

Did I just walk into a little love nest? Am I the king of all doofuses?

Ted's stomach did a swan dive into a gravel pit.

"How you doin'?" the man said, as if it were the most natural thing in the world to say under the circumstances.

Ted didn't answer. He heard Liz close the door.

"My name's Bill," the man said. "Liz's cousin." He stepped forward with his hand out.

Ted almost cried out with joy. A relative! A family member come to help Liz through this terrible, challenging time. Just like Ted! This man was not an interloper. He was not a rival.

Ted's stomach pulled out of the pit and settled. He shook the man's hand. "I'm Ted Gillespie. Great to meet you." *Hey. Bill and Ted. This is an excellent adventure!*

Don't be a nerd.

"Friend of the family?" the man named Bill said.

"I hope so," Ted said. He looked at Liz. She smiled at him. His heart thumped faster.

"Well that's just fine," Bill said. "What have you got there?"

The package. Ted had completely forgotten. "Oh yeah," he said, "a little gift. I thought Liz would like it."

"Well that's very neighborly of you, Ted," Bill said. "Let's have a look."

"Sure." Ted handed the package to Liz.

She took it, looking a little unsure of what to do. So sweet, Ted thought. What a gentle spirit she has about her. What would it be like to be married to a woman like this?

He could only hope. His last, best hope.

She tore off the brown paper. Then opened the white box. Took out the item.

"A clock?" Liz said.

"A Winnie the Pooh clock," Ted said. "I thought you'd like it. It's sort of a fun thing, you know? And when it ticks, he moves his honey jar."

For a long moment nobody said anything.

Then Bill said, "Did you notice Elvis over there?"

Ted cleared his throat. Bill was smiling, but his question seemed a little accusatory. Or was it just his imagination? "Yes, that's sort of why I thought Liz might like this one, too."

"The battle of the clocks, eh?" Bill said. "Winnie the Pooh versus Elvis?"

Ted tried a little chuckle. "Yeah, I guess."

Silence.

"Well that is just a very thoughtful thing," Bill finally said. "A really thoughtful thing to do. Ted, thank you very much."

"Yes," Liz said. "That was very thoughtful."

Yes! He was thoughtful. He was advancing. Good move. The Pooh clock was a very good move. He was on the upswing.

"Thanks so much for coming by," Bill said.

"Would you like something to drink, Ted?" Liz said.

"Sure!"

"Honey, we have to get going," Bill said. "Remember? We don't have much—"

"Just one drink, to say thank you," Liz said. "It's only right, since he took the trouble. As I remember it, Ted, you like ginger ale."

"That's right," Ted said.

"We'll have to make it quick, Liz," Bill said.

"You all sit down and get to know each other," Liz said, scooting into the kitchen.

Ted looked at Bill, who looked at Ted. Ted scratched his leg. His new Dockers were starting to itch. Bill said, "So I guess we should sit down."

They did.

"What's your line of work?" Bill said.

"I'm sort of looking right now," Ted said.

"Ah, footloose and fancy free."

"What do you do, Bill?"

"Me? I'm an accountant."

"Really? Now that's funny. I guessed that. You look like an accountant."

"Do I now?"

"Uh-huh. I sort of have a way like that. I can get pretty close to guessing what a person does."

"Well, that's just a great skill you have there, Ted. A really great skill." Bill looked toward the kitchen. "You about ready, Liz?"

Liz said, "Be right out."

"She's handling this pretty well," Ted said, just above a whisper.

"Handling what?" Bill said.

"Her husband's death."

"Oh right. Yes. Of course. What was I thinking?"

Ted sort of wanted to know that himself. Was Bill thinking of running interference for Liz? Keeping Ted away from her? Maybe that was why Bill was trying to hustle him out. Maybe there wasn't any real rush at all to go anywhere with Liz.

"Where do you hail from, Ted?"

"My dad was Air Force," Ted said. "We moved around a lot."

"What was your favorite place?"

"I don't know. Colorado Springs was nice. San Diego, too."

"Uh-huh?"

"Where are you from?" Ted said.

"Me? I'm from a little town I like to call Chicago." Bill sat back, crossed his legs. "Live there still. Do you know Chicago, Ted?"

"Um, not really."

"Great history there. Capone. The Cubs. Liz, you about ready with the drinks?"

"Coming," Liz said.

Bill looked back at Ted. "Yes, Chicago. The City of the Big Shoulders. Really sort of forgotten. Everything's New York or LA these days."

"Or San Francisco," Ted said.

Bill waved his hand. "Frisco's had its day. We need to look to the future, don't we there, Ted?"

Liz came in with a tray and three glasses with ice and ginger ale. "Here we go," she said. She brought the tray to Ted, who took a glass. Then Bill took one. She put the tray down on the coffee table and took her own glass.

"Cheers," she said.

They all drank.

It was almost normal. Ted thought maybe this was going to turn out all right after all. Eventually, Bill would have to leave, go back to where he came from. Chicago. That was far enough away.

Bill had just put his glass on the table when Ted saw the flash.

His mind told him instantly that what he saw could not be happening. It was not possible that Liz was holding a large knife in her fist, in plunging position, even less that she was bringing the blade down hard toward the throat of her cousin Bill.

But when the contact was made, he knew it was happening, really happening, though he could not begin to know why.

Ted Gillespie screamed.

11:14 a.m.

Mac knew something was wrong even before he turned into the church lot. It was like a vibe coming out to meet him in the street. He had a sense about things like that, even back in the Gulf.

He really honed the instinct in prison, when he could sense a Rambo coming up behind him, some punk who wanted to make trouble. Whenever that happened, his head would start to throb.

His head warned him like old farmers talked about their joints. They knew when a storm was coming because their joints started acting up.

Mac's head was acting up. The lot looked empty from the street, but then he pulled into the drive and saw the back end of a blue car behind the church. Between the church building and the shack euphemistically known as the home of Daniel Patrick MacDonald.

The door of which was open.

Mac gunned it to the blue car, stopped, and jumped out.

Inside, his place was just this side of a hurricane zone.

Most of his personal items were in a haphazard pile on the floor.

He heard the sound of a drawer being pulled out, all the way out. In his bedroom.

Where he found Slezak bent over a dresser drawer on the bed. Slezak was throwing underwear and T-shirts onto the floor. He looked up and saw Mac.

"Hey there," Slezak said.

Mac's head started pounding.

"Best thing I can do for you is help you stay clean, huh?" Slezak said. "Make sure you return safe and sound to the streets of our city."

The drawer was completely empty now. Slezak tossed the drawer itself on the floor and turned and pulled out another. Pants and a sweater in that one.

Slezak was smiling.

You could end this now, Mac heard a voice say. Not exactly a voice, but a part of his brain screaming for relief. *Just take the guy out and figure out your story later. It's just the two of you.*

Slezak emptied the drawer, threw that on the floor as well. "You got to do a better job of washing," he said. "Cleanliness is next to godliness."

Godliness. The word came crackling through Mac's fractured thoughts. He closed his eyes and prayed. He prayed the way Pastor Jon did sometimes. He prayed in the name of Jesus for protection from the Enemy. He prayed for the peace that passes all understanding. He prayed *the Lord is my shepherd, the Lord is my shepherd, the Lord is my shepherd.*

Slezak headed for the bathroom.

Just like last time.

He heard Slezak open the medicine cabinet and the metallic shuffling around. "You got any more of that Vicodin?" Slezak said.

Mac said nothing. *The Lord is my shepherd.*

"Hey, I asked you a question," Slezak said. "You got any drugs in this house?"

The Lord is my shepherd.

"MacDonald, I asked you a question."

The Lord is my shepherd.

"You want to go down for non co-op?"

"The Lord is my shepherd," Mac said out loud.

"What did you just say?"

"I think you heard me."

Slezak came to him, almost nose to nose. "Think you can pull the wool, huh? You can't. You're gonna slip or you're gonna crack, and I'll be there to take it all down and see you back where you came from."

In Mac's head the shrapnel glowed, and he thought he might hit Slezak. He wanted to. He wanted to knock teeth out or worse. But something held his fist back.

Then Slezak hit him in the gut.

11:18 a.m.

Ted shook. He could not stop. His voice was making little burbling sounds. He thought he would faint right there. "What—"

Then he felt Liz's hands on his shoulders and her blue eyes looking straight at him. He fell into her gaze.

"Ted, stop."

"—did you do? Oh, my—"

"Listen to me, Ted, listen!"

He stopped making sounds.

"I need your help," Liz said. "I need you to be strong. I know you are strong. You are the only one who can help me. Please."

She put her head into his chest and put her arms around him. He felt the electric charge of desire and male instinct to protect. He did not begin to comprehend why she had stabbed her cousin in the neck with a knife and was now covered with blood just as he was because she was holding him close. The warmth of her body, her breathing against him, calmed him.

He smoothed her hair with his hand, even though there was blood in her hair. He said, "I'm here. I'll help you. I'll help you."

She said nothing, but her hot breath lit a fire on his chest and in his chest and it spread all over him. He couldn't help himself. He grabbed her hair and pulled her head back and pushed his mouth on hers before she could protest.

She didn't protest but let him kiss her for what seemed like a whole minute. It must have been only a second.

Then she pulled away from him and said, "No, not now. Soon. But not now. We have to think."

"Yes," he said. "Yes."

There was blood on the floor, lots of it, and Bill was facedown in it. The bloody knife was on the floor next to him. Ted was still shaking, but the reaction was now a mix of desire and longing and some weird sort of excitement. He was intoxicated.

"Why'd you do it?" Ted said.

"Because he's a criminal. He came here to try to get money out of me. My life insurance. He knew about me."

"But he's your cousin."

"Of course he's not!"

She was angry with him now. *You stupid, stupid . . .*

"Listen to me," she said. "I had to kill him. He was going to kill me. He was probably going to kill you. Now we have to get rid of him."

"But how?"

"I know how we can do it," she said.

"But the blood . . ."

"We can do this. We can do this together. Why don't you come with me?"

Did she really ask him that? "Where?"

"I'm going to get out of here. I'm going to go away and start my life over again. Will you be part of that with me?"

This had to be a dream, an extreme dream, like the ones he had about jumping out of a plane with a snowboard and landing on the side of a snowy mountain, even though he had never been snowboarding in his life. He always thought it was a dream of something that would happen to him someday, and now he knew it *had* happened, only it was not a snowboard or mountain, it was a woman and a dead body and the chance to go away with her and feel alive.

"Yes," he said. "I'll go with you. I'll go anywhere with you."

"Then listen to me and do what I tell you."

"Yes."

"First thing, go in the garage, through the door in the kitchen. In the corner there's a big blue tarp rolled up with yellow rope. Go get that. We're going to put the body in it."

"Right." Easy, he told himself. Don't sound like you're a Cub Scout going off to get marshmallows for the campfire. Just do this thing and help her, and she'll give herself to you.

He kept telling himself that. He went to the garage and found the tarp. It was the kind somebody would put under a tent. He hauled it back into the living room where Liz was waiting.

"Now untie it and lay it out flat," she ordered. He didn't mind that she ordered. Still, he hesitated.

"You can do this for me," she said. "For us."

He felt her strength enter him like a river of liquid fire. As he untied the rope from the tarp, he was amazed at how easy it was to cooperate in a crime. This was a bad man she had killed, and she must have had a very good reason. But it was still a crime, and they were going to get away with it. He was going to help her get away with it.

For us.

He laid the tarp on the floor next to the body. Then he helped Liz roll the body onto it. Then they wrapped it up. Like we're about to take out the trash, Ted thought. Not so far off the mark.

"We've got to clean up the blood," Liz said.

"Yes," Ted said.

"You holding up?"

"Oh yeah."

She smiled at him. He drank it in.

"I can do anything," he said.

Liz nodded, then put her hands behind his neck, pulled, and kissed him full on the mouth.

11:29 a.m.

Don't get up, Mac told himself. Stay on the ground.

It had been several minutes since Slezak hit him. In that time he heard Slezak rifling through his things again, throwing drawers on the floor.

Baiting him.

He wants you to get up, Mac thought. That's just what he wants. For you to get up and take a swing at him. He wants you to take this to the next level.

He wants you back in prison. Or dead. Or anything in between.

The Lord is my shepherd.

The Lord is my shepherd.

Slezak did not say another word. He did not hit Mac again. Instead, he walked out, slamming the door.

Mac waited until he heard the car drive off.

How close he had come to defending himself. *Thank you, God, that I didn't.*

He thought of Jesus. Jesus got a whole lot more than a punch in the stomach and didn't rise up to defend himself.

Yeah, well, that was Jesus. Son of God. Not an ex-con with a head injury.

What did God want of him?

Anything?

Please, be something.

11:31 a.m.

"Does anybody know you're here?" Liz asked.

"Nobody," Ted said. His body, his nerves, his muscles, everything in him was alive. It amazed him that this was happening all at once — that she had killed a man, that she had kissed him, that she wanted him.

That this was a crime, that he was helping her in a crime, that he was *helping her.*

"Are you sure?" Liz said. "Are you absolutely sure?"

"I live alone in an apartment," he said. "It's a big complex. Nobody really looks out after anybody else."

"Good," she said. "What kind of car do you drive?"

"It's a Mercury," he said. "A Mercury Cougar."

"That'll do. I want you to look out the window and wait until nobody is around. No cars passing by. My next-door neighbor isn't here. She's in Europe or something. Her house is all closed up. The people across the street can't really see over here unless they're at the end of their driveway. So wait until you think it's all clear, then walk calmly to your car and bring it around to the back. We're up against the hill, there's nobody back there."

"Then what?" Ted asked.

"We put the body in, of course."

"My car?"

"If this ever gets out and the police come calling, they'll want to search my car. We'll have enough trouble getting rid of the blood in the house. I don't want it all over the trunk of my car. You'll be safe, because nobody is going to suspect you in this."

"All right," he said, willing to do anything she asked. She was smart. She was street smart. However she got that way, it was a complete turn-on.

The next ten minutes sped by. He got the car around the house to the back where the big curving driveway led him. Looking around, he could see there was no way for people to observe what was going on unless they were on top of the hill, looking down. No one was there.

They got the tarp-covered body into the trunk, slammed it shut.

"Now what?" he said. *Now what?* He knew what he wanted. He wanted to melt and stay with her always. He didn't care what that meant, he didn't even care if that meant his soul was damned forever.

"Inside," she said.

He followed her into the house. He would have followed her into the flames if she wanted him to.

"We have to wait," she said. "Until tonight."

Wait? With her? All day? Yes, yes, yes.

"I need a drink," she said.

"I'll get you some ginger ale," Ted said, starting for the kitchen.

"No," she said. "I want a real drink."

"Do you have something?"

"I do. You like bourbon?"

He smiled. "I'm more of a vodka guy."

"If I said bourbon is all I have and that I want you to have a drink with me, what would you say?"

His heart was running a one-hundred-yard dash. "I'd say that I was a bourbon guy."

"All right, then we've got some work to do. There's a bucket and bleach by the washing machine. And some rags. Bring them."

1:23 p.m.

Mac knew he could kill Slezak. His head wanted him to. The hate was building up inside like water against a dam. It was going to burst, just like it always had since he was a kid. Since his father died, in fact. He could trace it back that far.

He could barely remember his father's face. The man had brown hair, Mac remembered that much. And his voice. He thought, at odd times during the night, he could hear his father's voice, telling him what it was like to work maintenance on the MTA.

"You have to feel the vibration of the tracks. You have to listen to the rumble to know what direction that big old train is coming. You know what it's like? It's like walking around here at night."

"Around here" was a two-room apartment about ten minutes from downtown Newark. You just didn't go out at night, that's all there was to it.

Mac did remember his father had a laugh that seemed forced. It was like he knew life had delivered a bag of day-old bread to him, and that was going to be it. That's what he'd have to go on, but he didn't want his son or wife to know about it.

He died when Mac was eight. His dad was working repairs in the Hoyt-Schermerhorn station in Brooklyn. He and another guy were carrying a dolly across the G track toward the A and C. How they misjudged the G train no one ever knew, because both of them were killed instantly.

Mac remembered the funeral. A lot of people turned out. A lot of hands touched Mac's head and told him what a great guy his father was. He didn't know when it happened, but somewhere in there, sometime at the funeral, he started hating everybody. It came on him like a black fog. He didn't have a father, and all those people were all part of a world that took fathers away. No explanation, it just happened.

He lived in that fog until he was eighteen years old. He busted a lot of heads, bloodied a lot of faces. Once, when he was sixteen, he almost killed a kid from Great Neck who was visiting his grandmother. He just looked like a Great Neck kid, and that was all. That little episode got him busted into medium-security juvie at Burlington.

And that's where he might have graduated into the hard stuff if it weren't for the judge who told him he could choose between the Marines and more time.

Mac chose the Marines.

It did the trick for a while. All the hate got channeled into the places the corps wanted it to go. And after the Gulf, he thought he had it turned around.

But the headaches kept coming, and the VA kept jerking him around. He learned to hate again, this time the bureaucrats. He did manage to work in a couple of garages, got fired both times. Most of the nineties were lost to him.

Then he met a beautiful woman named Athena in Oceanside and that very night conceived a child. Three months later they got married. The child came. A daughter, Aurora.

Mac felt the promise of new life. It lasted about a month, which was when the money started running out. When fights with Athena started to get louder and made the baby cry.

One night he pushed Athena to the floor and ran out, got five bottles of tequila, and holed up in the Aku Aku Motor Inn for two days.

When he sobered up, he used a gun to hold up a liquor store.

2:05 p.m.

Geena was chattering away while Rocky tapped on her laptop. Trying to search and gather when Geena was around was like trying to do a crossword at a rave. A little distracting.

"—of the four harmonies," she was saying, just as Rocky was accessing the archives of the *Pack Canyon Herald*, such as they were. "They are actually the four humors the ancient Greeks found, only now we know what to do with them."

I'll tell you what you can do with them, Rocky thought.

"I can't remember what the guy's name was—"

"Hippocrates," Rocky said.

"What he said was, all of us have humor. There are four kinds of humor."

"Funny and unfunny," Rock said, reading the screen.

"Hmm?"

"Clean and dirty."

"What are you talking about?"

"The four humors."

"Really? No! They're liquid. Something like that. In the body. And Swami says if you have them in balance, you become like a liquid battery. Like car batteries with liquid gel or something like that."

"I don't find that humorous." Rocky was trying to read the story on Arty's death.

"So tell me more about this guy you met."

"Geena, do you mind?"

"I'll tell you about mine if you tell me about yours."

Rocky stopped reading. "What do you mean, yours?"

"No fair. I said you first."

"Geena, my humorous friend, I have *not* met a guy, okay? Mac's Arty's friend, that's all."

"Do tell."

"There's nothing to tell. Will you knock it—"

"You have no idea"—Geena did a spin move—"what is in store for you."

"Not romance, if that's what you're thinking. That ship has sailed. Crashed, burned, and sunk. Now can I get back—"

"His name is Leonard."

"Whose name is Leonard?"

"Leonard."

"I got that. Is this your guy?"

Geena did a spin move the other way. "Might be."

"Is he humorous?"

"He's smart, is what he is. Anything computer. Anything digi. Anything, anything."

"Anything?"

"Yeah. How 'bout that?"

"I'd like to meet this Leonard."

"You would?"

Rocky closed her laptop. "Like, now."

2:22 p.m.

"Lord," Mac said, on his knees, at his bed, Bible open, "please don't let me do anything stupid. Please keep me from doing something wrong. Please keep me from breaking the law. Please keep my head from hurting."

For the moment, while he was praying, while he looked at the Bible, his head was all right.

Maybe, he thought, if I walked around with an open Bible all the time, that would keep me out of trouble. Keep it tied to my face like a horse's oat bag.

Slezak. Slezak. You can kill him and get away with it.

Not God's voice. The con voice. He closed his eyes and put his head on the Bible pages.

"Make it take," he said aloud. "Make it take ..."

2:36 p.m.

"Ted?"

"Hmm?"

"How you doing?"

"Warm."

"Relaxed?"

"Oh yeah."

"Nerves steady?"

"Oh yeah."

"You're not going to bail on me, are you?"

"No way."

"I can count on you, can't I?"

"All the way."

The drinks had warmed him up. He never knew bourbon could make him feel so good. It was a nice, wood-fire kind of thing, right in the middle of his chest. And his head was happy. It all just made him feel so good.

That book is great, he thought. Mom said if I read it, it would make a difference. Boy, oh boy, was she right. Sorry, Mom.

"What did you say?" Liz was looking at him.

"Hmm?"

"It sounded like you said *Sorry, Mom.*"

"No," he said. "No way."

"I'll put on some music," Liz said.

"Oh yeah. Oh yeah."

"Who do you like?"

"Hendrix," he said. "Do you have any Hendrix?"

3:21 p.m.

When they got to the apartment on La Brea, Rocky almost had to hold Geena down, she was so hyper. Being stuck for a long time in LA traffic hadn't helped things. All the bubbling, vibrating, universe-vectoring energy that was Geena Melinda Carter was ready to burst forth like an electric storm.

It happened when the door opened, and Geena jumped the guy. He stumbled backward into his apartment.

So this was Leonard. A fuzzy-headed, sloe-eyed, lumbering sort with black glasses. He had a slight lisp as he said, "You must be Geena's friend."

Genius. Pure genius. Rocky grunted as she entered the apartment, which smelled of sandalwood incense.

"We met at the ashram," Geena said.

"Ah," Rocky said. "Another of Swami G's acolytes?"

"T," Geena said. "Swami T."

"If Swami T married Kenny G, what would they name their kids?" Rocky said.

Geena and Leonard just looked at her.

"You ever been 'shramed?" Leonard said.

Geena giggled and squeezed his arm. "He means *ashramed*. Doesn't he have a way with words?"

"He's a regular Hemingway. Now, can you help me with this?" Rocky pulled out the half cell phone she'd found in Pack Canyon.

Leonard took it. "That's half a phone," he said.

"Swami does it again," Rocky said.

"Isn't she funny?" Geena said.

"It's all good," Leonard said. "What do you want me to do with it?"

"Get me the information on it," Rocky said. "Who it belonged to. And anything else you can recover."

Leonard stroked his scraggle of facial hair. "Might be some cool ring tones on there," he said. "And games."

"Isn't he the cutest?" Geena said.

Rocky blew out a stream of tired air. "Oh yes. Cute would be the word."

"Let me keep this," Leonard said. "I'm late for my colonics appointment."

"You have a colonics appointment?" Geena said. "Can I come?"

"Sure," Leonard said. "How 'bout you, Rocky?"

"Um, can I say no?" Rocky said.

"You ever been hosed?"

"Thanks, Leonard, that will be enough."

"You haven't lived!" Leonard said.

"My problems are all behind me," Rocky said.

Geena giggled. "See? Funny."

5:21 p.m.

Liz felt completely in control. Even more, that she could shape events outside herself with a wave of the hand. She was driving as calmly as a deacon with a full tithe envelope. Ted was right behind her in his car with the incriminating cargo. It was almost as if he were on an invisible string. In a way, he was. A puppet, performing the dance she was choreographing.

Yes, he would do exactly as she said.

It's going to be all right, Mama, she thought. Then she heard her mother's voice saying, *I know, honey. I know you can do this.*

It was the same thing Mama said the night she killed Miller Jones.

Two days after he had come to Liz's bed, Mama seemed agitated in the trailer as they waited for him to come home. They were eating macaroni and cheese, and Miller Jones was out getting drunk as usual.

Mama didn't say much, except *Drink your milk* and *Wipe your face with your napkin and not the back of your hand.*

After dinner, Liz asked if she could watch TV and Mama said *fine.* They had a little black-and-white TV in Mama's room, and Liz liked to watch *I Love Lucy.* She thought Lucy was funny and Ricky kind of strange with that accent and hair. The character she couldn't stand was Fred. She hated Fred. She hated the way he wore his belt up to his chest. And she hated the way he treated Ethel.

Liz couldn't help it, but she always wondered why there wasn't a show where Ethel killed Fred and she and Lucy had to figure out a way to get rid of the body before Ricky got home.

What would they have done? It would have been really funny to see Ricky come home and find Fred's legs sticking out of a trunk. Ricky's eyes would go wide: "Lucy! What joo doo?"

But everybody would decide they were happier without Fred, and Ethel could marry a man who was her own age instead of an old fart who could have been her father.

This night it was an episode where Lucy and Ethel made bread with way too much dough and yeast, and this giant loaf came shooting out of the oven, pinning Lucy on the other side of the kitchen.

Now that was funny.

She heard Miller Jones come in.

Liz knew his walk, his sound, the way he closed the door, the way the trailer rocked with the weight of him. She knew his smell. It was bourbon, Mama said, and it was sour and could knock over a horse.

She heard his voice, too, thick with drink so the words came out like mashed potatoes.

"Neee sumthin' a eat ..." he said. This was followed by some curse words. Liz thought it was because he had trouble getting into a chair.

Mama's voice was soft tonight. Liz thought that was odd, because usually Mama screamed at Miller Jones when he was like this, making demands on her. Mama would scream until her husband hit her. Then it would stop for a time and then start again.

It got real quiet then. Liz turned the sound down on the little TV and peeked out the curtain of Mama's room. She saw the back of Miller Jones slumped in a chair. Both his arms were hanging at his sides. Mama was at the little stove, spooning out the last of the mac and cheese into a bowl.

Liz thought that was nice. Maybe they'd get along with each other for once. Maybe they'd have a quiet night.

Usually when Jones was like this, he went right to sleep and snored loud. He wouldn't be bothering her this night.

She was just about to go back to *I Love Lucy* when her mama did something strange. She stepped around behind Miller Jones, holding a knife behind her back.

Even before Mama did it, everything that happened next seemed to come to Liz like a movie preview.

Not just the bloody death of Miller Jones, but what she and Mama were going to do about it.

Liz didn't even scream.

When Miller Jones's body was finally still in a bloody heap on the floor, Liz came out.

Mama said, "It's done."

Liz nodded.

"He ain't never gonna touch you again. Now you got to listen to me."

Liz said, "Yes, Mama."

"We're gonna go over and over what happened, and you're gonna tell it just the way I say to tell it. Can you do that with me?"

"Yes, Mama. I can do it."

"I know, honey," Mama said. "I know that you can do this."

I know that you can do this.

Liz checked her rearview mirror. Ted was still right behind her, more obedient than a bloodhound.

She could do this indeed.

Liz found the driveway off Mulholland Highway, turned into it. The sun was going down, and it was perfect lighting for what they were about to do.

The small lot at the end of the drive had spaces for six cars. It was empty.

She parked, got out, and waited for Ted to pull up. She left her car and got in with Ted. His car smelled like old cheese.

"Now I want you to drive all the way up," she said.

"What are we going to do?"

"We're going to take a dirt road I know about." Arty had showed her once, on a day hike.

"What about tire tracks and all that?"

"What are you talking about?"

"You see that all the time on TV."

"Leave it to me, will you? I know what I'm doing."

"I know you do," Ted said.

"Then drive."

He hesitated. What was he doing? "Go on," Liz said.

"Would you do something first?"

"What?"

"Would you kiss me again?"

"Now?"

"Yeah. I can't stand it."

"All right," she said, "but after this you do what we talked about."

"Yes."

She leaned over and kissed him on the mouth, and tried not to think about it as she did. It was like kissing liver. She didn't think she could do it again.

"Now drive," she said.

"Oh yeah."

5:39 p.m.

Mac saw Henry Weinhouse, owner and operator of Pack Canyon Market, rearranging some tomatoes in the produce section.

Henry was a friendly ex-firefighter who'd moved to Pack Canyon back in the eighties, when houses were cheap and the market wasn't really making it. He bought it and turned it around, so Mac had heard, with something innovative: personal service. He knew what his customers liked and even extended credit.

He'd done that for Mac on more than one occasion. Which was why Mac refused to shop anywhere else. You could go to the Food 4 Less or Wal-Mart and save money. But there was something called loyalty, and that was in short supply, so Mac always came to Henry Weinhouse's store.

"How're them tomatoes?" Mac said.

Henry, who wore an old-fashioned grocer's apron, turned and said, "Lycopene, baby. Got to have your lycopene."

"What I want now," Mac said, "is milk and Oreos."

"Having a party?"

"For myself. Thought I'd rent me up a good ol' John Wayne movie."

"Can't go wrong with that," Henry said. "Hey, how you getting along? I mean, with Arty dying like that?"

"It was a shocker, that's for sure."

"Saw his widow this morning. She came in to get a paper."

"Liz was here?"

Henry nodded. "She looked out of it, to tell you the truth. I tried to talk to her a little. Has she got any family?"

"She's got a church. My church."

"That's a good thing. A church is a good thing. Can I send her anything from the store?"

"That's real nice of you, Henry. How about I let you know?"

"You'll be going to see her?"

"I'll look in on her. Maybe tomorrow. I think she needs a little breathing room. She's had a rough few days."

Henry nodded. "She'll make out. She's got some grit, that girl. She'll make out just fine."

5:45 p.m.

"Over there," Liz said, pointing. Ted saw the dirt road. More like a dirt path. It headed off into some trees.

"Is this like a park?" Ted said.

"Something like that. Go on."

"What if somebody sees us?"

"Then we make out until they leave."

That made him hope somebody would see them. The path twisted around a couple of times. It was clearly a hiking trail, not meant for cars. But there was no law here. Only the law of the jungle, he thought, and almost laughed. How far he'd come since he was eight years old and stole that bike.

He was with his friend Brett, and they saw this very cool bike leaning against the wall of the 7-Eleven without a lock.

Brett said, "Let's take it."

"But what if they see us?" Ted had asked, scared.

"I'll go in and see if the kid is there and what he's doing. Look at the front. If I wave at you, take it and ride it four blocks down that way. I'll find you."

"But—"

Brett turned and went into the 7-Eleven. Ted stood there looking around, thinking hidden cameras were all over, watching him. But he felt excited. This was the most exciting thing he had ever done. Or was about to do. The anticipation was the thing. The almost doing it was what got him juiced.

And Brett did wave at him out the front door. Without another thought, Ted got on the bike and rode as fast as he could to the street, turned right, and pedaled hard exactly four blocks.

He found a house with some ivy in front and put the bike in the ivy. Then he sat on the curb and waited for what seemed like an hour. Until Brett showed up, breathing hard and covered with sweat.

"So where is it?" Brett said.

"It's right here," Ted said. "Let's just leave it."

"Are you nuts?"

"We don't need it. They'll probably find out we took it."

"Come on!"

But the excitement was over. The taking of it was over. There was a letdown, and Ted didn't want to do anything else. He just got up and started walking away, even though Brett called him a whole bunch of names.

Now, driving with Liz, he didn't want to stop. He didn't want to call it quits before going all the way. There was a new resolution in him. *Brett, buddy, if you could see me now.*

"Stop here," Liz said.

They were in a little clearing. Ted could see that the path narrowed and wouldn't be able to accommodate his Cougar.

"It's getting dark," he said.

"Yes," Liz said.

"Hey."

"What?"

"A shovel. Don't we need a shovel?"

"No," she said. "We won't need a shovel."

"But what are we going to do with the body?"

She didn't answer. She had a strange, faraway look in her eyes.

"Liz, do you need me to do some thinking for us?"

She whipped her head around. "Don't you ever say that to me."

"I'm sorry, I—"

"Don't you *ever* say I don't know what I'm doing."

"I didn't mean that." *Don't. Let. This. Slip. Away.*

"Keep on," she said. "Turn to the right."

"Off the path?"

"That's what I said. Didn't you hear me?"

He did as she asked. Just a little longer, just a little more, and this would all be over and they'd be together. They could go back to the house. They could stay there for a long time, just the two of them.

He moved slowly, because the ground was bumpy and he had to avoid some big rocks. He wondered what would happen if he got a flat tire.

She'd get them out of it. He wasn't going to do anymore thinking. Not yet.

"Stop," she said.

He stopped. Just ahead of him, two trees stood like armed guards, blocking the way.

He really wondered what they were going to do with the body. If she wanted to bury it, they needed that shovel. He didn't have one. She might have one, but she left her car in the parking lot.

She wasn't saying anything. She had the faraway look again.

No, that wasn't it. A frozen look. Her eyes were still and cold. They were looking at him, and then he saw a knife in her hand and wondered, *Does she intend to cut up the body with that knife?*

It was the last thing he ever wondered.

6:02 p.m.

Mac drove by Arty's house, thinking he might stop in and see how Liz was. He did want her to have some breathing room. But he didn't want her to try to carry the load all alone.

As he cruised past, he didn't see any lights on in the house. He didn't see her car in the driveway. Arty's old BMW was probably still in the garage.

That's one thing he could do. Just day by day, help her get things in order. Things you never think about when your husband is still alive. Like deciding what to do with his car, paying outstanding bills, getting a death certificate to the bank.

Lots of things.

Mac decided to wait. She was probably resting, or maybe she had gone to be with some friends.

He'd have plenty of time in the days ahead to make sure everything was all right. And in making them all right for her, they'd be all right for him.

6:07 p.m.

As she walked back along the path toward her car, Liz could barely see. It was dusk, and the trees made it even darker. She had only one thing left to do, and she'd have to do it without much light. If she moved fast, she could—

She stopped at the edge of the paved parking area.

Another car was parked one space over from hers.

Through the windows, in the last light, she thought she could see two silhouettes. Two heads. The heads came together and moved around.

Tongue tango.

This was not in the plans.

Don't worry, Mama. I can do this.

Yes, just like when Mama and she rehearsed the story, over and over again. How the drunk Miller Jones had pulled a meat cleaver on both of them. The meat cleaver with only his prints on it that the police found in his dead hand. Mama had used a dishtowel and placed it there.

Then she used the dishtowel to try to clean up some of the blood after they called the cops.

Liz turned on the tears, too. They came easily as she told the story she'd rehearsed with Mama. When the one officer, the older one, tried to dig a little further, Liz cried a little harder. And he backed off.

The town knew about Miller Jones, so the questions were never very probing after that. Liz talked to a nice man from the district attorney's office and repeated the story, and he was satisfied.

They never talked about Miller Jones again, she and Mama. That name was never spoken aloud between them.

But every now and then, Mama would stop what she was doing and stroke Liz's hair and say, "You can get anything you want in this life, little girl. Anything."

So a couple of snoggers weren't going to get in the way now.

She heard a grunt behind her.

Turning, she saw a large backside and a figure in the unmistakable position of a male relieving himself.

He grunted again, dipped a couple of times, then turned around and looked at her.

She couldn't make out his face. He, apparently, couldn't make out hers. Because he was staggering as he walked.

"Oh hey," he said. "Nature callin'."

Liz turned, went to her car, got in. She had blood on her clothes. Even though she'd given Ted the knife under the ribs, not the neck, there was still the blood to deal with. She would burn the clothes later.

Right now she didn't need any conversations with some *crunk*, a crazy drunk.

She closed her eyes. The crunk was probably in the car with the makeout artists, and maybe they'd—

Bam, bam!

Liz almost jumped through the windshield.

The crunk was pounding on her roof, standing at the window.

"Hey, what time izzit?" the guy shouted. His big moon face was staring in at her.

Liz shrugged and motioned she didn't know. Now get out of here, she thought.

Bam, bam!

"Hey, what time izzit? You got da time?"

"No," she said.

"Huh?"

"No!"

"You all alone in 'ere?"

"No help here. Good-bye."

The guy didn't walk away. He stayed outside the window, swaying. She didn't want to look at him. She didn't want him to get a look at her face, even though he was blitzed.

"Come on," he said. "I gotta have a time. What time izzit?"

He pounded on the roof again.

Liz started the car, backed away from him. Her headlights were on auto. The beams hit the guy, and he covered his eyes.

She paused and watched him move around like he was trying to get out of a spotlight. Then a girl got out of the other car and yelled at him. For a moment, the guy teetered between them. He looked back and forth between the girl and the headlights. The girl went to him, grabbed his arm, and pulled him toward the other car.

She opened the back door of the car and practically pushed the crunk in.

She looked toward the headlights herself. A short, dark-haired girl. A little too curious.

Liz knew what she'd have to do if it went on much longer.

The short girl turned and got back in the car, and the car started and drove out of the parking lot.

Liz let out her breath. She'd been tighter than she thought. She parked again and got to work fast.

She got the can of gas and a couple of rags out of her trunk and ran back to Ted's car. She almost stumbled over a rock she couldn't see in the dark. She cursed and went on.

She got to the car and took Ted's wallet out of his back pocket, careful to use a rag so she wouldn't leave prints. She wrapped the wallet in the rag and put it under her arm. Then she poured gas over Ted's body, lying on the front seat.

She popped the trunk and soaked Bill's body. Then she spread gas all over the car. She soaked the rag and threw the gas can into the car.

She took a box of matches out of her pocket and lit the rag on fire. It caught on good. The flame licked her hand. She let the rag go, and it fell across Ted's dead legs.

The fire started slow, then spread fast. Liz ran back to her car. Just before she started the car, she heard the explosion and saw a flash of orange light.

Friday

9:32 a.m.

Rocky took the call on her cell phone. Not someone she expected to hear from.

"I need help," Mac said.

Rocky said, "What kind of help?"

"You're an investigator type, right?"

"You could say that."

"I need that kind of help."

"You want to hire me?"

"*Hire* may be a creative word for it. I really can't afford to hire anybody."

"What exactly is it you want me to do?"

"Find out about a parole agent named Slezak. My parole agent."

"A parole agent? Like for the state of California?"

"Yeah."

"It's not magic what I do," Rocky said. "I can't just snap my fingers and know about this guy, especially if he's government."

"Can you do more than snap your fingers?"

"What exactly are you looking for?"

"Anything. I want to be able to see my daughter again. This guy is making it so I won't. He wants me to crack. He wants me to go back to prison."

"Any idea why?"

"I've tried to think, but nothing comes to mind," Mac said.

"So what can I do?"

"If you can find something on him, some dirt—"

"This is a state employee," she said. "I could get into trouble for that."

"Has trouble ever stopped you before?"

She couldn't help smiling. "Let me get this straight. You want me to investigate a government employee, without anyone finding out that I am, and without paying me anything. Is that about it?

"Deal of a lifetime."

"Oh yes."

"Opportunities like this don't come along everyday."

"Golden, it's just golden."

A pause. Then Mac said, "Forget about it. I'm just a little desperate here."

"I can relate to desperate. All right. What have you got? I'll need some information."

"I'll come to you. Name the place."

9:47 a.m.

One drink, Liz told herself. That's all I need. One drink and that's it. When I get back, then I get the sacks. I put them in the trunk, under the mat, where the spare is. Then I tell them I need to get away and clear my head. Visit someone. Yes.

Over and done.

One drink.

This time, Liz chose the Pavilions store a few miles from home. It was bigger, served a different community. She could get in, shop, get out, come home, begin.

Maybe wait just a couple of days. Look normal. Quietly pack some things, then go. *Don't rush it. When you rush it, you make mistakes.*

Liz took her time shopping. No one would think it odd that she had decided to take a trip.

No one at all—

The man at the meat counter was looking at her. He was slender with a hawk-like face, and his look lingered on her too long.

What did he know? How could he know?

No one had seen her, she knew that. No one had come knocking on her door. She had gotten away with it.

Liz pushed her cart down an aisle, then made a beeline for frozen foods.

Where Arty was waiting for her.

She almost screamed.

It wasn't him. It wasn't even a man. It was a woman with short hair who didn't even look like Arty.

What were her eyes doing to her?

She needed a drink. Well, why not? She was alone in the house now. No Arty to frown at her. She could take a drink and not fear the wrath of Arty, the frown of Arty.

If only she could quit thinking that Arty was out there somewhere, able to see her.

What did that even matter? He couldn't do anything. Ghosts couldn't do anything.

Her pulse was pounding. Now why was that? Why on earth was her body doing that?

Because you killed two people yesterday, that's why. You killed them without so much as a second thought. Do you realize that?

Do you realize that after what you did to Arty you were able to kill two other people? And do it pretty skillfully?

She almost fainted. She held on to the cart. She was in front of the Lean Cuisine case. She took a long, slow breath.

Do not let this happen, she told herself. This is a form of weakness, don't you see that? They are fighting you. There're fights all around. Don't fall for them. They tried to fight you when you were little, but you showed them, didn't you? Didn't we, Mama?

In a few moments she felt calmer. Stronger. She also had a dryness in her throat, and that sent her toward the liquor aisle.

There she selected a fifth of Jim Beam, old reliable, and put it in her cart. *Enough, enough.* She headed for the checkout. As she was putting the bottle on the belt, she heard a woman's voice behind her.

"Well, well, well."

Liz turned.

Mrs. Axelrod, that infernal busybody from the church, was smiling at her through thick red lipstick.

"Oh," Liz said. "Hello."

"How nice to run into you, dear," Mrs. Axelrod said. "I wanted to invite you to my house for dinner this week."

"How nice, but I—"

"Won't take no for an answer, I ..." She stopped, looking down.

Liz realized she was homing in on the Beam.

"My, my," Mrs. Axelrod said.

"What?" Liz said.

Mrs. Axelrod snatched the bottle.

Liz opened her mouth to protest, a curse curling itself around her tongue, but then she remembered she was redeemed now.

Mrs. Axelrod placed the bottle on the edge of the counter. "Let's talk, shall we?"

The cashier, a woman, said, "Will there be anything else?"

"I should say not," Mrs. Axelrod said.

Torture must be like this, Liz thought, as Mrs. Axelrod left her own cart and walked Liz outside. She proceeded to sit Liz on a bench by a floral display and start a lecture.

"It all goes back to our sin nature, you see," Mrs. Axelrod was saying. But every word was like a hammer on Liz's eardrums. If this didn't stop soon, she'd scream and stuff some carnations in the old lady's mouth.

"—power of the Holy Spirit in us, you see—"

Liz stood up. "Mrs. Axelrod, I have to go. I'm sorry."

"Go?"

"I promise, I won't drink."

"Come to my house tonight and—"

"I really do have to go. Thank you for caring."

Liz started for her car, but Mrs. Axelrod grabbed her arm. "Don't try to run from the Holy Spirit, my dear. It can't be done."

And then Liz almost did scream.

10:49 a.m.

Rocky said, "I haven't been able to find out anything yet. I'm a little nervous about this."

"Can you keep trying?"

Mac had come all the way to Geena's apartment. Geena was out catching vibes or looking for a job, or maybe both. They were seated at the kitchen table, where Rocky had her laptop set up. Some office, she thought.

"I do have a life, you know," Rocky said.

"I'm sure you—"

"No," she said, sitting back. "That was a lie. At least you're giving me something to do."

"What about your singing?"

"In the toilet. A toilet makes more music than I do."

"No boyfriend?"

"Stop getting personal."

"I was just asking."

"Don't ask. I don't care to talk about my luck, or lack thereof, at the moment."

"Maybe you shouldn't rely on luck," Mac said.

"Life is all about luck, my naïve friend."

"I don't—"

"It was bad luck that I have a father who hates me. Big deal. And why'd you bring up luck anyway?"

"I didn't—"

"Forget it."

"I'm sorry," Mac said.

"And quit being sorry. I'm not sorry. I just feel like Michael Jackson's nose right now, okay?"

Mac let out a huge snort-laugh.

"What's so funny?" Rocky said.

"What you just said."

"It seemed like the best image at the time, okay? Quit laughing!"

But he was convulsed. He doubled over in his chair, the chortles pouring like rain.

Unable to stop it from happening, Rocky started to laugh, too.

"This is so absurd," she said.

"I will never," Mac said between breaths, "be able to think about Michael Jackson again without thinking about you."

"Just great. My legacy."

When they calmed down, Mac said, "There was this guy in the joint, a real hard case. At least that was his rep. He didn't seem like all that much. In fact, he looked like he could be taken out by a lot of the other cons. But he was F-14 Bulldog."

"What's that?"

"Street gang. Inside and out. Very bad. So this guy, he had a patch of turf in the yard, and you didn't go inside that without his say. Now it didn't matter if you only believed it a little bit, you knew the odds of surviving were better if you went along with it. Faith is like that. It's better than luck, I'd say."

"So your faith is sort of like a prison?" She was goading him, but it did seem like a good question.

"It's more like a fortress," Mac said. "And we all need that."

"What if there are no fortresses?"

"You got to believe."

"What if you can't?" she said.

"It's something you choose to do."

"Oh yeah?" Rocky said. "I heard some cluck say God chooses who goes to heaven and who goes to hell, and there's nothing you can do about it."

"That's not what Pastor Jon says."

"Is he the pope?"

"No, but he knows his Bible. And he says you can believe even if your faith is just a little thing. God'll take you from there and help you along."

A quick knock on the door was followed by the sound of the door opening. She hadn't locked it after she let Mac in. Good job security-wise, she told herself as she went to see who it was.

It was Boyd Martin.

11:00 a.m.

House.

No one.

Alone.

Good.

I did it, Mama. And there's no catching up with me. There's no hell to pay, like Miller Jones used to tell us. Remember that, Mama? Remember?

There isn't a hell, Mama, but if there was he'd be there. That's the only place for a man like him. And if there's a heaven, well then I guess Arty deserves to be there.

Where does that leave us, Mama? Where do we go when we die?

Pushing up daisies, like they say?

I think we just go to sleep and don't wake up.

They never thought we were good enough, you or me. Remember that? They never thought we were good enough to walk in their air or rub up against them.

Remember the time that lawyer from the center of town came in when you were working at the diner? I was there, drinking a Coke in the corner and looking at my schoolwork.

That lawyer, everybody knew him, but I can't even remember his name now. I just remember how he used to walk up and down the street, going to the post office, talking to people, only it seemed like he was letting the people talk to him, just talk to him.

When you gave him the eggs, they weren't just right, the way he wanted them to be. And he yelled at you, Mama. Remember? He screamed his head off and treated you like dirt.

They can't do that to us anymore.

Never, never, never. I will never let them. Never, never, never.

And then she heard the rain.

It started out like tiny tap-dancing feet on the roof, then quickly turned to a million marbles.

Liz ran to the window and looked out. This didn't happen in LA. This was a Mississippi storm.

So quick and hard.

The mud.

The jewels.

She had to get the jewels *now*.

Liz cursed at the sky and ran for her keys.

11:01 a.m.

"Who's in there?" Boyd said.

"A guest," Rocky said. "Now get out."

"I want to meet your guest," he said and started past her. She stepped in front of him. He had beer breath. He had crazy eyes, too. He raised his hands like he was about to push her.

From behind her Mac said, "How you doin'?"

Boyd's half-sotted face grew hard. "A guy, huh?"

"Boyd, this is Daniel MacDonald. He's a friend."

Mac stuck his hand out. Boyd ignored it.

"Tell him I want to talk to you alone," Boyd said.

"He's here on business," Rocky said. "And I don't want to talk to you anyway."

"Come on, babe, I came all the way — "

"It's okay, friend," Mac said. "Tomorrow is another day, like they say. She'll call if she wants to see you."

Boyd just stared at him. Rocky couldn't help noticing they were almost exactly the same height and build. She could almost smell the testosterone shooting into the room, like gas through a pipe.

Then Boyd said, "Why don't you get out?"

Rocky said, "Boyd, please — "

"I'm talking to him."

"Now look," Mac said.

"You look," Boyd said. "You don't get out, I'm gonna get mad. You want to see that?"

"I don't want to fight you," Mac said.

"Just go!" Rocky said. She put her hands on Boyd's chest and tried to turn him around. He didn't turn. He grabbed her shoulders and pushed her into the wall.

The moment she hit it, the side of her head thunking, she saw Mac move like a big cat. With an almost balletic grace, he grabbed Boyd's right arm and twisted it behind his back. Mac's left arm wrapped around Boyd's neck.

It was obvious Boyd was rendered fully and completely powerless. The only thing he could do was curse, which he started doing in earnest.

Mac pulled with his left arm, choking off the words.

"No more of that," he said, then started guiding Boyd toward the apartment door. He called to Rocky to open it for him.

She did, then followed as Mac escorted him to the stairwell.

As they went, Boyd fought to say something or do something. But each time he did, Mac would apply some kind of pressure and Boyd would stop.

"Now you just listen," Mac said, heading down the stairs. "No hard feelings here, but you have to stop this kind of thing."

Boyd grunted, fought, was restrained again by Mac.

Mac said, "Believe me, pal, I know what you're going through."

More struggle, more pain for Boyd. They reached the bottom of the stairwell.

"And the only thing that helped me," Mac said, "was admitting to myself that I was a permanent jerk, and if I didn't turn my life around, I'd be dead."

Mac aimed Boyd toward the double front doors of the apartment building. Rocky hurried over, opened them. A hard rain was coming down. Mac marched Boyd into it and released him with a hard push.

Boyd shot halfway down the walk, slipped, fell into the grass patch. Cursing now without restraint, he got up and pointed at them.

"Take me inside," Mac said to Rocky.

"What?" she said.

He put his arm around her and turned them toward the doors.

"What's wrong?" Rocky said.

"Get me inside before I beat him to death," Mac said.

11:04 a.m.

Rain streaked the windshield. It was like that scene in that movie *Psycho* that scared her to death the first time she saw it. There was a woman who stole a lot of money and was trying to get away. And the rain came down and she could hardly see out the window of her car.

When she finally saw something, it was that creepy motel where she got cut to pieces.

It occurred to Liz that she was just like that woman in the movie. And she wondered if she would end up in pieces in a bathtub.

That was called fate, and that's what you couldn't get out of. Fate or luck, or whatever. That's what killed Arty and that's what was trying to get her.

She looked in her rearview mirror. She wondered if she was being followed. What if a cop was following her? What if they had her on the radar screen?

What if Arty was watching her?

Why did she keep thinking that? Okay, she told herself, it's all right to feel a little crazy. You just killed a couple of people. You burned up their bodies. You have all kinds of adrenaline rushing through your system. Don't worry about it. Move on.

Keep moving. Always.

She almost ran into the back of a Toyota pickup. She hit the brakes and skidded on the wet surface of the road. The car fishtailed. That took her into the opposing lane. Oncoming headlights in the overcast late morning almost smashed into her.

The angry honk of the furious driver shattered her ears.

It was raining hard. She kept thinking of the bags she had hidden being washed away in a torrent. She got back on the right side of the road and continued, keeping a steady pace of twenty miles per hour.

She turned into the entrance of Pack Canyon Park. There was nobody in the parking lot. Of course not. It was too wet for the park. Too wet to be hiking.

But not for her.

11:05 a.m.

"You wouldn't really do anything like that," Rocky said. Mac was sitting now, back in Geena's apartment, breathing hard. The red in his face was slowly fading.

"I could," he said.

"I just don't believe it. The fact is, you stopped yourself. You didn't go after him. You came inside with me."

"I was this close," Mac said, measuring with his finger and thumb.

"But you didn't, that's the thing."

"Yeah. I guess that's the thing. But every day I have to fight the thing."

"But that's what your faith does, right? Like Arty used to tell me." Rocky could hardly believe she was saying this. She, who didn't have his faith, telling him what it meant.

Heaven knows, anything goes.

Rocky's phone buzzed. A number she didn't recognize.

"This is Eric Lendsian," the voice on the other end said. "I'm with mall security at The Promenade."

"Security?"

"Do you know someone named Frederick Towne?"

Uh-oh. "He's my father."

"He's here, he's disoriented. He says he has a car, but we don't think he's in any condition to drive."

"How did you get this number?"

"He had a union card in his wallet. We called and got routed to another number, someone named Arty."

"My brother. He died."

"This was the next number on the contact sheet. Can you possibly come and get him? He wants to go, and we can't force him—"

Rocky looked at her watch. "Half an hour."

"Let me give you my number, and you can call me when you get here." Rocky wrote it down and clicked off.

She looked at Mac. "I have to drive to the valley. It's my dad. What else can happen today?"

"I'm going with you," he said.

11:42 a.m.

This is stupid! Liz thought. The rain was so hard it was almost coming through the umbrella. She had her Nikes on, and all they did was get caked with mud. She stopped every now and again and held her feet out in the rain to wash them off. Then she started walking again.

She reached the high point of the path in about twenty minutes. The place where Arty had fallen. In the gloom she thought she could see his body again, down below. But it was just discolored earth. She thought she heard a voice and spun around. But it was nothing. Just rivulets of water pouring down the hillside because of the rain.

She was cold. Cold and wet. Get the jewels, she told herself. Get them before you die from a stupid cold!

You'd like that, wouldn't you, Arty? You'd like it that I got dead because of what I did. They'd all like it.

11:54 a.m.

It was really coming down, the rain. It pounded the top of Mac's truck, but at least the traffic was moving a little.

And at least he was helping Rocky. He wanted to help her.

He found, in fact, that he just wanted to be with her.

But he told himself not to think that. Because he was not a good choice.

Choices.

He'd been thinking a lot about choices lately. The choices he made that were bad, that still haunted him.

Pastor Jon set him straight on that. While God forgives your sins when you confess Christ, you're not spared the consequences of your actions. Like King David, when the baby he sired in adultery was taken from him.

Choices.

He had a choice whether to hold up the liquor store that night. He'd had a fight with Athena about money a couple days before, right after he'd been given the runaround by the VA again.

He wasn't approved for any further surgery, they said. They'd done all they could, they said. Just treat the pain the rest of your life, pal, and good luck to you.

That's the way he heard it, anyway.

So it's Christmas, and you can't get anything for your kid because you blew your only employment right after Thanksgiving. You drink too much, and when your wife gets on you about it, what do you do? Put her in her place, that's what. Yeah. Because you're not gonna take that from anybody.

Find a motel. Don't tell anybody where you're going.

You've got that revolver your dad had, that Colt, and you've taken care of it, and it's sitting there, and you remember that little liquor store you were in once is an easy target. Older Korean couple in the place.

And as you're sitting there in the car, across the highway, watching the place, waiting for the right time, you think you hear a voice in your head. You get ready for the talons to dig in, but this time they don't.

This time it's an actual voice, and it says something like, *You don't need to do this.* That's it. You heard it in your head. And then felt a moment's calm like everything was going to be all right.

But just then the old Korean man decides it's the time to run out for something. He gets into an old car at the edge of the strip lot and drives away.

Choices. You chose to get out of the car.

Mac brought his thoughts back to Rocky. "You're right about me and Arty," he said.

"How's that?" Rocky said.

"It does change everything. Faith does."

Rocky nodded. "You know, it's funny. I have a friend who has tried just about every spiritual fad there is, and she hasn't changed a bit."

12:00 p.m.

Liz thought, Rain can drive you crazy. Like waterboarding. Like Chinese torture.

Like life. Stupid life.

I am not going to let water get the best of me. I'm not going to let lightning strike me, even if it comes from the hand of God.

Now how do I get to the stones without slipping and breaking my neck?

She was at the spot now where Arty had fallen.

Are you here, Arty? Leave me alone.

No such thing as ghosts.

Money is waiting. Money. You will never have to worry about living like a redneck again. You will be able to have what you want, when you want it.

She was about to start down the rocks, toward the hiding place. It would be a wet hike but so what?

Then: "Hey!"

It sounded like a rifle shot. Liz turned. In the misty rain, she saw him. Coming toward her.

It was Arty. It was him. He'd been waiting for her.

Ghosts couldn't hurt you if didn't let them.

"Hey there!"

Closer. He didn't look like Arty now. It wasn't him at all. No, another person. A man.

And they were all alone in the rain.

Don't be paranoid. Don't stop moving.

"Listen," the man said.

She didn't have a weapon with her. Funny, but now that she was a killer, her preferred instrument was the knife. She wished she had one. What if he tried something?

"You shouldn't be out here," the guy shouted.

A swift kick to the classified section might do it. But there was only so much damage you could do with tennis shoes.

The guy was short. Not much taller than she. Looked Latino. His black hair was pulled back in a ponytail. He wore a black jacket and jeans.

She got ready for the kick. The path was muddy. She'd have to be careful not to slip.

When he was about five yards away, he said, "I work for parks and rec," he said. "You shouldn't be out here."

A city employee. Ha. Liz said, "I like it out here."

"It's dangerous."

"Is the park closed?"

"It's gonna be. That your car in the lot?"

"Yes."

"Come on," he said. "I'll walk you back."

Rain pounded their umbrellas.

Liz said, "I'll come out in a bit."

"I can't let you stay."

"It's okay—"

"Come on." He motioned for her to follow. "Before it gets worse."

Clearly, he was going to stick around and do his duty. A real civil servant, this guy. A credit to his employer. Something to do on a rainy day. Hassle people who want to use the park.

A thought flashed quickly through her mind. Of him falling. In the same spot Arty did. If she could just manipulate him a little, it wouldn't be too hard.

12:22 p.m.

"Dad, it's me," Rocky said.

He looked at her, but his eyes weren't focusing. They were in the security office on the second floor of the mall. A modest box of a room with a desk and computer, a white board, a filing cabinet, and a bike that presumably belonged to the guard, a serious-looking man of about thirty.

Mac stood by the door, the security guard sat in a squeaky chair. On the only other chair sat Rocky's dad.

"Like I said," this security guard told her, "he looked really disoriented. He wouldn't let me call the paramedics."

"No!" her father said.

"I think you better take him to hospital," the guard said.

"Where's my sandwich?" her dad said.

"He thinks he's supposed to be served lunch here," the guard said.

"Where is it?" her dad said.

"Dad, it's me, Rocky."

"Where's Arty?"

Rocky looked at the security guard, who shrugged. To her dad she said, "Arty can't be here right now. I am here. Come with me, okay?"

"I want my sandwich."

"That's where we're going," Rocky said. "We're going to get a sandwich."

"We are?"

"Yes. A big, honking sandwich."

"What kind?"

"You'll like it," she said.

He hesitated a moment, then nodded. He tried to get out of his chair but couldn't on his own. Mac came over. He and Rocky each took an arm and helped her dad up.

"Rocky?" her dad said.

"I'm here."

"Where's Arty?"

"Maybe we should go find him," she said. "We'll go find Arty and then he can take care of you, just like you want him to, okay, Dad? Will that be all right with you, Dad?"

The security guard made a face, like he wasn't sure now whether to let her take her own father out of the office.

"We have a close, loving relationship," Rocky told him. "Just like so many other happy families."

"Eh?" her father said. "I want a sandwich. Who's that?"

"That's Mac," Rocky said. "He was a friend of Arty's."

"Where's Arty?"

She took her dad by the arm, which felt bony, and steered him out of the security office.

"Wait," the guard said, "I need you to sign something."

"I'll take him," Mac said. "We'll wait out here."

She was glad Mac was here. He was a steadying force. She went back into the office, read the waiver and signed it.

Then she and Mac took Dad to the elevator. Her dad was walking with a limp. She could tell, even in his disoriented state, that he was mad about this. He was always self-sufficient. He must really hate having her and Mac helping him.

They struggled with him to the first floor, then out the side doors to the parking lot.

It was still raining hard.

"I don't suppose you know where your car is, do you, Dad?" she asked.

"Huh?"

"Never mind. We need to get you to a doctor."

He pulled his arm away from her. "Don't tell me what to do."

"Dad, we need to take you to the doc—to get a sandwich. Come with me, please."

"Where's my car?" He looked around and started out into the rain. Mac caught him and pulled him back.

"Easy there, Mr. Towne," he said.

"Who are you?" Dad said.

"A friend," Mac said. "And I like sandwiches, too."

"Yeah?"

"Oh yeah. I'll make sure you get exactly the kind you want."

Dad looked at Rocky. He looked like he was trying to piece everything together, but the puzzle was scattered all over the lot. Then he said, "He's okay. Let's go."

12:41 p.m.

The parks-and-rec guy was still standing there in the parking lot, stupidly waiting for her to drive off. Earning his pay.

She would have to come back later, after the rains.

She cursed, slamming her hands on the steering wheel.

It was almost as if someone was trying to stop her. Arty.

Arty, do you think you can stop me?

She wondered then if she was losing her mind. Part of her knew she was.

No, I won't let it happen.

Tomorrow. You can come back tomorrow.

Don't try to stop me, Arty. It won't happen. Stay where you are.

Tomorrow, I'll get away from you. From all of you.

4:33 p.m.

"Thanks for being here," Rocky said. It was about time she thanked him. They were in the waiting room outside Emergency.

"Glad I can be."

"I think I'd go a little bonkers if I didn't have someone to talk to." The place was sterile, dull brown. A TV droned the local news. An older Asian man across the room was listening to the news. Or at least staring at the monitor.

"You can talk to me," Mac said.

"Okay. What'll we talk about?"

"How about tulips?"

She smiled. "Tulips are good. What about fuchsias?"

"Fuchsias? I don't know foxglove from fuchsias."

"Me either," she said. "I just like saying *fuchsias.*"

"It's good to say *fuchsias,* that's for—"

He stopped. Because she was crying now. She put her head in her hands. She was shaking. *Don't do this.* She couldn't stop.

She felt Mac's arm around her shoulder. She fought back against the tears. "I'm sorry," she said.

"Don't be," Mac said.

"I just . . . I just want to be able to do something to make it different. I want to be able to pull a string and have my dad want to talk to me again. But I can't."

He didn't say anything and she was glad. Just glad he was next to her now, not trying to talk her out of anything. Just *here*.

8:21 p.m.

Elvis on the wall. She hated Elvis on the wall. What was he doing up there on the wall but making time tick-tock to the rain? He was mocking her in the rain, a rain that was not stopping. The rain that was beating on the roof. It sounded like handfuls of uncooked rice, thrown down, over and over and over. She cursed at Elvis, she told him to shut up and then she went to the wall and pulled him down and threw him on the floor. His legs stopped moving. The clock stopped ticking.

Saturday

9:15 a.m.

Now, Liz thought. Now it is dry, and now is the time, and now I can do this.

She threw on jeans and a sweatshirt.

Now is the time, and I will get away with it. They are all against me now, but I will survive. I will—

A knock at the door stopped her as she was putting on her shoes.

Another knock. "Mrs. Towne? It's Detective Moss."

Moss!

Run. You can run out the back. You can—

—Idiot, be cool. Cool. And if you have to kill her, you will. You will do that before you allow yourself to get taken in and—

Knock. "Liz, can I talk to you for a moment?"

Drawing a deep breath, Liz made ready. She could do it in an instant. Her strength was greater than Moss's.

She opened the door.

"I'm sorry for coming over like this," Moss said. She was all soft and smiley. Dangerous.

"It's all right," Liz said. "What can I do for you?" And then she thought, *Why is she working on a Saturday?*

Liz came out and closed the door behind her.

"How are you doing?" Moss said.

"I have good days and bad," Liz said.

"Understandable. Completely. You look tired."

"What exactly are you here for?"

"Just some information I wanted to give you," Moss said. "Some things we've learned, and I'm hoping maybe you can help us."

"Me help you?"

"If you can. Would you mind trying for me?"

"I suppose, but I can't think of how."

"I just thought you might like to know that we identified the body that was found near where your husband died. His name is Denton Roberts."

Liz waited. Moss waited. Liz shrugged.

"We think he was in criminal activity. A jet boy, someone who gets away from a crime scene on a very fast motorcycle."

"He was a criminal?"

"He had a prior record, but he's been quiet for a few years."

"What was he doing in the canyon?"

"We thought he was working, so to speak. A week ago there was a jewelry store robbery at a mall in Glendale. About two million dollars' worth of stones taken at about three in the morning."

"Wasn't there security?" Liz asked.

"An alarm tripped, but by the time the security company and cops arrived, the thieves were gone. Outside cameras caught two men on a motorcycle speeding away."

"Wow."

"Wow is right."

"Was this man, this man you identified, one of the robbers?"

"If he was, he didn't have the take with him. Maybe somebody took it from him."

"This is all such a bizarre story," Liz said.

"It gets even more bizarre, Mrs. Towne. There's another connection to this whole thing that is very troubling."

"And what is that?"

"The man who helped you, Mr. Gillespie. Ted Gillespie."

Liz was aware that her hands were fisting. She kept her face perfectly calm as she relaxed them. "Yes, how is he?" Liz said.

"We were wondering when the last time was that you saw him."

"Well, let's see. He came by a couple of days ago, I think it was. He came by to see how I was doing."

"Was it two days? That would be Thursday."

"Thursday. Yes."

"Can you tell me what time?"

"Can I ask why you're asking?"

Moss took a slow breath. "We think something may have happened to him. I tried to reach him and couldn't. I spoke with his mother, and she hasn't heard from him."

"Something happened to Ted?"

"If you help me, maybe we can find out." Moss looked Liz in the eye.

"I don't know what else I can say," Liz said. "He came to my house and just wanted to know how I was doing. He seems like a nice guy."

"How long did he stay?"

"Let me think." And she did think. She had to make sure any timeline checked out. "I can't really remember. A while. We talked."

"About anything in particular?"

"No. He did bring me a gift. He brought me a clock. A Winnie the Pooh clock. I thought that was very nice."

"Yes," Moss said. "Very nice." But the way she said it made Liz think that she wasn't interested in the clock in the slightest.

"I don't know him," Liz said, "but I got the impression he was, I don't know, a little lonely."

"What gave you that impression?"

"I don't know, he just seemed sad. He's a very nice guy, though. I think he means well."

"You just talked?"

"Just talked. About his work a little. He's into computers."

"Did he say where he was going after he left?"

Liz shook her head.

"He just drove off?"

Trick question. What if there was a witness in Moss's back pocket? "No. I drove my car, too. He followed me. I was trying to show him how to get out of the canyon on the valley side."

"He followed you?"

"Yes."

"How far?"

"Only till we got to Topanga."

"Then he went off on his own?"

"That's right."

"And where did you go after that?"

"Well, I got on the freeway and drove into Hollywood."

"Hollywood? What was going on there?"

"Are these questions really necessary?"

Moss said, "It's just helping me to talk all this through."

"But you said something happened to Ted. Why does it matter where I was after I saw him?"

"Sometimes going through a whole time period jogs the memory. It's just the way the mind works."

Liz paused. "It's just so stressful, this whole thing. I feel terrible that something may have happened to Ted. He was just trying to be helpful."

"And in Hollywood, what did you do?" Moss said.

Liz closed her eyes and brought up images of Hollywood. "I wanted to go to the center, at Hollywood and Highland. And shop."

"What time did you get there?"

"I wasn't really watching the time. And I really don't think I can help you anymore. I just don't know what I can say. I'm very sad he might be in some trouble."

Moss nodded. "And you've been finding some solace in your time of loss?"

"Oh yes," Liz said, relieved. The conversation was just about over. "The people at Pack Canyon Community Church are just so loving and kind. It's been a real blessing."

"Well, that does it, I guess. If you happen to hear from Mr. Gillespie, you'll let me know, won't you?"

"Of course I will."

Moss put her hand out. Liz shook it. Moss held a beat longer than Liz would have. Then she left.

She suspects, Liz thought.

No. She knows.

10:10 a.m.

Mac was cleaning leaves out of the rain gutter when he saw Liz Towne pull into the drive. On his knees, on the roof of the shack, he waited until she got out and said, "Hello, down there."

"Oh," she said. "Hi."

"Nice surprise. Be right down."

He descended the ladder at the side of the shack and wiped his hands on his jeans. The cooler air this morning felt good on his head.

"Come on in," he said.

She smiled and nodded. He opened the front door for her and followed her in. He flicked on a light. The day was gray, and he thought there might be more rain coming.

"It's nice to see you," Mac said. "How — "

She turned quickly and faced him. "Mac, I'm just so anxious. Have you got anything to drink?"

"I'll take a look in the cave," he said.

"Cave?"

"More cave than refrigerator."

He went to the kitchen, wishing he had more to offer her. She must have trusted him a great deal to show up here. He did not want to blow that trust.

His refrigerator was, indeed, a picture of desolation. Half a slice of cheddar cheese in plastic. Soggy veggies in the crisper. Jam. Peanut butter. Hot sauce. He could put all those together in a bowl, he thought, and pretty much have all the food groups covered.

He did have Pepsi. "Pepsi all right?" he called.

"That's fine," she answered.

He took out two cans and put them on the counter. He got two non-matching glasses from a cupboard and poured the contents of the cans into each. No ice. The ice maker was on the fritz.

When he came back to the living room, he saw Liz looking at the one framed item he had on the wall. A gift from Pastor Jon.

"That's a prayer from Francis of Assisi," Mac said.

"Who?" Liz said.

"An early Christian. I don't know much about him, but I like his prayer."

"Me too," Liz said. " 'Make me an instrument of thy peace.' "

" 'Where there is hatred, let me sow love,' " Mac said.

Liz read more. " 'Where there is injury, pardon. Where there is doubt, faith. Where there is despair, hope. Where there is darkness, light.' "

" 'And where there is sadness, joy,' " Mac said. "Go on, read the rest."

" 'O Divine Master, grant that I may not so much seek to be consoled as to console; to be understood, as to understand; to be loved, as to love; for it is in giving that we receive, it is in pardoning that we are pardoned, and it is in dying that we are born to eternal life.' "

"Amen," Mac said.

"It's beautiful," Liz said.

Mac took it off the nail. "I'd like you to have it," he said.

"No, I couldn't."

"Please." He placed it in her hands. "I've got it memorized. Put it up in your house now."

"I really can't—"

"It would mean a lot to me," Mac said. "Truly."

Liz looked at the prayer. "Thank you," she said. "I wanted to ask you something. I'm having some trouble with the investigator who handled Arty's death. She just got through asking me a lot of questions."

"What sort of questions?"

"I don't know, this and that. I just can't help feeling she thinks I've done something wrong. It was an accident, what happened to Arty. Why can't she accept that?"

"They have a job to do," Mac said, "and they all do it differently."

"You mentioned once to me that you're on parole."

"Yeah."

"And that you're under a parole officer."

"Yes. A guy named Slezak."

"They can make life hard on you if they want to, can't they?"

"Oh yes, they can," Mac said. "They can search me anytime, anywhere. And Slezak loves his job."

"I hate to see that happening to you," Liz said.

"I'll be all right," Mac said.

"How do you live with that? I mean, knowing that it could happen at any time?"

Mac thought, She wants to know. She really wants to know. This was a moment he couldn't blow. He'd blown it enough times in the past.

He picked up his Bible from the coffee table and held it up. "This is the only thing," he said. "I have to depend on this every day. And I have to pray. Those two things keep me going."

She looked at the Bible like it was a curio. Mac watched her face, looking for signs. What did she want to know? What could he say that would make a difference?

"Is that all?" she said. "Just read and pray?"

"It's a start," Mac said. He sounded to himself like a leaden idiot.

"Arty tried to read his Bible to me. I wouldn't listen." She looked down.

He wanted so much to comfort her. He was stumbling this way and that in his mind. *Just get to the point, the point of Christianity.* "The Bible says we'll see our loved ones who have gone on before us."

"I guess that's just something I can't wrap my head around," she said. "It seems too good to be true."

"It's too good *not* to be true," Mac said. "I mean, if God promises all good things, then wouldn't we expect the best to be true?"

She thought about it. "Mac, would you mind terribly if I asked you to make some coffee?"

"Coffee? Sure, I can do that."

"And while you're doing that, I'm going to sit here and read this prayer again. Would that be okay?"

"More than okay," he said. And when he went into the kitchen, he was happy. Happier than he had been in a long time. Happy knowing that at last he was making a real difference to somebody.

Being able to get through to somebody about God. And not just anybody, but the widow of his best friend.

Yes, God is good, he thought, as he pulled out the bag of Canyon Grind Breakfast Blend and started preparing the brew.

11:23 a.m.

Franklin Towne's doctor was a compact Chinese American named James Chu. He had a comforting face, which Rocky was grateful for.

"You will notice," he said when Rocky returned to the hospital, "that some of what would be normal movements are off a bit. As when your father tries to bring food to his mouth, his arm may suddenly flex."

"Can he walk?"

"There does not appear to be any paralysis, but there is hypotonicity in the left leg. A weakness there."

"Will he get better?"

"The focus now has to be on prevention. I'd like him to stay put for a few days. Do some tests, an echocardiogram, ultrasound."

"Yes. Of course."

"You can see him now," Dr. Chu said.

11:26 a.m.

This time Liz ran.

She left Mac's place with that framed prayer deal, which she tossed in the trunk of her car. She got to the park and started running up the trail.

She did not care that her lungs were burning. She didn't care who saw her. If anyone tried to talk to her, she would run the other way. She didn't care.

Keep moving. Don't stop this time.

She had a bag with her. The kind with a leather strap. A big purse, really.

There was a guy on a dirt bike riding by. He waved at her. She ignored him. She went down rocks and kept going and found the field where she had put the sacks.

The ground was soft and mushy from the rain. Her feet made gooshy sucking sounds as she walked. She almost dove into the hole where she had buried the jewels.

She reached in with her hands through the tangle of weeds and grass. She grabbed the jacket and pulled it free. She opened it up. The sacks were all there. Waiting for her.

Mama, I'm doing it. They are not going to stop us now.

She put the sacks in the purse and the purse over her shoulder and headed out of the canyon. Overhead, a helicopter flew by. For a moment she thought it was a police helicopter, tailing her.

But it went on. It had a giant 7 on its side. News helicopter.

Well, no news here. Everything is quiet. Time to get ready to get out.

She passed a couple of kids with their dad, then got to the parking lot and threw the handbag in the trunk.

Then she drove right on through the canyon and out to the 7-Eleven on the other side.

11:30 a.m.

"Dad," Rocky said, "you remember that time we all went to Magic Mountain?"

Her father looked through her.

"Magic Mountain, out in Valencia?" Rocky said. "Had the great big roller coaster, and you wanted to sit with me on it, 'cause you thought I'd be scared?"

He frowned, but in a way that told her there were gears shifting in there. File cabinets of memory were being opened, photo albums inspected.

"Do you remember going there?" Rocky said.

"Magic Mountain," he said.

"Yes."

"Yeah. Arty was with us."

"Yes," Rocky said. "Arty was with us. Do you remember the roller coaster?"

"I think I do," he said.

"I remember every bit of it," Rocky said. "I remember when we got on, and you said you were going to sit with me. You held my hand. When they got us in, you put your arm around me. Do you remember that?"

No answer.

"You said, 'We're going to ride like the wind.'"

No answer.

"Then you said you used to go on a roller coaster when you were a little boy back in Ohio, and that you were scared of it at first, but you learned not to be scared. And you said I could learn not to be scared. Do you remember it, Dad? I want you so much to remember that."

"I don't remember that," he said and turned his head away.

"But it's true, Dad."

"My head hurts," her father said.

"Well it's going to hurt for a while. You had a stroke."

"I know. They told me. I'm really mad at that."

"You've always been a fighter. I know you're not going to give up now."

He didn't say anything. His eyes glazed over for a moment, then cleared.

"But you can't fight this one alone," Rocky said. "You're going to need a little help."

"I don't need any help."

"That's not what the doctor says."

"Doctors. They know less than you think we do. *They* do. Ahh." He waved his hand in the air.

"I'm willing to go with the docs on this one, Dad. Will you let me take you home? I'll get you settled, and then we can talk about what to do next, huh?"

"I don't want any fuss made," he said.

"It's no fuss," Rocky said. "It's what we do."

"We?"

"Family. You know, the people who're supposed to look out for each other? It's the latest thing, been in all the papers."

He didn't say anything. He seemed to be looking into a long, dark hallway, wondering which way to turn.

"I'm not going to be around much longer," he said.

"What are you talking about?" Rocky said.

"I mean, I'll probably be going to be … going *to* check out soon."

"That's pretty silly talk."

"I don't want to die, it's just in the cards. And I have to say …"

1:41 p.m.

It was Slezak.

And Mac was calm. It would be all right. No matter what, it would pass. *Let him beat me with a stick if he wants to.*

"I sure hope you don't mind that I dropped by," Slezak said.

"I know you're just doing your job," Mac said.

Slezak nodded. "Taking the easy approach, huh?"

"Nothing wrong with that," Mac said. "Life seems to go a little smoother if you remember that we're all neighbors underneath."

"I don't even know what that means," Slezak said. "Is that some Bible spouting?"

"As a matter of fact, it is."

"So you're still hanging in with that Bible and church stuff? Well, at least it's keeping you off the street."

"I don't have any intention of going back on the street," Mac said.

"Then you won't mind while I take my usual look around," Slezak said. "Because I just know you are aching to file a report on me, aren't you?"

"No," Mac said. "I will accept anything that comes my way."

"You ought to be on TV. One of those self-help shows. All right, have a seat while I look around. This shouldn't take long."

No, Mac thought, it shouldn't. And as Slezak went through the bathroom and kitchen, Mac noticed his head wasn't hurting.

Pray for him. That's what he should have been doing all along. Pray for your enemies, right? Pray for those who are against you. Something like that. Jesus said it. You're a Christian, then behave like it.

Mac silently prayed for Gordon Slezak.

Until Slezak moved the bureau that was sitting in the living room. He didn't go through the drawers, just moved the thing away from the wall.

Mac watched and waited. Slezak's only reward would be some dust. He hoped that wouldn't make the PO frustrated. He started praying for him again.

Slezak bent down and picked something up.

Slezak's back was toward him, so Mac couldn't see what Slezak was doing. He appeared to be looking at something.

He spent a long moment looking at this thing. Mac didn't dare ask him what he'd found. He'd find out soon enough.

Slezak put whatever was in his hands in his coat pocket. Then slowly turned around.

His face had changed. It no longer had a diabolical smile. He didn't look the way he usually did when he had nothing on Mac.

Slezak looked hard and serious. "Get up," he said. "And turn around."

"Why?" Mac said.

Slezak pulled his gun. "Get up and put your hands behind your back."

"What's going on? I have a right to—"

"Now," Slezak said.

2:15 p.m.

"I need to go away for a while," Liz said.

Pastor Jon, on the line, said, "Taking a trip?"

"Yes, just need to get away. Thought I'd go up north, Oregon maybe, visit family."

"Well, I think that's a good idea. Is there anything we can do for you while you're gone?"

"Oh no, really, nothing—"

"We'll be praying for you."

No, don't do that. Do not do that. I don't know what you think you're praying to, but I don't want to hear it.

"Thank you," Liz said. "I appreciate it."

She hung up and felt now she had a small window. To leave. To get out. To keep moving.

3:12 p.m.

"Do you know why you're here, Mr. MacDonald?"

The detective was a woman. Her name was Moss. She seemed focused, intense. And working with Slezak to send him back to prison for some sham violation.

He tried to convince himself that this was one of the "all things" Pastor Jon preached about. As in, all things work for the good of those who love God. But the thought was only tickling his frontal lobes. The rest of his brain was telling him to play it close to the vest.

"Because I'm under arrest," Mac said.

"You're not under arrest," Moss said. "Yet."

"Then I'm free to go?"

"You've been brought in as a potential parole violator."

"For what?"

"That's what I want to ask you about. Some questions about a man you might know."

"Who?"

"Theodore Gillespie."

Mac frowned. The detective's eyes were filled with certitude. "I don't know any Theodore Gillespie. And you can stop playing your cop games and tell me what this is. If you don't, I'm walking out. If you arrest me, I'm calling a lawyer. So why don't we just cut right to it, okay?"

The detective did not seem overly worried by the idle threats of a violated parolee. She sat back in her chair and said, "You know Elizabeth Towne, isn't that true?"

"What's Liz got to do with this?"

"You helped her along after her husband died."

"Yeah, of course. Arty was my good friend, she was hurting. Still is."

"You got her involved in your church, I believe."

Mac put his palms on the table. Like a magician getting ready to perform levitation. "What's that got to do with anything?"

"There's a connection between Mrs. Towne and Mr. Gillespie. He was the one who found her in Pack Canyon after the incident."

"Accident you mean."

"And there is a connection between you and Mrs. Towne, and also Mr. Gillespie."

"I don't know Mr. Gillespie. Never met the man."

"Mr. Gillespie is dead."

Mac shook his head. "What does that have to with Liz or me?"

"His car was found, torched, with two bodies inside."

"So?"

Moss said, "Would you please explain why it is that Agent Slezak found Mr. Gillespie's wallet in your house?"

A hundred lights went off in Mac's head. Like an airstrip in the desert at night. Darkness all around, with an eerie luminescence shooting up. But nothing seen in the light. The only possibility was—

"He planted it."

"You're saying Agent Slezak planted the wallet?"

"He had to. I don't know any Gillespie, and I never had his wallet. I don't know what you and Slezak are trying to pull here, but I'm not playing."

Mac stood up.

"I'm going to have to place you under arrest, Mr. MacDonald," Moss said. "I'm giving you a Miranda waiver to sign. Or you can call a lawyer."

4:32 p.m.

Pastor Jon was admitted to the lockup to see Mac.

Mac had not called his old lawyer, because he could not afford him anyway. Pastor Jon was the one who would help him most now.

"There's a classic frame going on," Mac explained. "You know about my PO, Slezak?"

"Sure. I even met him once, remember?"

"Right."

"You said he was on some kind of a rampage against you."

"Listen, there's a dead man named Gillespie. He was the one who helped Liz when she got hurt in the canyon."

"Yes, I know the name. You're saying he's dead?"

"That's what they're telling me. Somehow his wallet ends up in my house, and Slezak just happens to find it."

"The dead man's wallet was in your house?"

Mac nodded.

"How?"

"I don't ..."

"What's wrong?"

Mac looked at the blank wall behind Pastor Jon. A twisted picture was forming, one he wanted to fight. But it was coming on strong. And with it, pain in his head.

"Mac, what's going on?"

"When's the last time you saw Liz?"

"I got a call from her today, as a matter—"

"Where is she?"

"She said she was going to go up north, to see family in Oregon ..."

A slow-melting anguish trickled down the inside of Mac's ribs. "It could have been her," Mac said.

"What could have been her?"

"Liz came to see me. She asked me about Slezak. She had me make coffee. Moss said Liz had a connection with him. If she had this guy Gillespie's wallet, she could have been the one who planted it."

"But why would she do that?"

"Jon, get me a lawyer. Anybody. I've got to get bailed out. If I don't find her, this whole thing could come down on me."

9:28 p.m.

Arty was looking at her. She was sure of it now. Whether he was up in space or floating through the earth, he could see her.

She would not crack. That was not going to happen. Arty wasn't really there. But he was.

Trying to keep her eyes from closing, Liz pressed on through the desert night. Highway 15. East. Just going east. She would just drive and that would be that. Eventually, she'd have to stop and look at a map or something.

Arty, staring at her from the backseat.

She screamed.

She remembered a TV show she saw once, one of those *Twilight Zones*, in black and white. There was a creepy hitchhiker in it, and the girl who was driving her car kept seeing the hitchhiker. On the side of the road. In her rearview mirror.

What was that one about, anyway?

Death, wasn't it? Death following you. Death catching up to you. Death you can't avoid.

That's what it was. Death. That's what she'd been running from her whole life. When you stopped moving, they could kill you.

They will not get me, Mama.

Sunday

10:00 a.m.

Rocky took the call at Geena's apartment, which was Geena-less at the moment. She was at Leonard's. Which was why it was no surprise when Rocky heard Geena on the other end.

"Leonard wants to talk to you," she said.

"I hope it's just about the phone," Rocky said.

"You're funny. Hold on."

A second later, Leonard's voice came on. "Arthur Towne was the owner of the phone."

Rocky's skin started tingling.

"I printed out his call history," he said. "As far as it would let me. Incoming, outgoing, missed."

"I'm coming to get it," Rocky said.

"What's the dealio?" Leonard said.

"Don't ever say *dealio* again. Just have it ready."

"Shizzle," Leonard said. Geena giggled in the background.

11:43 a.m.

The town wasn't much to look at. Liz thought all towns pretty much looked alike now. As soon as they had over a hundred thousand people, they'd add a Jack in the Box or a McDonald's. Two hundred thousand and both would be there, along with a Wendy's and a KFC.

Keep going up, and you'd have an Orchard Supply Hardware, then maybe three different gas stations and a little shopping mall.

This one was at the OSH level, and she needed gas. She needed to eat.

She chose the Jack in the Box and went inside. She ordered a bacon-and-cheese ciabatta burger, curly fries, and a large Barq's. She asked for two ranch dressings and went to a table by the window. She unwrapped her sandwich and placed it to one side, then peeled back the top of one of the dressings.

She dipped a curly fry in the ranch dressing and popped it into her mouth.

Now she started to feel good again, human. Sleeping in the back of the car like some homeless person was ridiculous. She'd never do that again. Because she deserved to be happy. Deserved it, because she'd been through enough already. She was the victim. Betrayed by her past and by Arty, who promised her things he couldn't deliver. No, wouldn't deliver. Broken promises, and that's why he died. He had only himself to blame.

She realized she had taken a huge bite of her sandwich without knowing it.

Who put that bite in her mouth? Who was trying to control her thoughts?

Who knew everything she knew?

The man across the restaurant was looking at her. He had buggy eyes and no hair.

Why was he looking at her?

He was watching. He was watching to see what she'd do, a single woman at a Jack in the Box.

Voices.

Pastor Jon talking about that guy who got gripped and couldn't control his own actions, and wasn't that just another way of saying he went insane?

She should have a gun or something for people like the bug-eyed guy who might get too curious.

Arty, I'm sorry, but you brought it on yourself.

Curly fries are good with dressing. I need more dressing.

Sleep is what I need, I'm losing it here.

The whole mess was sloshing around in her stomach. She left the rest of the meal on the table and practically ran out the doors. She saw the liquor sign and made a quick purchase but did not like the way the man at the counter looked at her. Like she was some criminal on the run.

What right did he have to look at her like that?

12:11 p.m.

"I've advised Mr. MacDonald not to talk to you," Tito Sanchez said. He was a lawyer and a personal friend of Pastor Jon's, a sturdy Latino about the same age. That he was willing to come in on a Sunday said something about their friendship.

Detective Moss's presence, too, suggested she was more than a little interested in Mac's arrest. They were in an interview room at the sheriff's substation, a few miles west of Pack Canyon.

Moss said, "Do you understand what your lawyer just said, Mr. MacDonald?"

"Yeah," Mac said. "And I waive my right to silence. I want to talk."

"All right," Moss said. "If you'll sign the waiver, you can go right ahead."

Mac grabbed the pen and the Miranda waiver and scrawled his signature on the bottom. He pushed the paper and pen back to Moss.

"The person you need to be talking to is Liz Towne," Mac said.

"I have talked to her."

"And?"

"And what?" Moss said.

"Have you questioned her as a suspect?"

"Do you have any evidence that she is a suspect in something?"

"Yeah," Mac said. "The fact that I'm sitting here and she's not."

Moss touched her chin with the clicker of her pen. "She's free to go anywhere she wants."

"Don't you find it strange?"

"Mr. MacDonald, I have to work with evidence. Right now there is evidence pointing to you. If you're trying to give me a lead, you have to do it with something I can see or hold in my hands."

"Like a confession?" Mac said.

"A confession would be nice," Moss said.

Tito Sanchez said, "We can stop this anytime you say."

"I'll keep going," Mac said. "She was in my house a couple of hours before Slezak showed up."

"Yes?"

"I didn't have any wallet till after she came in. It had to be her or Slezak. And as bad as Slezak wants to bring me down, and he wants to bad, he's had plenty of chances to plant something before this. He could have lied up and down about me. Liz must have planted the wallet, then called Slezak. And I bet it was an anonymous tip. Did Slezak tell you that's what it was?"

"An anonymous tip is not unusual," Moss said. "Especially with parolees."

"Convenient, isn't it?"

"I have to look at the evidence."

"Have you dusted the wallet for prints?" Mac said.

"Not yet."

"You won't find mine," Mac said. "You can't link the wallet to me."

"Except that it was found in your house," Moss said.

Mac's head started feeling hot. No. Not now. He closed his eyes, trying to force back the fire.

"Listen," Moss said with an understanding tone, "Can you account for your whereabouts on Thursday afternoon? Anyone who saw you, who you were with?"

Mac thought about it. "I was in the market, the Pack Canyon Market. I talked to the owner, Hank Weinhouse."

"What time was this?"

"I can't remember exactly. Around five maybe."

"Where were you after that?"

"I was driving," he said.

"Driving where?"

"Just driving. For a while. Listening to the radio. I drove by Liz's house, I remember that. She wasn't home."

"How do you know that?"

"Well, the lights weren't on."

"You didn't go in?"

Mac shook his head.

Moss grunted.

"What does that mean?" Mac said.

"Can you understand my skepticism?" Moss said.

"Can you understand mine?" Mac's temples burned. His eyes started watering.

"Maybe we should take a break, huh?" Tito Sanchez said.

"No!" Mac slammed his fist on the table. "You have to go after her."

"I can't do that," Moss said. "I have no probable cause. Your statement alone doesn't provide that. And I'm afraid if that's all you've got, we can't move forward."

Mac grabbed his head.

"Let's call it," Sanchez said. "We need to get—"

"Get me bailed out," Mac said.

Silence.

Mac looked at Sanchez. "Well?"

"This is a homicide," Moss said. "A particularly bad one. There's no guarantee bail will be granted."

"She's right," Sanchez said. "So let's concentrate on the hearing."

"This is insane!" Mac said.

A knock at the door. Moss went to the door, opened it. Mac heard somebody say something. The detective turned back to Mac and Sanchez and said, "I'll be right back."

Mac looked at his lawyer, who shrugged. "What's that all about?"

Sanchez said, "We're being taped. Now is the time, if there ever was a time, for you to really and truly not say anything."

"I thought it was going all right," Mac said. "I think I'm getting through to her."

"My friend, it is never good to talk to cops. All they want to do is hang you, and they will make the rope from your words."

Mac said, "I know all that, but I'm not playing a game."

"They're not playing, either."

"I've got to tell the truth, that's it. And not just because I'm innocent, which I am. I don't even know if you believe me, but I am. No, because I made a covenant with God to play it straight, and I'm just gonna trust him on that."

"God made lawyers, too, my friend."

"Are you so sure about that?"

For a brief moment, they smiled.

Then Moss came back through the door of the interview room. She said nothing at first. She slowly sat down. She looked at Mac, then Sanchez, then Mac again.

Finally she said, "I want you to listen very carefully. I am not going to seek a filing yet."

"You're going to cut me loose?" Mac said.

"No, not loose. You are, as the department likes to tell the public, a person of interest. You are not out of the woods."

"What about my violation?"

"I am not reporting a violation. You're going back on the street, and you and your PO can work out your differences together. But I am not satisfied that my questions have been answered, so I'm advising you to stay available and keep in good graces with Mr. Slezak."

"He's not going to be happy about this," Mac said.

"That's not my concern," Moss said. "He brings violations to me, and I assess the evidence. Some new evidence has come to light. I want to follow it up before I make a decision about you."

"What new evidence?"

"I can't tell you," Moss said. "But I think you're going to find out."

Mac had no idea what she meant by that. But he did have a strange feeling that the detective was cutting him a break. Not one she normally would have. Because he'd been straight with her.

"Okay," Mac said to his lawyer. "Let's go."

Tito Sanchez looked utterly relieved. He picked up his briefcase and hurried toward the door.

Mac paused and said to Moss, "Thank you."

"Good luck," she said.

Outside the station door, Sanchez asked Mac where he'd like to be dropped off. Mac was about to tell him when he saw Rocky leaning on the hood of her car, arms folded.

"I don't think I'll need a ride after all," Mac said to the lawyer.

Sanchez shook his hand and headed for his car. Mac headed for Rocky.

"Need a lift?" she said.

"You got me out?"

She smiled.

"How?" Mac said.

"Liz lied to the detective about Arty's phone. I found it in the canyon."

"You were there?"

"I did a little sniffing around," Rocky said.

"How did you know it was Arty's?"

"I had someone examine it."

"Who?"

"You don't know him. He's a colonics and computer expert."

"Huh?"

"Haven't you heard? It's the latest thing. A real specialty. Anyway, he got the data. I called you but didn't get an answer, so I called your pastor. Imagine my surprise when he told me where you were. So I came down and gave the stuff to the detective. And now, here you are. My question is how you got here."

"Slezak. My PO. He found the wallet of a dead man in my house. The guy who helped Liz the day Arty died, a guy named Gillespie. He's apparently been murdered and his wallet showed up in my place right after Liz visited. Slezak found it."

"Liz put it there," Rocky said.

"Maybe. It could be Slezak put it there, but I wonder about that. He could have trumped something up before if he wanted to. But it's that Gillespie connection that points to Liz. Slezak wouldn't have any motive to kill him. But Liz might. Now what was it?"

"We have to figure that out," Rocky said.

James Scott Bell

"We?"

"That's right," Rocky said. "You and me. Two heads and all that. Like the song says, 'Two heads are better than one.'"

"I, uh, don't know that song."

"Well you're going to. Because we probably don't have that much time. Now listen, you know about that other body they found in Pack Canyon?"

"Right. A biker or something."

"What if there's a connection?"

"Between Arty and the biker?"

"Or between Liz and the biker."

"But the body was already there."

"Maybe there was something the biker had that Liz and Arty found."

Mac rubbed his chin. "And then what? Arty died over it?"

"Who knows?" Rocky said.

"That's a pretty wild theory."

"My job isn't to judge how wild a theory is. I've seen some pretty crazy scams tried against insurance companies."

"Liz said she's heading up north to see family. In Oregon."

"I didn't know she had family in Oregon," Rocky said.

"I don't think she does," Mac said. "It's another lie. She could be heading anywhere."

"Then we have to figure out where anywhere might be."

"You have any ideas?"

"Oh yeah," Rocky said. "Hop in."

1:15 p.m.

The pawnbroker was a heavyset man with thinning black hair. He sat behind an old-fashioned cage. Plexiglas has apparently not made its debut in this town, Liz thought. So behind the times.

She felt right at home in the shop. It had the feel of what she'd grown up with, charged with crosscurrents of legality and illegality. Not like in California, where the pawn industry was regulated heavily.

268

Here, business was a little looser. A little more Wild West.

Just what she needed.

The fat man was sitting on a stool, eating a sandwich. He had glasses perched on top of his forehead.

No one else was in this store. Shelves and wall mounts held everything from musical instruments to laptop computers to coats and VCRs. Televisions, cameras, and living room furniture. A glass case held watches, rings, and other jewelry.

"How we doing today?" the man said.

"Nice little shop you got here," Liz said

"I call it home. I live up above, which makes me very much a down-home business. That's why people come to me. Do a good exchange, but I don't recall seeing you in here before."

Liz went to the cage and fingered one of the bars, as if she were in jail.

"I'm just passing through," Liz said. "And I mean passing through. I will never come back to this town again, on purpose at least."

"Tourist? We don't get many of those."

"Not a tourist," Liz said. "I'm making a straight line back home."

"Where's home?"

"Florida," Liz said.

"Ah. God's waiting room." And the man laughed. His stomach jiggled under his wrinkled white shirt. A spot of mustard sat on the precipice of his ample belly. It bounced like a little yellow ball.

He put his sandwich down on a napkin on the counter and stood, not without effort. The stool under him squeaked with relief when his girth was fully removed. He brushed his hands, put his glasses down on his nose and said, "Now, what can I do for you?"

"I'd like to exchange something."

"Well, that's what I do. Let's see the merchandise and I'll value it for you."

"May I count on your discretion?" Liz used the code that pawn-brokers have heard in various languages and settings for nearly three thousand years. Mama had told her all about the history, about it going back to ancient China. Not as old as prostitution, Mama used to say, but it makes a good run for second place.

Liz watched the fat man's eyes.

"You not only can count on it," the fat man said, "you can wrap it up for Christmas and stick it under the tree."

"Because I would hate to have anything hinder what could be a very beneficial relationship between us."

"I am reading you. And now I'm asking you, are you a cop? Or maybe a federal?"

Liz shook her head.

"Because," the fat man said, "you don't survive in this business if you take a dim view of the law. I have been audited and investigated and looked upon, and I could name this place Smells Like a Rose. And I just don't want to take any chances."

"You really don't think I'm the law, do you?"

His eyes lingered on her for a moment. Then he cracked a smile, "No, I guess I don't. But that leaves you as someone who has been doing things you probably ought not to have done."

"Do you want to see what I've got or not? Do you want to do business or eat a sandwich?"

"You can always show, and then you can do."

"Then take a look at this." She handed him the diamond. One of the smaller ones from the sack. He took it in his sausage-like hands and raised his eyebrows. He rolled it around, feeling it. He lingered over it. He squinted, adjusted the lens, and looked at it some more. Then he put the diamond down on the counter and removed the eyepiece.

"I know I should not ask where you came by this stone," he said. "But sound business practice compels me to ask at least one question. Is this a hot rock? It will help me to put a proper value on it."

"We both know it's hot."

"I am prepared to offer you four hundred for this."

"And we both know that's a rip-off."

He smiled. "You know the business?"

"I do."

"Do you know the expression *Take it or leave it*?"

"Do you know the expression *Untraceable handgun*?"

He smiled. "Where were you forty years ago when I got married?"

"Yes or no?"

"You may hold the merchandise," he said and handed her the diamond. He came out from behind his cage and went to the front door. He flipped the sign around so "Closed" was showing outside. Then he bolted the door and went back to his spot behind the bars.

"If you'll wait here," he said, "I think I may have something that will meet your need."

He went through a curtained door behind him.

Liz waited, chewing her bottom lip.

Do you really want to do this?

Yes.

Stop now.

"Shut up," she said aloud.

The fat pawnbroker reappeared, holding a handgun in his open left palm.

"This here is a .45 caliber, Spanish made," he said. "On the streets of Detroit or LA, they'd call it a pocket rocket. Serial number's obliterated. You think you can handle that?"

He handed her the pistol through the cage.

It felt heavy, but good heavy, in her hand.

"Yes," she said. "I think I can handle that."

"Got a kick to it."

"I've handled guns before."

"Then you're going to need something to go inside it. It doesn't do much good without ammo."

"You have any?"

"I might."

She waited for him to move. He didn't. He raised his eyebrows instead. "You have more where this came from," he said, tapping the diamond.

"And?"

"One more will do. After that, I ask no questions and tell no lies. Except to the authorities."

She had no time to haggle. "Done," she said. She had one more little diamond in her pocket, a ring. She took it out and passed it to him.

He waddled back through the curtain.

Liz looked at the gun. Semiauto. She had handled guns in the shop. All sorts of them.

He came back with a red-and-black box. He passed it to her. As he did, he reached under the counter and came up with a shotgun.

"My security system," he said. "Just in case."

"It's almost like you don't trust me," Liz said.

"You could be my own daughter, if I had a daughter. And so I don't trust you at all. But I will say it's been a real pleasure doing business with you. My name's Casper, in case you ever have something you'd like to move along."

"There is one more thing you can do," Liz said.

"Name it."

"I need a little referral," Liz said.

1:24 p.m.

Mac's hands had the jail shakes. What you get when you've been in, just got out, and are doing something that might get you back in again.

He and Rocky were at the back of Arty's house, the locked back door. Though the terrain made them virtually invisible to prying eyes, Mac couldn't control the popping nerves.

Rocky had her bag with her, the one she said carried her implements of the trade. Which, he knew, were for advanced professional snooping.

"You're figuring you can break in?" Mac said.

"Not break. I've picked harder locks than this."

"What I mean is that we don't have a right to enter."

"And who is going to protest? Liz?"

"It's still breaking and entering."

"I'm Arty's sister."

"Arty's dead. The house belongs to Liz. I don't like the risk."

"Can I remind you that you're the prime suspect in a murder?"

"Work fast."

Rocky took a pick out of her bag. Mac was not entirely unfamiliar with the task. In prison he'd had a cell mate for a couple of months who was a safe cracker. His father had been a legendary lock picker in the forties, and Junior was trying to keep the family business going. He did pretty well until he ran into a sophisticated alarm system that sent him packing at state expense.

Junior gave Mac a short course in all things pick—wardeds, tumblers, mortises. Mac had never put any of it to use, but watching Rocky, he had no doubt she'd learned well. The door was open in about thirty seconds.

Mac followed her in.

She reached into her bag and came out with a box of rubber gloves. "Put these on."

"You think of everything."

"Compliments later. Now let's think about this. The only thing I know about Liz is that she was from the south, Alabama or Mississippi."

"Mississippi," Mac said.

"When I first met Liz, her last name was Summerville. I don't know if that was fake or not, but look around for papers that might have that name on it. I'm going to see if I can crack the computer."

"Right, chief," Mac said. "Can I call you chief?"

"Start looking." She headed toward the small study where Arty had his computer.

Mac put the rubber gloves on and made for the bedroom.

It looked like a room rushed out of. Clothes were tossed on the bed. The chest of drawers had various items, including a small teddy bear, scattered on top. The closet doors were open.

He pulled out the top drawer of the bureau, revealing underwear of various colors. He gave a quick look for something else in the drawer. Found nothing.

This went for the rest of the drawers, which had brassieres, a couple of sweaters, nylons, nighties, and a few other items. No papers. No smoking gun.

He went to the closet. Arty's clothes on the right side, Liz's on the left. Shoes down below. On the shelf, more clothes and some baseball hats. Two LA Dodgers caps, a Cardinals cap, and two or three others without any logo.

An open shoebox on the shelf held shoe polish and a buffing rag. That was not going to do them much good.

Mac started to feel the static of desperation. This was needle-in-the-haystack time. He began to repeat *Please, please, please* in his head.

Please for everything. For now, for tomorrow, for Aurora and justice, and to stop Liz wherever she is. Stop her from doing something crazy, and bring her to her knees.

Please, please, please.

2:15 p.m.

The cycle shop Casper told her about was at the far end of town. Liz lingered over a line of Yamahas just outside the store's plate-glass window. Waiting. *Let them come to me.* That's how you played these things.

The way she learned to play back in Jackson. Liz had done the outlaw thing, when she was running with some of the bands in the underground music scene.

Temptation Beaters, London Radio, Square Root of Yes.

Then with the guys at the motorcycle shop.

If you wanted to know how to get something on the down-low, Sonny's Cycles was the place to go.

By that time, Liz had learned that the way to get something from a guy, any guy, was to give him a little something in return. Which she did, always in control.

All that served her well. She held the lure, the baited hook that would get her what she wanted from the males of the species.

The first one out of the shop was a kid with a shaved head. Looked like a student in a high-school play about street cred. His skinny, tattooed arms hung out of his T-shirt sleeves like rope.

He said, "You in the market for a fine bike?"

"I might be," she said. "But I came to see Chris. He around?"

The kid looked through the window. "Yeah. He's with somebody. I'll tell him you're out here."

"Thank you." She smiled at him.

A few minutes later, a bandana with a head under it walked out. He was big and bearded. The bandana was a Confederate flag, which didn't exactly go with his black Raider Nation T.

"Help ya?"

"Maybe," Liz said.

"Now there's an answer," Bandana Man said. He had a deep voice and seemed to like the sound of it. "Did you know there are 4,628 known species of mammals in the world?"

"Excuse me?"

"There was 4,629, but one of 'em went extinct. The extinct one is the uncurious male."

"Which makes you a little bit curious," she said.

"More than a little. When a nice lady I've never seen before shows up, asks for me personally, I can't help wondering how I can help her?"

"That's just wonderful," she said. "Are you Chris?"

"If I wasn't, I'd sure want to be."

"Very smooth," she said.

"How'd you happen to select yours truly?"

"Casper gave me your name."

Chris smiled. "Well, I guess I owe Casper big time. What would you say if—"

"He told me you were the one to talk to if we wanted to keep something off the books."

He lost his easy smile for half a second. He slapped it right back on. "That all depends."

"Now there's an answer," Liz said.

"You're not from around here."

"If you're not the one to talk to, why don't you tell me who that might be?"

He spread his arms. "Now, did I say anything about not being someone you could talk to? But until a man hears what the terms are, he can't make the call."

"Why don't we talk about that?"

Chris gave a quick look inside the store. "I have to make it look like I'm showing you something. Or the boss man, he might think I'm slackin' off."

"I want a great, big bike," Liz said. "One with big old pipes."

He put his hand on the seat of a yellow Yamaha and said, "This is a nice little bike. Good for your size. And what's this little something you need?"

"How do I know I can trust you?" Liz said.

"What is it? You want somebody iced?" He chuckled.

Liz pressed her top teeth on her lower lip.

Chris's eyes widened. "Wow."

"Relax," Liz said with a smile. "I don't want anybody dusted."

"You were messing with me?"

"How'd I do?"

He snorted a laugh. "You did good, little sister. But just to let you know, I know people who know other people."

"Then maybe you really can help me." She looked him up and down. "Where can we talk? Private."

He looked at his watch. "An hour. In the middle of town, there's a place called The Hammer. Everybody knows it. They know me. We can get a booth."

"I look forward to it."

"You and me both, little sister."

2:18 p.m.

Mac thought, She is something, this Rocky Towne. A tech-savvy angel from heaven.

In her car, heading back to his house, he said, "Did you need more time with the computer?"

She shook her head. "I copied a ton of files onto a flash drive. Now I just have to look at it, figure out how to get into anything that might tell us where Liz's mother is."

"What are you going to do?"

"I'll take it to Geena's. She has that boyfriend."

"What boyfriend?"

"The colonics expert."

"I still don't know what you're talking about, but it sounds painful."

"Trust me," Rocky said.

He did. He liked it that he did.

"It's a long shot, I know," Rocky said, as she pulled into the drive next to the church. "So you do the praying and I'll do the prying."

He didn't want the car to stop but knew it had to. If only he wasn't toxic, he could allow himself to love this woman. But he was, and he couldn't, and he got out of the car quickly before he made a fool out of himself.

"One more thing," she said. "Remember you wanted me to look at your PO?"

"Yeah."

"I found something." She handed him a sealed manila envelope through the car window. "I'll call you later."

She drove off, the car kicking up the gravel.

Mac went inside and sat in his old wingback. It felt like freedom. A few hours ago he'd been in jail. Now he was here, thanks to Rocky Towne. He was here and he was free, yet he was not, because a murder charge was hanging over him, ready to drop. Until he was free of that—

He opened the envelope.

Inside was a print out of a webpage, a story from the *Orange County Register*.

An obituary.

A soldier who died in combat in Afghanistan. Four years ago. Twenty-two years old. Left a wife and two-year-old son.

Thomas "Tommy" Slezak.

Marine.

3:14 p.m.

Chris had a big grin on his face when he met Liz in the lounge. She was waiting for him in a booth of red vinyl and Formica.

"Cozy little spot you have here," she said, and not in a friendly way.

"You like it?" he said.

"What's not to like?"

"I can hear it in your voice." He winked and slid into the booth. A little too close. She slid away.

"You have that out-of-town way about you," he said. "Where you from? The big city?"

"Does it matter?" she said.

"Just making friendly conversation before we talk business."

"Let's talk business."

"Don't you want to have a drink first?"

"No."

"Mind if I?"

"Fine, but make it fast."

He slid out of the booth and ambled off toward the bar, calling out hello to some guys sitting on stools. They laughed and clapped each other on the back. The smell of stale beer and body odor filled the place.

Then it happened again. The feeling she was being watched. She looked around the bar. A few heads were turned in her direction. Somebody put on music. It was disco. Disco! The place was in a 1970's freeze.

And *she* was in a freeze. Frozen in the moment like an insect in amber.

Like she'd been placed right here in this spot by some giant set of hands. Trapped.

Trapped because there is no way back. Not ever. *Arty, why'd you make me? No, don't think that way. You had to do it. You're given cards, the game is rigged by fate. Why fight it? Just keep moving and outsmart it. Like you're going to outsmart this punk.*

When Chris got back with a pitcher of beer and two glasses, he said, "Hope you don't mind."

"You going to drink all that yourself?" Liz said.

"Thought maybe I could get you to join me after all." He started pouring the suds into one of the glasses. His hands were still dirty from his day at work.

"I said nothing for me." Liz turned the other glass over on the table.

"Now that's just not in the spirit of things," Chris said.

"You want to do business or don't you?"

He poured himself some beer and took a long sip, looking at her the whole time. Some of the foam stuck to his mustache. He wiped it with the back of his hand. Then he said, "What if I want this to be the start of a friendship?"

"All right, Chris, I'll tell you what. You show me what you can do, and then we'll talk."

"Why don't we do the friendly things first? Get to know each other?"

Liz put her elbows on the table and her palms together. "Listen, Slick, I'm only going to say this once. You want some action, you earn it. Let's see what you're made of first."

A smile sneaked through Chris's facial hair. "Okay, little sister, you got my attention. And just to let you know, I like to collect."

"Save that for the local Susies, will you? Here's what I want, and you get it for me or you can drown in your beer. I want a car. I want a car that's untraceable. Fake plates. I will pay you for it. I want it delivered in a place where we won't be seen, and I want the plates taken off my car and then I want my car torched. Now, do you think you can handle that?"

He didn't answer for a long moment.

"I can do that," he said. "Only thing is, I'd like to know why."

"You don't have to know why. You only have to know that you'll be paid."

"How much?"

"A lot."

"How much is a lot?"

"How much do you want?"

He looked at her over his glass of beer. Now he was thinking. Now he was getting to be dangerous. "I'd say for a thing like this, ten thousand wouldn't be asking too much."

"Okay," she said. "That's what you'll get."

"You really have that?" he said.

"Can you deliver?"

"Oh yeah, I can—"

"In four hours?"

"Four?"

"That's the deal. If you can't deliver, deal's off."

"When do I get paid?"

"On delivery."

He thought about it. "I want some up front."

"No," she said. "On delivery."

"What if I go to all this trouble and you don't pay off? What if you decide to take the car and shoot me or something?"

She smiled, sighed. "Chris, do I look like a killer to you?"

7:18 p.m.

Rocky, at the computer, rubbed her eyes.

She did not pause to linger over all the docs and e-mails. Leonard had been helpful recovering some of the deleted files and putting them in a readable format. Now she was alone, looking for something, anything, about Liz's mysterious past.

Liz, who had seemed to want to prevent anyone from looking into it. The secret Liz.

Who are you, really?

I'm going to find out.

7:37 p.m.

Liz parked her car on the little patch of brown grass Chris had described to her. The place he chose for them was three miles outside the town limits in a grove of birch trees.

The moon was bright and full. It was a night you could see things. Good. That would make the transaction a whole lot easier.

She got out and heard, faintly, the sound of a river.

She liked rivers. They washed things clean. If only life was a river. If only she could be clean.

No, don't think that, don't think that. They'll get you if you think that.

Don't hope to be clean, you can't be clean, you don't want to be clean.

She heard the sound of a car coming, then the headlights.

She waited.

The lights cut. Liz saw a silhouetted figure emerge from the driver's side. And another, from the passenger side.

"I said to come alone," Liz said.

"Gary's a buddy of mine," Chris said. "We've known each other since we were kids."

"Why is he here?"

"Just to make sure nothing goes wrong."

"What could go wrong?" Liz said.

"Maybe you try to get away with something, maybe you try to gyp me. I don't know. I just know that you can't always trust the ladies."

His companion smiled and nodded.

Liz said, "That thing run?"

"Clean and neat," Chris said. "Rebuilt engine, too. Fake plate, so you don't get stopped crossing the state line. Maybe we can sell yours for a few hundred."

"Mine?"

"You won't be using it anymore."

"No," Liz said, "I want it destroyed."

"I don't see where that gets anybody. We can at least strip it for parts."

Liz shook her head. "No deal."

Chris looked at Gary. Gary shrugged. Chris looked at Liz. "You're the boss. Now, what about the payment?"

Liz said, "Ask your friend to go wait by the car."

Chris stuck out his lower lip. "That's not very nice."

"I'm not very nice," Liz said. "You can have your pay, but I deal only with you."

"She's tough," Gary said.

"I like that," Chris said. "I really, really do. Tough is good."

For a moment, nobody moved. Then Chris nodded and Gary turned and walked back to the car.

"That better?" Chris said.

"Give me the key," Liz said.

"Now tough is one thing, but dishonest is another. Let's do a fair exchange. Same time. Just like a kidnapping."

"Throw the key on the ground," Liz said.

Chris laughed. "You have this all figured out, don't you?"

"Key."

He reached in his pocket and tossed a key near her feet. "Now you," he said.

Liz reached in her pocket and pulled out a diamond ring. A particularly impressive one. She held it out. Chris frowned, put his hand out. Liz dropped the ring in his hand.

He looked at it. Then said, "What's this?"

"A diamond," she said.

"I don't want no diamond."

"It's worth over ten thousand dollars."

"So you say. It doesn't even look real."

"It's real."

"What is it, some family ring?"

"Yes. It was my mother's engagement ring."

"Was it now? And you're willing to part with it?"

"Go get it appraised."

"Yeah, and you'll be long gone."

"Trust me," Liz said.

"That's gonna get me in a lot of trouble, I think. You know what else I think? I think you're trying to con me."

"I don't care what you think." Liz bent down to pick up the key. But Chris stepped on it with a black boot.

"Hold on there," he said.

Liz straightened up. "What are you doing?"

"I want to know where this came from," Chris said. "I don't believe any engagement ring story. I'm thinking maybe there's more of these."

"Come on, you've got your payment. Let's get on with it. I want you to torch my car and—"

Chris backhanded Liz across the face. His knuckles felt like marbles on her flesh. She almost went down.

"That's enough," Chris said. "You're going to do what I want from now on."

Then he waved at his friend to come join him.

Gary bounded from the car like a golden retriever about to go for a walk.

Liz allowed herself a little sob, to set things up.

"You think you ever had me punked?" Chris said.

Gary was almost to them. Liz put her left hand on her cheek and said, "Please …" She reached behind her with the right, turning slightly so Chris would miss it.

"Don't be so worried," Chris said. "We know how to treat the ladies." To Gary he said, "Don't we know how to treat the ladies?"

Gary said, "I don't know about you, tubby, but I got it goin' on."

Chris said, "Yeah, right. Watch and learn."

They both looked at Liz. She brought the gun around and pointed it at Chris's face and fired.

As Chris fell to the ground, Gary yelped like a dog. One quick, high-pitched *yap*, and then turned and ran.

Liz got him in the back. He went down.

He was crawling and crying when Liz finished him with one to the back of the head.

More fire needed now. Burn them up. Fire, always fire.

Flames erupted. In the trees. All of them, all on fire, flames licking the sky.

The fire had voice, telling her to put the gun in her mouth. It was the only way, the only way.

"No!"

Liz's scream died in the sound of the river.

The flames disappeared with it, leaving her in silence.

Monday

9:30 a.m.

Sheriff's Homicide Detective Kathy Moss stood at the front of the room. The gathered men and women of the sheriff's department listened attentively as she held up the picture.

"This is Elizabeth Towne," she said. "You know that her husband was killed in Pack Canyon. Supposedly an accident. But it wasn't an accident. He was pushed. Pushed by his widow, who is waiting to collect a nice life insurance claim. But there's more to it than that."

A young deputy in the front row raised his hand. "Is there sex and violence involved?"

The others in the room laughed.

"Oh, she used sex all right," Moss said. "She used it on a man named Theodore Gillespie. She had him wrapped up like an early Christmas present, to the point where he would do anything for her. And one of the things he did for her was help cover up the killing of another guy, a well-known heist man. A man who liked to call himself Bill."

"Not too original," said the young deputy.

"Which is exactly why it works, Einstein," Moss said. "Our little lady Liz Towne used a knife on this one."

"Sweet," the young deputy said.

"It gets sweeter," Moss said. "She got this Theodore Gillespie to help her take the body to a little park out there in Malibu Canyon, and then she used the knife again. On Gillespie. After she killed him, she doused him and his car with gas and set the whole thing on fire. Oh yes, she is a sweet one, she is."

Silence in the room.

Moss gestured toward a square-jawed man leaning against the wall. "This is Special Agent Victor Voltaire, FBI. He's going to take it from here."

The heads turned to Agent Voltaire. "It's not that hard," he said. "She has crossed state lines. She is a fugitive. But we know the make and model of her car, and the license plate—"

No!

"—and we know the direction she's heading. We have ordered checkpoints—"

"No!" Liz screamed. She gripped the gun. She would shoot them before they stopped her. Her head felt fuzzy. The gun felt smooth.

She looked at it, and the gun turned into a bottle, a nearly empty bottle, and she realized it was night and she was in the backseat of her car. Her head felt like two halves of a tomato.

Between the two halves was this crazy dream.

She was sweaty and hung over. Asleep in her car. Where? She couldn't remember.

But the dream had reminded her she had better keep moving.

Thank you, dream. Thank you for that much. Maybe there was fate, and it was on her side. That's what it was. The whole thing is fate, and you fight it, and if you do it respects you and gives you a break.

I'm close now. Close. Yes. Keep moving. Yes.

She started the car. Where was she? Off the highway, yes, on a dirt road. It's a wonder what you find when you're desperate and drunk.

She drove randomly. Then remembered, back the other way. Back to the road. Find a bathroom, coffee, a breakfast burrito.

Now that you've done it again, two more times, does it scare you?

Scared of what?

Divine retribution.

No, I am not scared of that.

Are you scared that you will never be able to stop thinking about these things?

No, I am not scared of that.

Are you scared they will find you out because you get careless?

No, no, no! I am not scared of anything now. Stop it, stop it, I don't want to hear.

The car she bought with the lives of two men was a junker. It smelled like grease and old clothes. It smelled like death. Death in a small town.

Are you scared you'll end up like them back there?

No, I am not scared of that and stop it, shut up, stop it.

They are making the connection back there, aren't they?

No.

They are linking up all the evidence. They are finding blood in your house, and the blood will tell them you are the one.

Are you scared?

Yes, but I won't let it stop me. I won't let them take me. They've been trying to take me all my life. I won't let them take me.

10:16 a.m.

Mac waited for Rocky out back. By the crocuses. Or crocuses-to-be. If they came up at all, maybe it would be a sign of some kind.

But he couldn't wait for them. He needed something now, and Rocky said she had it.

He heard a car on the gravel of the church lot. A few moments later, she was there. And she was beautiful.

He made coffee and they sat at the kitchen table. Rocky had a shoulder bag with her, took out some papers and spread them on the table. "Are you ready?" she said.

"What've you got?"

"An address for a Rose Summerville. Last known. It's about ten years old."

"Liz's mother?"

"I'm guessing. I looked up the address on Google Earth and got a trailer park. I tried to find a phone number, got nothing. I could make some calls, but I think going local would be better."

"Actually going there?"

"It's faster," Rocky said. "You can get more accomplished with face time. All it takes is money."

"I can scrape up a little."

"You don't have to go. This might lead to nothing."

"You kidding? I'm there."

"What about your parole?"

Mac nodded. "Then it *better* lead to something."

Mac heard the sound of a car outside. Near the church. Could be anybody, but that vibe kicked in, that something-was-wrong vibe. He got up quickly, went to the front window and looked out.

And saw Gordon Slezak getting lazily out of his car.

"He's here," Mac said, in a voice almost outside himself. "Slezak."

Rocky was next to him in a moment. "He's got nothing."

"Doesn't matter," Mac said. "I don't want you involved."

"But I am. Can you stall him?"

"Stall him?"

"Just for a minute."

Steps came up to the front door. Then a knock.

Mac looked behind him, saw Rocky throwing the papers in her shoulder bag, then fishing for something.

Another knock. "Hey, Daniel," Slezak said. "Let's have a talk."

Mac looked at the door. Back at Rocky. Now she was heading to his bedroom. She nodded at him before disappearing.

Mac opened the door.

"It's really disappointing," Slezak said. His face was flushed as he breezed past Mac.

Mac closed the door.

"Yes, very disappointing to have the sheriff's office be so lax," Slezak said. "So put your hands behind your back."

"Gordon . . ."

"Don't call me Gordon. Ever. Do you understand?"

"I know about your son," Mac said.

Slezak's eyes stilled for a moment. Lights out. Then quickly flashed with rage. "You are not worth the dirt under his fingernails. You know nothing, are nothing."

"I was a Marine, too."

With one step, Slezak was to him. And drove his fist into Mac's midsection.

Mac doubled over.

"I'll kill you," Slezak said. "I will make sure you go back inside, and I'll make sure it's done there. You don't deserve to be alive. You should be the dead one. Now you get on the floor facedown."

Mac, hands on his stomach, stood and faced him. He would not let Slezak hit him again.

Slezak looked over Mac's shoulder. Mac turned. Rocky was in the doorway.

"Who are you?" Slezak said.

Rocky said, "You've just committed a criminal act, Sir."

Mac watched as Slezak fought for control. He could almost see the demons poking his face from inside.

"Nice try," Slezak said, his voice coldly efficient now. He looked like he wanted to pull his gun and shoot them both and be done with it. He did have a rim of sweat on his forehead. His face was slightly flushed as he turned and left the way he had come in.

Mac waited until the car drove out of the lot before turning back to Rocky.

"Now you're on his bad list," Mac said.

"He can't do anything to me," she said. "Or you either."

"He can do plenty."

"You could have used more makeup," she said.

He looked at her and thought she had a slight smile on her face. "What are you talking about?"

She went to the table in the corner of the living room, the one by the TV. And there she picked up something Mac hadn't noticed before. A pair of sunglasses.

"Also, be aware," she said, "that the camera adds ten pounds."

"Camera?"

"Let's get this to your lawyer," Rocky said. "You may be able to buy a little time after all."

1:35 p.m.

One more leg, Liz thought.

"One more leg," she said aloud.

The car was moving. It would make it. It would make it to Jackson. *Make it, car.*

She saw Mama then, as clear as anything. She was in the distance, on the road, waving at her. *Come home, daughter.*

Big surprise, Mama. You'll get a big surprise when you see your daughter and see what she has.

You'll be happy, and that'll make up for all the bad things they did to you.

I'll go see Old Dane and set it up, I'll set it up for me forever, and then you'll see, then you'll—

Liz screamed.

It was not her mother. It was Arty.

She jammed the brakes.

Behind her, the sound of tires, an angry horn, a shouted curse.

She fought for breath and closed her eyes. When she opened them again, Arty wasn't there.

2:55 p.m.

In Tito Sanchez's office on Burbank, Rocky played the sunglasses video on her computer. Mac thought it unfolded exactly like all those hidden-camera-reveals-undercover-reporters used in sting operations. It not only made Slezak look guilty, but also it made it look like he was born to play the part.

Some of his expressions, on pause, even made him look crazy.

Maybe he was.

Sanchez sat back and said, "Wow."

"What can you do with it?" Mac said.

"I'm not sure," Sanchez said. "Get it to the Department of Corrections."

"ASAP?"

"I'll make some calls."

"I need it to be immediate," Mac said.

"Why?"

"I've got to leave town for a few days."

The lawyer shook his head. "You can't do that."

"I know. But I'm doing it."

"But—"

"You can stall Moss if she has any questions."

"I can't lie to her."

"Did I say lie? And you can stop Slezak. Get a temporary restraining order or something, right?"

"Well, I can try—"

Mac shook his hand. "I got faith in you."

"You hardly know me."

"You're a friend of Jon's. That's good enough for me."

Sanchez ran his hand through his hair. "I hope it's good enough for the both of us," he said. "I still advise you not to skip out."

"Noted," Mac said. "See you in a few days."

Tuesday

4:38 p.m.

Los Angeles to Houston.

Houston to Jackson.

Two hours sleep.

Mac was amazed he could remember his own name.

Rocky Towne, on the other hand, looked like she did this every day. Amazing indeed.

But was this the worst idea in the world?

No. It got him out of LA for a while. It gave him the feeling that he was doing something.

And he liked being with her. He liked the fact that she had gotten the goods on Slezak. He liked the fact that she was not pretentious or sold on herself.

She rented a car at Jackson – Evers International Airport. Drove out into a thundering rainstorm.

"Southern living," Mac said as Rocky drove.

"We only have earthquakes," she said.

"Where to now?"

"To find Rosie Summerville Jones," Rocky said.

"I was hoping you'd say find some chicken-fried steak."

She looked at him.

"Kidding," he said. "Drive on."

5:15 p.m.

Driving, blinking, fighting off sleep. Fifteen hours on the road this last stretch. Just two stops. Not bad.

Almost home, Mama. You'll see, and you'll know.

5:20 p.m.

The rain was pounding when they hit the trailer park.

Rocky was glad Mac was with her. His steadiness was comforting, even in the face of their long odds.

All they had was a trailer number. No phone. No other means of contact.

Finding it in the dark and the rain wasn't easy. Some of the long boxes had less-than-complete numbers. Other trailers didn't have numbers at all.

And there were bikes and balls and cars strewn in random fashion all over the grounds.

But cool estimation brought them to space number 17, which happened to be one of the more pristine. At least she could clearly see the red numbers in front.

"Of course we didn't bring umbrellas," Rocky said, pulling to a stop.

"We're from LA," Mac said.

Rocky got out. There was a small awning over the trailer's door. It took three long, sloshy steps to get there. She knocked on the door. Mac joined her for the second knock.

The large woman who opened it issued a loud curse against someone named Cody, as if expecting him to be standing there.

Then she cursed at Rocky and Mac. The curses had a sing-song, deep southern accent to them. Rocky thought of that cartoon rooster, Foghorn Leghorn.

Rocky held up the case with her investigator's license in the display. She flipped it open and showed it to the woman. "We're looking for Rosie Summerville Jones," she said.

The woman, who might have been thirty, wore a large yellow T-shirt with an oak tree on the front, green sweatpants, and red slippers. The oak tree was stretched at the roots by her girth.

The woman said, "Whuz the name again?"

"Rosie, or Rose, Summerville Jones."

"Don't know nobody by that name."

"She used to live here."

"She ain't livin' here now."

"Any idea where she moved?"

"I said I don't know her."

"How long have you lived here?"

"I don't see as I got to answer that."

"Now look—" She felt Mac's hand on her arm.

He said to the woman, "You don't have to answer that, but we've come a long way and it's important for us to find her. That's all. It's about her daughter. She may be in trouble. Is there a manager on the grounds?"

"Ain't no manager."

"Who's your landlord?"

"The county," she said. "They own the place. Try gettin' anythin' from 'em 'cept trouble."

Mac said, "Is there anyone you know who's been here a long time?"

"You might could try across the way, in thirty. Miss Boaz. Only don't say I sez so."

"Thank you," Mac said. "You've been very helpful."

The woman closed the door.

5:25 p.m.

The old house was just like Liz remembered it. Overgrown grass and a kudzu wall all the way around. Made the place seem like a green fortress. The old wood frame itself looked like it could be blown over.

But still, there it was, with a light burning in the front window.

Liz knocked. The rain had soaked her during the little run up to the door. She wondered if Old Dane would even recognize her.

If he even let her in. She saw his wizened face look out the window at her. She must have looked like a drenched rat.

"Whatta ya want?" His voice strained through the dirty window.

Liz indicated that he should look at her face.

He squinted. Then smiled. His teeth were as brown as ever.

When he opened the door, the smell of pipe tobacco burst out like a padded fist, followed by his high-pitched voice. "Lizzie!"

He practically pulled her in.

Old Dane Lowery was not really that old, maybe sixty. But ever since Liz could remember, that had been his nickname. His hair was the color of hickory nuts and he had wild, furry eyebrows over blazing blue eyes. He was thin and sinewy, like her own mountain forebearers. But there was no hint of hillbilly about him. Liz knew he had killed two men, both criminals, who had tried to cheat him.

The bodies were never found.

She was like him, she knew, in more ways than shared heritage.

He was also the best fence in the South. No one knew better how to move hot property.

He sat her by the fireplace and got her a towel.

"Now, little girl," Old Dane said, "what's got you to my door on a night like this?"

"You know," she said. "I need your services."

"Last I heard, you were gone to make your fortune in LaLa Land. You thinking of settin' up here again? 'Cause I could—"

"No! I'm getting out. As soon as I can. Soon as you fence what I've got. I want to go away. I want to go somewhere. Out of here. Mexico. A place where I can live like I want. A place where they won't get me. I want to—"

"Easy, girl, easy. Let me get you something warm to drink."

"Whiskey," she said.

"Natcherly," Old Dane said. "Then you can tell me all about your merchandise."

"It's big," she said. "Really big."

He raised his substantial eyebrows. "It sounds big."

"Bigger than that," she said.

5:29 p.m.

The old woman at the door looked suspicious.

As well she should, Rocky thought. Two wet strangers in the night, knocking.

"Miss Boaz?" Rocky said.

"Who wants to know?"

"We're looking for Rosie Summerville Jones."

The woman was in a bathrobe that might have been fresh in 1978. She said, "You're a friend of Rosie's?"

"Her daughter," Rocky said.

"Lizzie? Is she out here?"

"That's what we think."

"That girl is trouble, always has been. Runs in the family."

"Can you help us?" Mac said.

"You want to find Rosie, do you?"

"Yes."

"I can help you with that. Oh yes, I can."

5:42 p.m.

"Help me!"

"Easy girl," Old Dane said.

"Don't tell me to take it easy! Don't tell me that anymore. I've got to go."

"It's pouring out there."

"Help me!"

"You're just plum exhausted. You drink up and sleep. I'll take the couch. Tomorrow is time enough —"

"Help me stay out of hell!"

Old Dane put his arms around her and stroked her hair. It felt like flames of fire licking her head.

"You just quiet down now," Old Dane said. "You just rest now."

Wednesday

10:32 a.m.

The grass was still wet, with drops sparkling in the sun. The smell of moist leaves, along with the scent of mud, filled Liz with a kind of earthly comfort.

She drank it in.

Mama was resting peacefully under the plain brass plate.

Liz laid a diamond ring on top of the plate. The simple grave was in a row under some willow trees, dripping with the remnants of rain.

"I made it, Mama. You knew I would. It was tough there for a while, but I did it. You always said I could, and I did. But there's something real big about it this time. I got some luck. Did you know Arty died? I didn't really want him to, but once it happened, what could I do?"

Some leaves blew across the grave. One of the leaves landed on Mama's first name.

Liz took the leaf, wet and brown, and lifted it to her cheek.

"Did I do it right, Mama? Did I get what was coming to me?"

She took the diamond ring and pressed it into the soft grass below the plate. She pressed it with her thumb as far as she could. Then she pulled her thumb out with a *goosh* sound.

"Mexico maybe, Mama. I'll live like you wanted me to."

Good luck. Now the seed had been planted. Mama had the ring and that meant good luck forever and ever.

"Hello, Liz."

She shrieked at the voice and spun around.

10:34 a.m.

Mac thought, She looks like a wounded animal.

A dangerous, wounded animal. With crazy eyes.

No quick movements, he told himself. She might snap.

Liz looked between them. Mac sensed Rocky's tension, but she was letting him do the talking.

For the moment.

They were three people alone in a cemetery. A hundred yards away, a man was mowing some grass. The steady hum of the mower was the only sound.

Liz started shaking her head. No words. Just swiveling with a mad uncertainty.

Mac said, "Whatever's happened, it can be made right."

The head shake grew more pronounced. Then stopped as she stood up. She reached into her purse. She pulled out a gun.

They were ten feet apart.

Mac stepped in front of Rocky. "Liz, listen to me. I'm not out to get you. I want to help you. So does Rocky."

"No," Liz said.

"Yes, Liz, we do. We came here to help."

"Not her."

Rocky moved to Mac's side. "Yes, Liz, me, too."

Pointing the gun at Rocky now, Liz shook her head. "You hate me."

"I don't know you," Rocky said. "And I never gave you a chance."

"Both of you hate me."

She's getting close to crumbling, Mac thought. No sudden moves. He said, "We're family. We need to work this out together."

"Not family," Liz said. "Can't be fixed, can't be fixed. Can't put it back together."

"Put the gun down," he said softly. "Let's talk it out."

A beat.

Then another.

No one moved.

Then, slowly, with a look of astonishment, Liz began to lower the gun.

Rocky took two steps toward her.

Something didn't look right. Mac was about to yell *stop* when Liz whipped the gun up again.

Mac pulled Rocky behind him.

Liz put the gun to her own temple.

Mac jumped, without thinking, hands out, grabbing, contact.

And heard the shot, as if in the distance.

As if in a dream of death.

Saturday

The skies over LA were, at last, blue again. The city woke up to the weekend tentatively, almost as if it expected the rains to return.

This despite what the cheery meteorologists on the local broadcasts had been telling them for the last few days.

Yet gradually there was, in the early morning activities of Angelenos, a sense of new beginnings.

But not all was rosy.

The *Times* carried a story about the fear of a hellish fire season a few months hence, because of all the new growth that would be caused by the rain. A scorching summer was expected, the story said, and fierce Santa Ana winds would turn the hills into tinderboxes.

"We could be getting the worst fire season in a decade," Los Angeles Fire Department Assistant Chief Wayne Gregg was quoted as saying. "But then again, they're all bad."

In the *Daily News*, the lead story was about the mayor's new proposal to quell gang violence. He was calling the plan "Love 'em Early," and in a tearful news conference promised to reach at-risk kids at ages eight or nine instead of fourteen or fifteen.

It was only going to cost twenty-four million dollars.

And the *Pack Canyon Herald* burst forth with an across-the-page headline — its first in many years — announcing the closing of Pack Canyon Park.

The city of Los Angeles had closed the park after state toxics regulators warned of a positive test for lead at a former skeet range, an area that now had a grass field and basketball court.

An environmental consultant hired by the city found that one-third of the samples it took contained lead that exceeded health standards.

Mark Young, captain of Rolling Thunder, a wheelchair rugby team that used Pack Canyon Park for practice, was upset. "We have three practices a week. Park space is hard to find. Now what are we going to do?"

Los Angeles Parks and Recreation General Manager Glynnis Kirk was quoted as saying, "The safety of our park patrons always comes first, and while we understand a park closing is inconvenient, this was mandated by the State of California."

The California Department of Toxic Substances Control ordered a chain-link fence erected at the entrance to the park, with a red warning sign prominently displayed.

HAZARDOUS MATERIALS! DO NOT ENTER!

At 9:31 Saturday morning, members of the Los Angeles County Sherriff's Crime Scene Unit completed the first phase of their investigation of 871 Feather Lane, Pack Canyon. Luminol procedure had revealed blood spatter and a footprint.

Sheriff's Homicide Detective Kathy Moss, just three hours after her return from Mississippi with a prisoner, confirmed that the size of the footprint matched the shoe size of one Theodore Gillespie.

9:52 a.m.

"You were gone," her father said.

"I had a little business to attend to," Rocky said.

"Working?"

"Actually working."

"Getting paid?"

"You always know the right thing to say."

His face clenched. At least he was in his own house now. His neighbor, a woman named Jesse, had been checking in on him.

"I don't know anything," her father said.

Rocky said nothing. She had the urge to hold his hand. She didn't, though. She didn't know if he wanted her to.

"I need to tell you something," he said. "Before I die."

Rocky wanted to cry out. *Do not die, no, not before we make things right, not before we have one last chance.* But she thought words like that might pierce the thin tissue of connection he was obviously trying to make.

They sat in silence for a long moment. He was on the sofa, propped against pillows, looking gaunt. His pipes were in their carousel, looking cold. The tobacco smell in the house was stale.

Finally, he said, "I'm afraid of it."

"Of what?" Rocky said.

"Dying."

It was the first vulnerable thing he had ever said to her that Rocky could remember. A hairline crack in the hard-shell enclosure of his emotions. She could hardly speak, then heard herself using the old name. "Daddy," she said, "you're not going to die. Not yet."

"I have to say something." His face held torment. Rocky thought he must be suffering discomfort of some kind. *Or, please, no, not another stroke.*

"What is it?" Rocky said. "Can I get you something?"

"Listen to me."

Rocky leaned forward.

"If I don't say this, I might go to purgatory or something."

Purgatory? Where had that come from? He wasn't a religious man.

"I don't know what's out there," he said. "I'm afraid of it. But I have to try to say this. I have to try ..." He looked straight at her then. His eyes were damp.

"Go ahead, Pop. I'll listen."

Another long, leaden moment passed. Rocky felt a sudden loss of breath, as if she had to expend all her strength to keep the channel with her father open. Or else the door would slam shut too soon.

Then her father said, "I didn't fix the fence."

"Fence?"

He took a deep breath. "The dog got through. The dog. I knew he could get into the yard. I didn't fix the fence. I didn't ..."

And then he was full-on crying. An old man, aging before her eyes, face wet, voice weak.

The dog. The dog that had mauled her.

It was clear to her in that moment that this was his plea for absolution. He had carried the guilt of her scars all these many years. He had hidden behind a rock wall of denial and, at times, neglect. It was why he had not wanted to be with her. It was why he had withheld his love.

It was both a shock and relief. To finally know why he had treated her the way he had. And it was devastating, too, all the lost years. She saw instantly how bitter she really was about it. Now here was his confession. And she could choose to give him what he asked for or leave him to die in his remorse.

She went to him, put her arm over his bony body, and rested her head on top of his. She let him cry it out, and by the time he was finished, she found she was embracing him, and he was letting her.

She took his hand. His grip was firm, as if holding onto life itself.

They stayed that way for a long time. His breathing normalized. Then he said, "Do you still sing?"

"Yes, Daddy. In fact, I do."

He nodded, like he was trying to remember something. "You did when you were little. You liked to. I remember that."

"I still like to."

"Would you sing something for me?"

"What, now?"

"I'm not going anywhere."

She swallowed. Her throat was dry. She was amazed he was asking this. "What ... do you want me to sing?"

"Anything."

" 'Anything Goes?' "

He smiled then. "That's a good old song. You know it?"

"I can give it a try."

"Please try," he said.

Softly, Rocky sang.

10:57 a.m.

"I just acted," Mac said. "I just jumped. It was the wrong thing to do. I should've kept talking to her."

"You haven't got a whole lot of time to consider your options when somebody has a gun to her head," Pastor Jon said.

They were sitting in front of Mac's place. The sun felt good on Mac's back. The events of the last three days had left him feeling cold inside. As if a dark, cool void had taken permanent residence in his chest.

Now, warmed by the sun and his pastor, the cold was slowly melting away.

But not all of it. There was still Liz.

"She went away right before my eyes," Mac said. "Like there was a place inside her brain where she was going to take up residence. Not exactly like being in a coma, but close."

Jon nodded, steepling his fingers. "This is a spiritual battle, first to last," he said. "I have a friend, a guy I went to seminary with, who is a psychiatrist now. Ray Vickers. I'd like him to come see Liz. He recognizes the spiritual. He's kind of a rebel that way, in his profession. He has a theory he calls 'sin dissociation.'"

"Sounds heavy."

"He explained it to me once. Sin's real, even if you don't believe in it. And it affects the mind. If you ignore it, you dissociate, you try to compartmentalize it. But the guilt seeps through, and if you don't turn it over to God, it will turn on you."

"How?"

"If it's bad enough, it makes you paranoid, for one thing. Full-on mental illness in extreme cases. It can result in conduct you try to justify in your own mind. You begin to think anything you do is all right, that you're entitled. So if you get caught, you withdraw. Into your own little world, so you can still be in control."

Mac thought about it, about Liz's almost lifeless eyes. "I have to see her," he said. "I have to let her know I'm here."

Monday

10:39 a.m.

Tito Sanchez was almost laughing over the phone. "They've suspended Gordon Slezak immediately, pending review."

"You have got to be kidding," Mac said.

"Not me," Sanchez said. "I'm the most serious guy in the world. But this has me, I don't know, just laughing."

"I'm glad I could brighten your day."

"That girl, what's her name?"

"Rocky. Roxanne."

"Rocky Roxanne?"

"Just Rocky."

"She's awesome, what she did. She could be up for an Oscar for best documentary. I e-mailed the video straight to the Department of Corrections' oversight office. They called me back in an hour. They pleaded with me not to release it to the news. I think that might not be a bad idea, to get—"

"No," Mac said. "I don't want you to. Let them handle it. The guy's going to suffer enough."

"But this is the way it's done now," Sanchez said.

"It's not the way I want it done. Are we clear?"

"Okay. You're the client. Speaking of which, the child-custody papers. I filed them on Friday."

Mac said nothing. He felt nothing.

"You okay with that?" Sanchez said.

"I'll let you know," Mac said.

When he clicked off, Mac sat for a long time, looking at the wall.

11:02 a.m.

"You're welcome to stay, you know," Geena said.

Rocky kissed her cheek. "I know. But it's time to get back to my own place."

"What about Boyd?"

"I'm not afraid of Boyd. I don't even think he'll come around."

"And if he does?"

"I'll take care of it then."

"Maybe your boyfriend can throw him out on the street again."

"Geena ..."

Geena smiled. "Come on. You hauled in a criminal together. He's just right for you, he's—"

"Stop. Okay? Just stop. And don't vibrate about it. Don't visualize or verbalize or any other kind of -ize. Just leave it alone."

"There are some things you can't control," Geena said. "Some things just happen."

1:28 p.m.

Mac sat across from Liz, looking at her through the visiting-room glass at the Century Regional Detention Facility in Lynwood. Her eyes were empty. Vacant.

Or maybe looking at something so far away that only she could see. She was in a jail-issue, neon orange jumpsuit. Her hair was stringy.

"I came to see how you're doing," Mac said.

Liz took a breath. "You look weird," she said.

Mac smiled, trying to reassure her. "But how are *you*?"

"There's fire."

"What?"

"Fire."

"Where?"

"All around. It's in the trees and the birds."

Gripping the handset, Mac prayed silently and said, "Liz, I want to say something to you, okay?"

"It's in the rocks."

"Liz, just listen."

Her eyes met his.

"Do you remember being baptized?"

She said nothing.

"Do you remember saying you wanted it?" Mac said.

Silence.

"You can call on the name of Jesus, Liz."

A low candle flame flickered in her eyes. "It's too late," she said.

"No, it is never too late."

"Arty knows. He knows what I did."

"Arty forgives you."

She shook her head. "It's too late. You can't go back. You are what you are. Never change. Can't."

"No," Mac said. "You can choose, right now. You can choose—"

"Too late!"

Liz screamed. Her face twisted. She threw the handset at the Plexiglas and stood up, defensive, as if Mac was going to bust through and grab her.

Two female deputies rushed over, and that was that. They dragged Liz, literally kicking and screaming, from the visiting room.

Just before she disappeared through the door, she caught Mac's eyes once more.

They were wide with a kind of fear that reminded him of something.

Then he knew what it was. It was like that Iraqi kid soldier who had screamed *I love you!* as the Marines tied him up.

4:29 p.m.

"Bedford–Mulrooney."

"May I speak to Athena, please?"

"Who's calling please?"

"Mac."

"May I tell her what this is regarding?"

"Aurora."

Pause. "One moment."

Classical music. Then: "Mac, I'm not supposed to talk to you. My lawyer said—"

"You won't need the lawyer."

"What?"

"I'm not going through with it."

"Do you mean that?" Athena said.

"I don't want Aurora to be in the middle of a war."

"Mac, I ... I don't know what to say."

"You don't have to say anything. I know she doesn't even know who I am."

Athena was silent.

"Is Tony a good father?" Mac said.

"He's a very good father," Athena said.

Mac took a long, deep breath. He closed his eyes.

"I'm glad," he said.

"I believe you," Athena said. "I really, really do."

7:31 p.m.

"This is strange," Mac said.

"What is?" Rocky said.

"Not feeling afraid that somebody could show up at any time and try to knock my head off. They haven't given me a new PO yet. I almost don't know what to do."

Rocky smiled and almost said the same thing. She and Mac sat with feet up on the outside deck of the Canyon Grind. The evening was warm, only a hint of a breeze through the mountains.

The lights of the city were spread out as usual, way down below. They still comforted Rocky, still offered up a hopefulness that once she had only pretended to believe in.

"Are you going to see Liz again?" she said.

"If she'll let me," Mac said. "They put her on suicide watch."

Rocky shook her head. "I should hate her."

"But you don't."

"What's going on in her head must be pretty bad."

"It is."

"Insanity defense, you think?"

"No doubt."

He reached over and took her hand. That surprised her. She saw his face in the light of the table candle.

He said, "You did good."

"Lucky, I guess."

Mac shook his head. "The insurance company for the stones, they're going to love you. They're not going to think it's luck."

"I might pick up a file or two out of it."

"Maybe you'll need some help," he said.

"You looking for work?"

"Anything to keep me in crocuses."

Rocky smiled and looked out again at the valley. A plane was starting its descent into Bob Hope Airport in Burbank. Blinking lights, smooth line. People coming back home.

She kept hold of Mac's hand. He didn't let go.

8:19 p.m.

They want you to eat this.

Poison.

Don't do it.

They won't get to me.

It had to be this way.

Step by step, I had to do it all.

Arty, stop it! Get away.

If I hit the wall and bleed, that will be good. I can go to sleep that way. I can bleed.

Tuesday

2:34 p.m.

This was not why Larry Mesa went into medicine.

He wanted to heal. He wanted to spend time with the sick. He wanted to be a doctor who made a difference.

What he didn't want to be was part umpire, part politician, part circus ringmaster.

And only occasionally a doctor of medicine.

Dr. Larry Mesa had chosen LA County – USC Medical Center, with its fading green walls and yellowing ceilings, precisely because he could be where he was needed most: among the poor of the city, the ones most citizens would rather forget.

Here were the John and Jane Does, the homeless, and yes, even the gangbangers. He wanted to heal them all without judgment.

The higher-ups would not make it simple. Especially when there was a big county screwup. And especially when they told you, a doctor of medicine, how to handle a coma patient.

That was the game, when the politicians and lawyers got involved. They could crush you if you didn't play.

Dr. Larry Mesa played, because he wanted to keep his job.

But all those concerns went away, for one sweet moment, when he saw his coma patient fluttering his eyes.

"Hello there," Dr. Mesa said, hope swelling in his chest. To pull a patient out of a coma was one of the most awe-inspiring things a doctor could do.

The eyelids fluttered again.

"I'm Dr. Mesa. Can you hear me?"

The eyelids slowly opened, closed, opened again.

Dr. Mesa forgot all about potential lawsuits and politicians and life's disappointments, and whispered a silent thanksgiving to God.

Right now, everything seemed worth it.

"You can hear me, can't you?" Dr. Mesa said.

The eyelids blinked, this time with definite alertness.

Now it was just doctor and patient, man to man. The antiquated equipment and sour hospital smell could not stand between this transaction.

"Yes, yes, you're back. Come all the way."

"Muh ..."

He was trying to speak! There was no uniformity about comas. Someone could be out for a day and never come all the way back. Others could be gone for a decade and one day wake up and recite the *Gettysburg Address*.

It was part of the marvel of biology and, perhaps, some Power beyond medical science's limited ability to comprehend.

But there was no doubt here. This man was trying to communicate.

"I'm Dr. Mesa. Can you hear me?"

"Myn ..."

Mine?

"Yes?" Dr. Mesa said.

"... name ..."

"Yes?"

"Ar. Thur."

So that was it. *Arthur.* The real name. The information Dr. Mesa now had to keep away from any other staff. The patient had an identity now. But who was he in the larger scheme of things? He'd come over as a John Doe, and there were no prints or DNA in the databases that matched.

One of the lawyers working for the county supervisors had filled Mesa in on what was at stake. This was a case of thanatomimesis, which had happened before in the chaos that was the county morgue. A body thought to be dead is discovered, just before an autopsy — or, horror of horrors, during it — to be alive.

Barely, but alive.

But there was more. They'd nabbed a medical assistant in some sort of bizarre scheme. A body switch. The lawyer didn't give Dr. Mesa all the details—and he really didn't want to know, to tell the truth—but whoever was behind the mess had put a false Doe tag on this Arthur.

Why? Did somebody discover he was alive and want to cover it up somehow? Then there was the other part of this strange tale. The lawyer wouldn't say much, except that there was a pushed-through autopsy and a cremation that shouldn't have happened. Some other poor John Doe had gone to the crematorium. Mesa had heard of the mortuary in question and knew it was not one of the more reputable in town.

If any of this broke, it would be major lawsuit time. *60 Minutes* time. *Geraldo* on steroids.

Those were the lawyer's exact words. *Geraldo on steroids.*

Mesa told himself to be very, very careful.

"Arthur?" Dr. Mesa said.

Eyelids blinked.

"I'm Dr. Mesa."

"Arthur."

"Yes?"

"Towne."

"Town? You're in Los Angeles."

"No."

"No?"

"Arthur. Towne."

"Arthur Towne? That's your name?"

The patient's eyes grew wider, life seeming to pour back into him by the second. "My wife," he said. "Where's my wife?"

The Whole Truth

James Scott Bell,
Bestselling Author of
No Legal Grounds

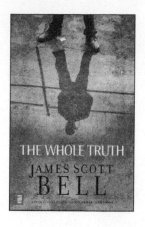

At the age of five, Steve Conroy saw his seven-year-old brother kidnapped from the very bedroom they shared. His brother was never found. And the guilt of his silence that night has all but destroyed Steve's life.

Now thirty years old with a failing law practice, Steve agrees to represent convicted criminal Johnny LaSalle, an arrangement sweetened by a lucrative retainer. It's not long until he discovers that this con man might just be his missing brother.

Desperate for his final shot at redemption, Steve will do anything to find the truth. But Johnny knows far more than he's telling, and the secrets he keeps have deadly consequences. Now Steve must depend on an inexperienced law student whose faith seems to be his last chance at redemption from a corrupt world where one wrong move could be his last.

Softcover: 978-0-310-26903-8

Pick up a copy today at your favorite bookstore!

No Legal Grounds

*James Scott Bell,
Bestselling Author of
Presumed Guilty*

How far will a man go to protect his family?
Attorney Sam Trask will go farther than
he ever dreamed, even in his worst nightmare. Because his worst nightmare is about
to come true...

At age forty-seven, attorney Sam Trask finally seems to have his
life in order. The dark years of too much drinking and all-consuming
ambition have given way to Christian faith. His marriage is strong
again. Everything seems finally on the right track.

Then a voice from the past comes back to say hello.

Suddenly Sam faces a danger more real than he ever imagined
— danger from someone who will not rest until Sam's life comes
crashing down around him. Desperate, Sam seeks protection from
the law he's served all his life. But when the threats are turned
on his family, and the law seems powerless to protect them, Sam
must consider a choice that strikes at the heart of his life and
faith — whether to take the law into his own hands.

Softcover: 978-0-310-26902-1

Pick up a copy today at your favorite bookstore!

Sins of the Fathers

James Scott Bell,
Bestselling Author of
Breach of Promise

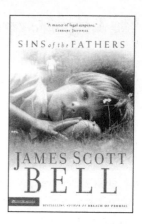

A parent's worst nightmare.
 A lawyer's biggest challenge.
 A young boy's life on the line.
 The unimaginable has happened. A
thirteen-year-old boy has fired a rifle into
a baseball game, killing several of the kids on the field. Parents are
devastated. The townspeople are horrified.

When public opinion swells to an enraged cry for justice, an
ambitious deputy district attorney sees his opportunity—a sensa-
tional trial that will catapult him into the D.A.'s office in the upcom-
ing election. There's just one obstacle: the boy's defense attorney,
Lindy Field.

To all appearances, the case is a slam-dunk. Convict the killer,
make him pay. But it's not that simple. Lindy's young client is
unwilling—or unable—to help Lindy defend him. And as the case
progresses, it becomes clear that someone doesn't want the truth
revealed.

As Lindy delves into the haunted world of her client's torment,
she finds a spiritual darkness that dredges up her own troubled
past. And when dangerous forces close in around her, Lindy must
fight for answers not only in the justice system, but in the very
depths of her soul.

Softcover: 978-0-310-25330-3

Pick up a copy today at your favorite bookstore!

Deadlock

James Scott Bell,
Bestselling Author of
Breach of Promise

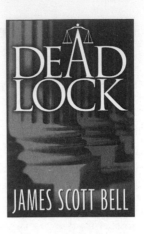

She is a Supreme Court Justice. She is an
atheist. And she is about to encounter the
God of the truth and justice she has sworn
to uphold.

For years, Millicent Hollander has been
the consistent swing vote on abortion and other hot-button issues.
Now she's poised to make history as the first female Chief Justice
of the United States Supreme Court. But something is about to
happen that no one has counted on, least of all Hollander: a near-
death experience that will thrust her on a journey toward God.

Skeptically, fighting every inch of the way, Hollander finds herself dragged toward belief in something she has never believed
in—while others in Washington are watching her every step. Too
much is at stake to let a Christian occupy the country's highest
judicial office. Even as Hollander grapples with the interplay between faith and the demands of her position, and as she finds answers through her growing friendship with Pastor Jack Holden, a
hidden web of lies, manipulation, and underworld connections is
being woven around her. It could control her. It could destroy her
reputation. Unless God intervenes, it could take her out of the
picture permanently.

Softcover: 978-0-310-24388-5

Pick up a copy today at your favorite bookstore!

ZONDERVAN®
.com

Breach of Promise

*James Scott Bell, Author of
the Bestselling* City of Angels

How far will a father go to get back his only
daughter? And how will he survive in a
legal system that crushes those who can't
afford to fight back?

Mark Gillen has the storybook life other
men dream of, complete with a beautiful
wife and an adoring five-year-old daughter.

Then his wife announces she's leaving him. And taking their
daughter with her.

The other man is a famous film director with unlimited funds
and the keys to stardom and wealth for Paula. How can Mark begin
to compete? But the most bitter blow comes when he is kept from
seeing his daughter because of false charges … and a legal system
ill-suited for finding the truth.

Forged in the darkest valley Mark has ever walked through,
his faith in God may ultimately cost him everything in the eyes
of the family law system. But it is the one thing that can keep him
sane — and give him the strength to fight against all odds for what
matters most.

Softcover: 978-0-310-24387-8

Pick up a copy today at your favorite bookstore!

Presumed Guilty

James Scott Bell,
Bestselling Author of
Breach of Promise

Murder, betrayal, and a trial that feeds a media frenzy.

Can one woman stand against the forces that threaten to tear her family apart?

Pastor Ron Hamilton's star is rising. His 8,000-strong church is thriving. His good looks and charisma make him an exceptional speaker on family values. And his book on pornography in the church has become an unexpected bestseller. Everything is perfect.

Until a young woman's body is discovered in a seedy motel room. The woman is a porn star. And all the evidence in the murder points to one man: Ron.

With the noose tightening around her husband's neck, Dallas Hamilton faces a choice: believe the seemingly irrefutable facts — or the voice of her heart. The press has already reached its verdict, and the public echoes it. But Dallas is determined to do whatever it takes to find the truth.

And then a dark secret from Dallas's past threatens to take them all down.

As the clock ticks toward Ron's conviction and imprisonment, and an underworld of evil encircles her, Dallas must gather all her trust in God to discover what really happened in that motel room ... even if it means losing faith in her husband forever.

Softcover: 978-0-310-25331-0
Audio Download, Unabridged: 978-0-310-27819-1

Pick up a copy today at your favorite bookstore!